RED-HOT AND ROYAL

susanna carr

A SIGNET ECLIPSE BOOK

SIGNET ECLIPSE
Published by New American Library, a division of
Penguin Group (USA) Inc., 375 Hudson Street,
New York, New York 10014, USA
Penguin Group (Canada), 90 Eglinton Avenue East, Suite 700, Toronto,
Ontario M4P 2Y3, Canada (a division of Pearson Penguin Canada Inc.)
Penguin Books Ltd., 80 Strand, London WC2R 0RL, England
Penguin Ireland, 25 St. Stephen's Green, Dublin 2,
Ireland (a division of Penguin Books Ltd.)
Penguin Group (Australia), 250 Camberwell Road, Camberwell, Victoria 3124,
Australia (a division of Pearson Australia Group Pty. Ltd.)
Penguin Books India Pvt. Ltd., 11 Community Centre, Panchsheel Park,
New Delhi - 110 017, India
Penguin Group (NZ), 67 Apollo Drive, Rosedale, North Shore 0632,
New Zealand (a division of Pearson New Zealand Ltd.)
Penguin Books (South Africa) (Pty.) Ltd., 24 Sturdee Avenue,
Rosebank, Johannesburg 2196, South Africa

Penguin Books Ltd., Registered Offices:
80 Strand, London WC2R 0RL, England

First published by Signet Eclipse, an imprint of New American Library,
a division of Penguin Group (USA) Inc.

First Printing, June 2008
10 9 8 7 6 5 4 3 2 1

SIGNET ECLIPSE and logo are trademarks of Penguin Group (USA) Inc.

LIBRARY OF CONGRESS CATALOGING-IN-PUBLICATION DATA:

Carr, Susanna.
Red-hot and royal/Susanna Carr.
p.   cm.
ISBN 978-0-451-22399-9
1. Princes—Fiction. 2. Princesses—Fiction. I. Title.
PS3603.A77435R43 2008
813'.6—dc22   2007047677

Set in Bembo
Designed by Alissa Amell

Printed in the United States of America

Praise for Susanna Carr's "Sizzling"★ Romances

"The guys are hot, and the sexual tension is unbelievable!"
—*New York Times* bestselling author Sabrina Jeffries

"A must read for everyone."   —Fresh Fiction

"Be sure not to miss out on this one. After all, being wicked and being in love can fall hand in hand. This is a keeper, definitely.
—The Romance Readers Connection

"I can't say that I have ever laughed so much while reading erotica, but Susanna Carr definitely delivered. I love this book. It was an enjoyment to read such a change from the average erotica."
—Romance Readers at Heart

"Delightfully humorous, with sizzling chemistry between the characters, great secondary characters, and a love story that won't be soon forgotten. A definite recommend!"   —★Love Romances

"A hilarious romantic read that will have you turning page after page…a must-read story."   —Romance Junkies

"Carr's stories are full of well-matched characters, exhibitionist-style lovemaking, and some wedding faux pas that are sure to entertain married and single women alike."   —*Romantic Times*

"Witty and sexy."   —Just Erotic Romance Reviews

"Sexy, sassy, delicious fun."   —Shannon McKenna

"Delivers exactly what readers want."   —*TwoLips Reviews*

Other Signet Eclipse Titles
by Susanna Carr

Pink Ice
Bad Girl Bridesmaids

To the very tenacious and always supportive Jenny Bent

PROLOGUE

"POOR HUGO." Prince Zain of Mataar shook his head. "Who would have thought he would have been the first to go?"

His friend Prince Santos swiveled his head in surprise. "You didn't see it coming?"

"No."

"The extreme sports? The gambling?" Santos tugged impatiently at his shirt collar. "Let's not forget the women. That was his ultimate downfall."

"The paparazzi must be really mourning," their friend Crown Prince Rafael of Tiazza added before he took another sip of his drink. He leaned against an ornately carved pillar and watched the other guests.

Zain surveyed the crowd, wondering what captured his friend's attention. It was probably nothing. As the heir to the throne of a European principality surrounded by powerful countries, Crown Prince Rafael was always alert and watchful.

As far as Zain could tell, there was nothing unusual going on. Not that there would be. All of the guests were royal, dressed appropriately and well-behaved. It was nothing new to someone as sophisticated and world-weary as Rafael. The only unusual event was that their friend Santos wore a suit.

"He should have listened to the warnings," Santos decided as he loosened his tie a little more. Zain knew his friend spent most of his time barefoot and shirtless on Isla de la Perla, unlike his own desert kingdom, which required everyone covered up. As much as he understood that Santos was not used to wearing formal clothes, if the guy continued to fidget, Zain was going to grab the tie and give it a good yank.

"He should have gotten his act together before the warnings," Rafael said with no hint of sympathy. "He's supposed to represent stability and honor, but he's always on the front page of the newspapers causing one scandal after another."

"That's Hugo," Zain said. "His motto was always 'faster and harder.' He was famous for pushing the limits. But this?" He gestured at the room. "This doesn't make sense."

"What did you think would happen?" Rafe asked.

Zain shrugged. "I don't know. Anything but marriage!"

The three men turned and watched the bride and groom receive more guests in the reception line. Hugo stood ramrod straight, his expression stoic, but those who knew him well could see the strain around his eyes and mouth. Zain noticed how Hugo didn't interact with his bride. He stood as far away from her as politeness allowed. He wasn't going to pretend he was happy with his father's choice.

Santos shuddered. "Better him than me."

"Hugo is lucky to have Agnes as his wife," Rafe argued. "She is everything a princess should be. She's regal and honorable, and she has always done the right thing."

"She'll keep Hugo in line," Santos predicted.

Hugo was going to be bored to death. Maybe that was the plan. Zain could see it now. Slowly and methodically, every bit of freedom was going to be curtailed and before he knew it. Hugo would turn into a mindless zombie.

Zain's sigh came from deep inside him. "Poor guy." He downed his drink in one gulp.

"You know," Santos said, rolling his shoulders as if he was trying to get used to the fit of the exquisitely tailored jacket, "the bookmakers are placing bets on which one of us will be next."

"Who's leading?" Rafe asked absently, as he continued to scan the wedding reception.

"Zain."

This was news to him! "Why me? Rafe is a crown prince." Zain motioned at his friend with the jerk of his thumb. "He needs to get married."

"First of all, I don't need to." Rafe's voice roughened with annoyance. "Second, it's going to be a while before I find a suitable bride. There are requirements for the woman I marry. Do you know how hard it is to find a proper woman, let alone one who has been trained to behave like a queen?"

Zain rolled his eyes. Like Rafe was looking. Ha. Right. "You're not going to find such a woman at your usual hangouts."

"I have no interest in visiting a place that is crawling with virgins." Rafe couldn't mask his displeasure over the idea. "I'll marry when I can't hold off any longer. Santos here will marry before me."

"That won't happen for a while. The Castle is too busy with their new pet project." For a moment Santos's constant smile disappeared. "They want to turn me into a gentleman."

Zain couldn't prevent sharp laughter from bursting out, causing a few hats and tiaras to turn his way. He couldn't help it. Santos looked more like a surfer than a sophisticated man. The idea was ridiculous. Even Rafe cracked a smile.

"I'm serious," Santos said, two words he rarely used together. "My country needs to work on international diplomacy, and I'm stuck with the job."

"That's not as bad as it sounds," Zain insisted. "You know how to be social. Isla de la Perla is famous for its hospitality."

"But now I have to do the meetings and"—he made quotation marks—"functions. I have to wear medals and sashes."

Rafe's eyebrow lifted. "You're kidding, right?"

"I wish I were. Sashes! What man willingly wears a sash?" Santos rested the back of his head on the pillar. "But it can't be that bad. You guys can be gentlemen when the occasion calls for it, so I can do it, too. Can you see me in white tie and tails?"

Zain knew his jaw had dropped. He gave a quick glance at Rafe, whose expression was suspiciously blank.

Santos lifted his head when no one responded. "Well, come on, you guys. What do you think? Can I pull it off?"

Rafe shook his head. "You're screwed."

Santos winced. "Yeah. I am, aren't I? This is what I get for being fourth in line for the throne. I get the dirty work. The stuff no one else wants to do."

"All you need is a few lessons," Zain said. He wanted to be encouraging, but Santos was raw energy and restless when indoors. He would not survive in the refined world of operas and waltzes.

"That's what the Castle decided. Just an intensive course. I have to meet an image consultant in California next week, and my first embassy dinner will be in Los Angeles. I heard this consultant is about as strict as an army sergeant, but the Castle made sure I have access to a beach. As long as I'm near the ocean, I'll survive."

"I'm going to be in America, too, with some agricultural businesses," Zain said with a smile. "But I'll be surrounded by miles and miles of cornfields."

Rafe gave him a suspicious look. "Why does that make you happy? Is there something about corn I should know about?"

"No woman is going to find me there." He didn't have any public events, and the press office did everything possible to keep his upcoming trip to Illinois as quiet as possible. The chances of a woman seeking and finding him were very slight.

"Huh?" Rafe looked at Zain as if he were crazy.

"My birthday is coming up. My thirtieth birthday," he added meaningfully.

"Oh, yeah. The royal prophecy." Rafe shook his head. "You still believe in that?"

Zain chose not to answer. Rafe didn't believe in anything that didn't provide concrete evidence. "It doesn't matter what I believe. Every woman in my country knows about the prophecy."

Santos looked back and forth at them. "What prophecy?"

"Don't you remember?" Rafe asked. "The woman who kisses a bachelor prince at midnight on his thirtieth birthday is destined to be his bride."

"Oh, yeah." Santos turned to Zain. "Now that sucks."

"Tell me about it. And if a woman kisses me at that moment, and I don't follow through by marrying her, I lose my royal status."

One kiss had the potential to ruin his life. He would not give up his title with dishonor, but he didn't want to be stuck with a woman not of his choosing. Zain glanced over at his friend Hugo and shuddered. He wasn't going to let that happen to him. It was best to hide out until the time limit for the prophecy expired.

"But why do you have to go across the world to hide?" Santos asked. "They have women around cornfields."

"But it's highly unlikely that any woman in Illinois will know about the prophecy. Those farm girls aren't going to make a point of getting a kiss at that moment. They can get as close as they want before or after my birthday."

"You're better off taping your mouth shut," Santos said, showing no signs of awe over his plan. "Or better yet, develop a rash on your lip. Something that oozes."

"You think that's going to stop a woman who wants to be a princess?"

"No. You're right," Santos replied, his tone weary. They all knew what it was like being pursued by women hungry for the title and the tiara.

"I'm telling you, going to the heartland of America will keep this prophecy from happening," Zain said, deciding that his business trip to Illinois couldn't have happened at a better time. It was almost providential. "No woman there will try to kiss me at midnight. I can guarantee it."

CHAPTER ONE

PRINCE ZAIN
Deep in America's Heartland

EVERYTHING WAS GOING WRONG. As usual.

Lauren Ballinger pulled the crumpled paper from her borrowed evening bag. The people on the crowded dance floor jostled her as they shimmied and swayed to the primitive beat. She felt them closing in but refrained from hunching her shoulders. She wanted to leave, but she couldn't. Not yet.

She squinted at the picture while the colored lights pulsated above her. Her stomach made a funny little flip. Zain, Prince of Mataar, was very handsome.

He looked like a sly charmer. The square jaw and the slashing lines of his cheekbones should have been intimidating, but the dimple in his cheek and the laugh lines fanning his eyes ruined the effect. Lauren also noticed the naughty gleam in his brown eyes and the wry tilt of his lips. It was the prince's mouth that captured her attention. It promised pleasure.

A shiver tripped down Lauren's spine, and she straightened her back. It was too bad she couldn't find the desert prince anywhere at this stupid nightclub. She could have sworn he'd be here. It was the only place in a hundred-mile radius where someone of his stature would celebrate his birthday.

Lauren still couldn't believe her luck that a prince was visiting nearby. She needed to meet someone royal and her only hope was to visit one of the kingdoms. That was way out of her price range.

For two months she had been racking her brains, trying to come up with a plan that would allow her to get up close and personal with a prince. When she found out Prince Zain was in the area—from a boring document she scanned at the office, of all things—she knew she had to act fast. An opportunity like this would not come twice.

She glanced around the undulating mass of shadowy, sweat-slicked bodies, ignoring the throbbing beat that she felt through her strappy heels. No one matched the picture. All of the guys looked ordinary. Not one appeared remotely royal.

Maybe she was wrong about the prince. Lauren considered the possibility as she shoved the picture back into her tiny purse. Prince Zain might be a homebody and hate the club scene.

After all, what kind of man would choose to hang around farm country where there was nothing to do? Someone from the desert might find small farms in Central Illinois exotic, but she doubted it. She couldn't imagine royalty wanting to visit on purpose.

Maybe he really wasn't a prince.

Lauren gritted her teeth. He had better be a prince. She had done her research on the Internet. The computer had done a horrible job at translating, so she didn't understand a lot, but the man was definitely a prince. She had to stop worrying about every little detail.

She exhaled sharply, blowing the hair away from her forehead. Why did she even agree to do this? Lauren placed her hands on her hips and scanned the crowd again. She shouldn't have to do this. She had won the competition fair and square.

This was what happened when she won. Someone would inevitably decide that the rules weren't hard enough.

But one couldn't argue with the rules made ten years ago. They had been written after high school graduation by Lauren and her four friends. They had scribbled down their dreams and goals, predicting where they'd be ten years from that day. After stuffing the scraps of paper in an old thermos, they had buried it under "their" tree.

She had forgotten about that makeshift time capsule until her friend Stacy dug it up two months ago and presented it with a flourish at the booth in the bakery where they sat every morning. Trust Stacy to remember. The woman made everything into a Kodak moment.

Everyone squealed and hurriedly looked for their list. Everyone but Lauren. Dread punched her in the stomach so hard she felt sick. She was afraid to see what she had written down. Scared to see that she failed once again.

She finally grabbed the paper, knowing that if she didn't, her friends would read it out loud for her. She reluctantly read her list and felt a moment of disbelief. She had completed everything. Everything!

Okay, so there were only three items: get a full-time job, get a place of her own, and get a car. But she completed it! Relief poured through her tight muscles, and she slowly breathed out. In fact, she had finished her list within three years of graduating from high school.

"That's not fair," Tanya complained when she found out Lauren was the only one who had completed her goals. She swiped the paper out of Lauren's hand and skimmed it. "This isn't a life list. It's a to-do list!"

"Who cares?" Renee asked, flipping her blond hair over

one shoulder. "Look at this." She waved her paper in Tanya's face. "I should have been a millionaire by now."

"So what?" Tanya said, unimpressed. "I should have *married* a millionaire by now."

"Guys, look." Stacy pointed at the remaining paper on the Formica tabletop between the coffee cups and plates. "It's Cheryl's list."

The women immediately stopped and stared silently at the paper. Lauren wanted to look away, but couldn't. Suddenly their dreams and how far they were from achieving them didn't matter. Cheryl had never got a chance to dream.

"Has it been ten years since she died?" Renee asked softly.

Ten years? It was hard to believe. "That car crash seemed like it was yesterday," Lauren said.

Renee picked up the paper.

"What are you doing?" Tanya whispered fiercely as she made a failed grab for the paper. "Those are Cheryl's dreams."

Renee rolled her eyes as she unfolded the list. "It's not like they're sacred."

"Yes, they are," Tanya insisted.

Renee read the list and gave a low, long whistle. "Wow. She had big dreams."

Tanya slouched in her seat. "And she didn't get to go after one of them."

"She didn't have a chance," Lauren said.

Stacy suddenly slapped her hand on the table. "So we'll do it for her."

Lauren froze. "Say what?" Was Stacy suggesting they fulfill Cheryl's wishes and dreams?

"Renee, how many dreams are on there?"

The blonde quickly counted them. "Ten."

Ten? Lauren's mouth dropped open. She had only had three, and they had been purposely vague. Who in her right mind could list ten dreams at the drop of a hat?

"And there are only four of us." Stacy pursed her lips. "Doesn't matter. We'll do what we can. Each one will get two of Cheryl's dreams. And we'll complete it for her."

"Are you kidding me?" Tanya squawked.

Lauren was glad she wasn't the only one who felt that way. Cheryl had been a dreamer who wanted to believe the world was sprinkled with pixie dust.

"I haven't had a chance to get through mine." Tanya thrust her hands into her short hair. "Now I have to put mine aside to complete Cheryl's?"

"Okay, okay," Stacy said impatiently as she relented. "We'll put a time limit on it."

"Another ten years?" Tanya asked hopefully.

Stacy shook her head, her curly ponytail bouncing against her shoulder. "How about a year?"

"How about Cheryl's birthday?" Renee suggested.

"That only gives us six months," Lauren quickly pointed out.

"We can do it," Stacy decided, determination glowing in her eyes. She reached out into the center of the table, palm down. "Are you guys in?"

"I'm in," Tanya agreed, clasping her hand over Stacy's.

"Me, too," Renee said, slapping her hand over Tanya's.

Lauren wasn't so sure. What were the pros and cons? What were the rates of success and failure? "I don't even know what the dreams are."

"Does it matter?" Stacy asked. "It's for Cheryl."

She had a point. And, unfortunately, one that couldn't be argued. "Fine. Okay." Lauren reached over the table and put her hand on top. "I'm in."

"Great." Stacy's smile was wide with anticipation. "Everyone, pick a paper."

Lauren grabbed the smallest slip of paper. She felt guilty for doing that, but she didn't know what she was getting in to. Cheryl's plans were always outrageous and ever-changing. One moment she wanted to climb Mount Everest, and the next she wanted to learn a musical instrument. There was no telling what Cheryl wanted to do right after graduation, when she felt that the world was her playground.

Unfolding the sliver of paper, Lauren was hit with a wave of nostalgia. The lined school paper was faded, but her friend's handwriting was large, confident and girly. Lauren blinked back the tears and tried to swallow, but her throat felt tight. She read the dreams she had to complete.

To kiss a prince
To win a million dollars

Lauren's eyes bulged until they stung. No way. *No way.* They were impossible! Literally, statistically, absolutely impossible. There was no way she could do this. Not in one year or ten. And she was supposed to get this done in *six months*?

"Uh"—Tanya gnawed on her lip and looked up from her slip of paper—"I think mine is illegal. Can I switch?"

"I want to trade, too," Lauren added quickly.

"No trading!" Stacy commanded.

Lauren crumpled the paper in her fist. "I can't do these things."

"We'll help each other," Renee said, "but no trading."

Lauren's eyes narrowed as she studied her friend with suspicion. "You got the easy ones, didn't you?"

Renee raised one eyebrow. "Do you think Cheryl knew how to dream small?"

Lauren was abruptly pulled into the present as a dancer bumped into her. Disoriented, she looked around, the kaleidoscope of colors and rays of pulsing lights not helping her. She wanted to run from this place, but she wouldn't get anywhere near finishing Cheryl's list.

Who was she kidding? There was no way she could get one thing done on the list, but at least this time, no one could accuse her of giving up too early. She would prove that she hadn't taken the easy way out.

None of Cheryl's dreams were simple and easy, Lauren decided as she stood on her tiptoes to look over the dancers in the nightclub. But she guessed that had been the point. Cheryl believed the impossible could be achieved if given enough time.

Cheryl, you have a lot of explaining to do.

Where the hell was the prince? She had to find him tonight because this was the closest she'd ever get to him. Lauren checked the dance floor again, hoping he wasn't with another woman. How could she possibly kiss him if his girlfriend was right there?

And that was her plan: get in kissing zone with the prince, plant one on him, and get out before security grabbed her. It was a simple plan, if she could get near the prince.

Which, of course, was the kicker. She'd seen enough tabloids to know what kind of girl a prince hooked up with: someone who was gorgeous, filthy rich and didn't understand the concept of failure. The kind of girl who always had a date, never had a pimple and had money thrown at her like confetti.

She was not one of those girls.

Maybe she should act like one though. That might draw the prince out. Lauren gave a snort at the random thought. *Riiight.* Like she could pull that off.

But this was her only chance to get close to the prince. Lauren bumped into the raised platform in the center of the dance floor. Scantily clad women shook their hips and whatever else they had, trying to show off and gain attention. Some were just posing, while others were dancing badly.

The platform was the way to go. If she wanted to find the prince, she needed to get up there and show off. Dance like she'd never danced before and show him what he was missing.

Lauren cringed at the thought. What if her moves weren't enough? No, she had to think positively.

Even if she didn't catch Prince Zain's attention, at least she'd get a bird's-eye view of the crowd. She'd spot him and go for Plan B, whatever that was.

Lauren hooked the thin metal strap of her purse over her shoulder, allowing it to lie flat on her hip. She marched up the steps and onto the platform. The women dancing there weren't ready to give up space for her, but she wasn't going to let that stop her. Lauren turned to face the crowd. She paused.

It'd been a while since she'd danced on a stage, probably ten or eleven years. There were times when she danced for herself, when the stillness in her body was too much to bear. Then she turned out all the lights in her home, cranked up the music and danced until the exhaustion hit.

Tonight was different. Tonight she had to give a performance. Something sexy and provocative.

Lauren rolled her hips tentatively, letting the aggressive song pulse through her. She felt the rhythm, but it wasn't enough. She needed to feel the music.

She placed her legs farther apart, the hem of her dress rising up her legs. Lauren dragged her hands along her bare thighs to her waist and curves of her breast. The music snagged into her blood. It was hot and prickly. She smiled as she felt the kick in her veins before it whooshed into her bloodstream.

Lauren brushed her hands along her neck and face before spearing her fingers into her hair. Her surroundings began to recede as the music got louder. She stretched her arms and reached as high as she could.

She closed her eyes and began to move.

"Look at her."

Zain was about to take a drink from his beer when he turned to where his private secretary pointed. He had heard the awe in Ali's voice, but he hadn't been prepared. His hand froze, the amber bottle suspended, as he saw the slender brunette in the silver dress.

Her moves were hypnotic and fluid. Sensuous and feminine. She didn't bump and grind like the other women fading in the background. This woman was like dancing fire.

He set the bottle down hard. Zain felt the pull and he didn't want to resist. It was an elemental call, something ancient and imprinted deep inside him, telling him to move toward her.

He wanted to get closer and play with her brand of fire, to harness her intensity for his sole pleasure. His skin felt drawn tight against his bones as he watched her. He longed to feel her move just like that underneath him.

A part of him knew he should play it safe. Tonight of all nights was not the time to lay a claim on her, no matter how fascinating she appeared. He knew to hang back, but his instincts were to go after her. He had to capture her before she flitted away.

Her long brown hair swayed and fanned against her face and

shoulders. The silver dress pulled and tugged against gentle curves. A sheen of sweat glowed against her toned arms and legs.

The woman's eyes were closed, but her mouth curled up with a secret smile. She looked lost in her own world, dancing for her own satisfaction. His chest tightened at the deep roll of her hips. White heat flashed through him, and Zain bolted from his chair.

"I'll be back," he said, his eyes never leaving the woman. There was no chance of losing her in this crowd. She radiated with power and sexuality.

"Your Highness," his secretary warned, "wait until after midnight."

"Don't worry, Ali." He waved off the man's urgent words. The man was more superstitious than he was. "I'm only going to dance."

He hadn't forgotten about the prophecy. His small entourage already thought he was pushing his luck celebrating at a nightclub. But no one recognized him around here, and this woman wouldn't know who he was.

He wasn't looking for a kiss from her anyway. That was too tame and didn't offer enough contact. He wanted to feel the woman's body against his and create some sparks.

Zain pushed his way across the crowded dance floor. The closer he got, the more impatient he became. The woman opened her eyes and pushed the long hair away from her face.

Her gaze skimmed the crowd and suddenly connected with his in a jolt. Her electric blue eyes had the ability to hold him immobile.

Her dancing changed subtly. It was as if his attention set her ablaze. He found it difficult to breathe as his chest rose and fell sharply with anticipation.

Watching her dance wasn't enough. He ached for more. Zain wanted her to perform only for him. Dance against him, skin against skin.

As if she could read his mind, the woman reached for him. He took her hand, almost expected her touch to singe. Instead he felt a zip in his blood, the hot sensations curling around him. The woman's hand felt delicate and warm under his fingers.

Zain helped her down the steps, noticing her graceful movement. She was much shorter than he expected, only reaching to his shoulders. He could tuck her against him easily.

Careful . . . The warning was like a wisp of smoke. He should finish this dance. He should turn away now. What he was doing was dangerous. He had gone halfway across the world to play it safe.

The woman looped her arms over his shoulders and pressed her curves against his body. The contact was almost too much. He drew in a shallow breath and inhaled her spicy scent.

He wrapped his arm around her waist, his hand spanning her hip. His eyes widened when the woman glided her bare leg against his jeans before hooking it against his hip.

His cock lurched against her hot center.

She arched her back, pressing her breasts against his chest. He felt the pounding of her heart. Or it could have been his. They followed the same beat.

Zain pressed his other hand against her spine and felt that the back of her dress dipped low. He swallowed roughly as his fingers flexed against her warm, silken skin.

She tilted her head, her hair falling back like a curtain. The woman smiled at him, her confident invitation beckoning him closer. His attention zeroed in on her mouth and his lips tingled.

Her fingers cupped the back of his head and he shivered as

her nails raked through his hair. The music dimmed when he dipped his head. The smoky lights in the nightclub flashed as colors swirled around them.

The woman leaned closer and paused. Zain's chest tightened with a mixture of disappointment and regret. He didn't want her to pull back now. Thrusting his hand at the base of her head, he tangled his fingers in her soft hair.

She couldn't escape now, but getting away was obviously the last thing on her mind. She offered no hesitation as he pressed his mouth against hers.

The kiss wasn't exploratory or tender. It was hard, primal and searing hot. Heat licked his body, flushing his skin. His knees buckled as his mind went blank.

She deepened the kiss, holding him tight as if he might step away. Like that was going to happen. He couldn't move. He felt like he was disintegrating as a flood of raw energy coursed through him.

The woman suddenly pulled away. She looked as dazed as he felt. She pressed her swollen lips together. Zain's hand tightened against her hip.

She easily glided from his hold and dove into the crowd. It was as if she disappeared right before his eyes. Zain followed, but he lost her trail in the spinning lights and dark shadows.

"Your Highness?" Zain's private secretary pushed his way through the crowd and stood a step behind him. His eyes were wide with shock and worry. "What happened?"

"I'm not sure." He stared in the direction the woman went, but he couldn't see her anymore. She had vanished.

"Who is she?" Ali yelled over the music as his gaze frantically darted over the crowd. "Where is she?"

"I don't know." Zain shrugged, not sure what had happened. What did he do to spook her?

"We have to find her."

"Good luck on that." Zain ran his hand through his hair. His heart continued to thump against his ribs.

"We have to," Ali insisted. "The prophecy has been fulfilled."

The prophecy. The watch on his wrist suddenly felt heavy. Zain slowly raised his hand and looked at the time. It was three minutes past midnight.

His head snapped up. "Do you mean that woman . . . ?"

Ali nodded. "She is destined to be your bride."

CHAPTER TWO

CROWN PRINCE RAFAEL
East Coast of the USA

SHAYLA PENDLEY LOOKED at her reflection in the bathroom mirror and flinched. "Okay, so maybe I can't pull off the dangerous-woman look," she admitted.

"Could you have found this out sooner?" Luca asked as he paced behind her, worry lines marring his boyish good looks. "I need my brother to think I'm caught by a gold digger. We need you to look stunning and sexy this afternoon."

One miracle coming right up . . . She pulled the hairpins out, and one corkscrew curl sprang against her darkly rouged cheek. "We have tried everything from femme fatale to the trashy-tramp look. None of it worked. Do you have anything else?"

Luca stopped abruptly and glared at her. "I don't keep women's clothing in my apartment."

"Good to know, but we could have used some backup." She tossed the pins in her seldom-used makeup bag. She scrunched her hair in her hands. Thanks to all the spray, gel and cream, she had the Medusa look going. Unfortunately that wasn't the kind of dangerous-woman look she was striving for.

Luca leaned against the wall, the back of his head hitting the tiles with a thunk. "I don't know if I can do this."

If *he* could do this? Shayla rolled her eyes, which felt heavier than usual thanks to the layers of eye shadow and mascara. Luca didn't have anything to do other than stand there and look pretty. "You should have thought of that sooner. Or asked someone else."

"There is no one else," he said in something that sounded suspiciously close to a wail.

"You mean no one else who would agree with this plan," she corrected him as she gently pushed him out of the bathroom.

"And wouldn't go behind my back and sell the story," he added as she closed the door in his face.

Shayla grinned as she shimmied out of the borrowed red dress. What Luca said was true. Here she was, alone with Prince Luca of Tiazza in his apartment. She was half naked, doing him a favor, but money and sex were the last things on her mind.

But she was Luca's tutor at Wolfskill University nestled in the Shenandoah Mountains. She was his friend, too, but at twenty-five years old, she felt more like an older sister always looking out for him. Luca was considered a great catch, or an easy way to make money off of an exclusive tell-all, but she didn't see him that way.

It was yet another sign of what was wrong with her. Money didn't motivate her, and sex was too easy to find anywhere on campus. But romance? Love? That was different.

She was a hopeless romantic and proud of it. A fan of chick flicks, romance novels and slow songs, she had plenty of knowledge to use when matchmaking or helping star-crossed lovers.

Shayla yanked on her worn jeans and oversized college sweatshirt as she remembered all of the couples she had helped. As much as she believed in the power of love, sometimes it needed a little guidance or a mighty shove. Everyone on campus came to her for advice or a shoulder to cry on.

Okay, it was romance and love for *other people*, but she was happy on the sidelines for now. She hadn't found anyone who made her want to suffer through the messy emotions and uncertainty.

Shayla's favorite heroine said, in her beloved *Pride and Prejudice,* that she wouldn't marry unless she experienced deep love, and Shayla felt the same way when it came to a serious relationship. One day she'd find her Mr. Darcy. And when she did, she'd know how to handle him, thanks to all of her experience.

She balled up the sassy red dress and swung the bathroom door open. Shayla jumped back in surprise when she saw Luca leaning against the doorjamb, barring her exit, his arms stretched across the doorway.

"Okay, let's go over this again," he said wearily.

She ducked under his arm. "Kid."

Luca's squawk made her swivel around. "Don't call me 'kid!'" he exclaimed. "That will ruin everything!"

She held up a placating hand. "Sorry. Luca, darling," she said in a low purr.

Luca shuddered. "Eww."

"There is such a thing as being overprepared," she advised him. "If we even sound rehearsed, your brother is going to smell a rat."

"Wait, wait, wait." He waved his hands for her to stop. "*You* are accusing *me* of being overprepared?"

"Shut up." As his tutor, she had met her match. Luca was disorganized, and forgetful, and he was far too interested in experiencing life away from the supervision of the palace.

"By the way"—Shayla silently braced herself for the news—"what did you get on the history quiz?"

"That's not important!" he exclaimed as he tossed his hands in the air. "Not when my love life is under attack!"

"I'll hunt down your professor," she warned. A wave of curls fell over her eyes and she flipped them back. "Did you ever think that your big brother is visiting because of your school performance?"

"No." Luca readily dismissed that idea. "The palace doesn't care about that. It's not like I'm the heir to the throne. Rafael must have heard that I have a girlfriend. I tried to keep it a secret. Cathy's the first woman I've been serious about."

Shayla gave him a disbelieving look.

"Well, the first one my family hasn't known since birth," he clarified. "And I really love Cathy. She's wonderful."

Oh, here we go. Shayla liked helping couples—she really did!—but she could do without the way they often listed all the attributes they loved about each other. It could get sickening and a little weird. It also got boring real quick unless it was about you.

"And your family will see that she's wonderful," Shayla agreed, stopping Luca from rhapsodizing about his girlfriend again. "You have to give them more credit," she decided as she stuffed the dress into her duffel bag, which was stretched to the seams with other discarded outfits.

"The palace will try to break us up because she's not from my world," he insisted.

"You know, you could be completely off the mark. Your brother might just want to see how you're doing." She doubted it, though. The visit was unexpected and occurred just when Luca and Cathy were getting serious.

"Oh, Shayla." Luca's *tsk*ing made her turn to face him. "You have so much to learn about the world."

Her eyes widened. "Excuse me? This from the man who couldn't find North America on the map?"

"I can find it now, thanks to you. And I promise"—he held

his hand up as he pledged—"once Rafael leaves, I will be your best student."

Uh-huh. Right. For about a day, until another drama distracted him. "Promises, promises. Don't worry, Luca. I'm happy to help. And it's going to be fun."

"Fun?" Luca reared his head and stared at her incredulously. "My brother has handled delicate peace-treaty negotiations, and now I'm trying to pull one over on him. How is this going to be fun?"

Shayla shrugged. "I've never played the other woman before, and they always have more fun. All we need is the right outfit."

She was startled at the sharp knock on the front door. There was something imperious about the sound that alerted Shayla. "Are you expecting anyone?" she asked in a low voice.

Luca shook his head, his gaze never leaving the door. "Cathy agreed to keep clear."

He reluctantly walked to the door and looked in the peephole. Luca hurried back to Shayla. "It's Rafael," he whispered fiercely. "He's early!"

A wave of panic crashed through Shayla. "What are we going to do?" she squeaked out as Rafael knocked louder.

"You get it." He pointed at her.

"No, you get it. He's your brother," she reminded Luca in a hiss.

"He's your target."

There was another knock on the door.

Shayla pressed her hands on her cheeks, trying to come up with an idea. She wondered if the crown prince had done this on purpose. It was like he wanted to catch them off guard. Well, he was going to get more than he bargained for.

"Just a minute!" she called out. "I'm naked."

Luca looked like he was going to have an aneurysm on the

spot. His legs were frozen as Shayla pushed him into the bedroom. "Strip down to your underwear."

Those words snapped him out of his catatonic state. Horror flitted across his face. "Are you kidding me?"

"Do you want this to work?" she asked as she rushed to his closet and grabbed the first shirt she could find. "Once you get your clothes off, get into bed and roll around," she ordered as she turned her back on him and whipped off her shirt and bra. No need to shock him beyond all reason.

"You . . . what . . . I . . ." Luca sputtered.

"Just do as I say." She pulled his dress shirt on, thankful it hit midthigh. For once she was glad she was so short. She slid off her jeans and panties. "Try not to make a lot of noise. Muss up the hair and then stagger out of the bedroom like you've just woken up from a wild night."

"What . . . I . . ." Luca watched with incomprehension as Shayla whirled around, trying to button the shirt as quickly as possible, but his long sleeves were getting in the way. "What are you doing?"

"Making a first impression." She kicked her clothes under Luca's bed. "Wish me luck."

Shayla hurried to the door, her bare feet slapping against the wood floor as another impatient knock echoed through the apartment. "Hold your horses!"

Nervousness swamped her as she reached the door. She closed her eyes and pushed her wild hair back. She took a deep breath, opened her eyes and unlocked the bolt. She swung the door open and her breath snagged in her throat when she came face-to-face with Crown Prince Rafael of Tiazza.

The first coherent thought that came into her sluggish mind was *Whoa*. Rafael was tall and whipcord lean, but she sensed a restrained power lurking underneath the sculpted mus-

cles. The man possessed a sophistication that she couldn't begin
to imagine. His expensive dark gray shirt, black pants and black
shoes didn't have to clue her in on that. It was his commanding
presence and the way he immediately filled her senses.

He was nothing like Luca. There was a faint family resem-
blance, but Rafael wasn't classically good-looking. His features
were too sharp and weathered. His black hair was ruthlessly
short and nothing like the luxurious waves of his brother.

While Luca had the fun-loving boyish look down pat, Rafael looked like a fallen angel. It must have been the dark winged
brows or his brown eyes, which concealed more than they revealed. No, it was his full, unsmiling lips that made her want to
commit a few sins.

Shayla grabbed the doorknob as her world slowly shifted
sideways. She blinked as everything inside her went quiet. The
truth dropped with a boom. She felt the explosion ripping
through her stilled body with a ferocious speed. It took all of
her strength to remain standing, but she didn't fight against the
invasion. She accepted the truth.

This was the man she had been waiting for all her life.

And she was wearing nothing but his brother's shirt.

The man took a long look at her from her unvarnished toe-
nails to her wild mop of hair. Heat coiled deep in her pelvis, and
Shayla pressed her thighs together. She grabbed the oversized
collar of her shirt and pulled it closed. That was probably a bad
move as her tight nipples pressed against the thin material.

She wasn't sure what to do about the way Rafael looked at
her. It was almost as if he liked what he saw. Her pulse fluttered
with excitement.

No! Her wandering mind hit the brakes with a screech. He
wasn't supposed to like her. Damn.

Shayla leaned against the door, grateful for the support.

"Can I help you, honey?" she asked as she batted her eyelashes, feeling slightly out of control and not sure what to do next. "You look lost."

He seemed affronted at the possibility that he might have made a mistake. "I'm trying to locate my brother," he said, his deep voice making her toes curl. "His name is Luca—"

"You've come to the right place. Hold on." Her heart pounded in her chest as she tried to appear casual. Shayla called over her shoulder, "Luca, baby! Are you out of bed yet?"

She heard a muffled groan and pivoted on her bare foot. Luca hadn't quite followed her instructions. He stood at the bedroom door wearing a pair of unzipped jeans.

Luca also had the deer-caught-in-the-headlights look. Flustered and completely at a loss for words. Apparently Rafael had that effect on everyone he encountered.

Luca was so lucky she had watched every romantic movie and read lots of romance books. She knew how to handle every kind of guy from Scottish warriors to best male friends. She could manipulate an alpha male like Rafael. At least in theory. She'd never seen one up close and personal until now.

Shayla smiled at Luca as she silently willed him to come closer. "You didn't tell me your brother was as cute as you."

Luca whimpered.

Okay, so much for help from that corner. "You'll have to excuse him," she confided to Rafael, leaning dangerously close to the man. "He isn't much of a conversationalist when he first rolls out of bed."

Rafael showed no expression at that tidbit of information, but Shayla felt the temperature in the apartment cool.

"Luca." Rafael gave a curt nod to his little brother.

Luca crept closer, folding his arms tightly across his chest. "Rafe."

They turned and looked at Shayla. She knew this was her cue. She had to be the other woman.

What would Scarlett O'Hara do? She would make the conversation all about her. Shayla gritted her teeth and tried to channel the spoiled Southern heroine.

"Hi, I'm Shayla Pendley," Shayla said as she grabbed Rafael's hand. Her pulse gave a jolt when she touched him. She didn't know if he felt her reaction. His large hand closed over hers, and for a moment, she felt trapped.

"Nice to meet you," she continued in a rush, doing her best not to struggle out of his hold. "Rafe, is it?"

"Rafael," he corrected.

He released her hand, but her skin still tingled. "Please sit down," she offered, wishing Luca would jump in at any time. She gestured at the one chair that wasn't cluttered with books and dinnerware. "Would you like something to drink?"

"No, thank you." He looked around as if he were in danger of catching something.

She paused, channeling Scarlett once again.

She should flirt.

Her spine went rigid as she considered this and then chickened out. This man was way out of her league. Any attempt she made to be sexually attractive would only amuse him.

"Well, I'm sure the two of you have a lot to catch up on." She took a step back and then another. "I'll be in the shower."

Luca gave her a look. *Coward.*

Yeah, she probably was. She hurried into the bathroom, mindful of how little Luca's shirt covered. Her skin pricked with awareness until she locked the bathroom door behind her. Leaning heavily against the thick wood, she took a shuddering breath, grateful for the reprieve.

She made her shower last as long as possible. Even when the

water turned icy cold, she hesitated to get out. She reeked of Luca's shampoo and soap, but she didn't care.

It had been more important to her to get rid of all hair gunk and makeup. She needed to wipe away her failed attempts to look like a dangerous woman. She should have known she didn't have it in her. She was destined to be a man's good friend or, worse, invisible.

Wrapping a large fluffy towel around her, she belatedly remembered that her clothes were under Luca's bed. Shayla tiptoed to the bathroom door, held her breath and flattened her ear against the wood.

She didn't hear anything. No voices. Nothing. Luca must have taken his brother out. He was probably giving him the grand tour around campus like he had discussed.

It was a good plan to do it now. That would give them time to reassess and regroup. Shayla unlocked the door and strolled to the bedroom.

As she tucked the towel firmly between her small breasts, she heard a sound that made her stop in her tracks. Oh, crap. She was not alone.

"Miss Pendley?" Rafael said.

Heat flashed through her body. She slowly turned around and saw him rising from the sofa. "Please," she answered hoarsely as her blood raced through her veins. "Call me Shayla."

He gave a nod. "Shayla."

Ooh. She shivered at the sound of his voice. She liked how he said that. Made her feel all warm and—

"How much are you getting paid?"

CHAPTER THREE

"P-PAID?"

Rafe was quite impressed by Shayla's expression. She appeared stunned, her brown eyes wide with confusion. She acted like she didn't know what to do next.

She had the innocent look down pat. Her face was fresh and clean, and he saw a sprinkle of freckles along the bridge of her nose. Her long black hair fell past her slender shoulders in wet ropes.

He watched as a drop of water slithered along her collarbone before spilling down her cleavage and disappearing beneath the white towel. Desire rolled through him, and he curled his fingers into his palms, refraining from touching her.

Rafe had to give her credit. She was good. She looked vulnerable and defenseless. Young and unworldly. She changed her look like a chameleon, predicting what persona would work best for each man. Her strategy might have worked on Luca, but it wouldn't work on him.

Shayla carefully scanned the apartment and pulled her towel closer. "Where's Luca?"

The tighter she held the towel, the better he could see her curves. His hands itched as he imagined her breasts spilling out of the towel and into his hands. He blinked hard and tried to clear his mind.

What had she asked about? Luca. Rafe had realized his brother didn't want him alone with Shayla. That had made him even more determined to send Luca on an errand. "He went to get coffee."

She bit her bottom lip and slid a glance in the kitchen area. "There's coffee here."

His body seized up as he watched the edge of her teeth sink into her plush lips. "Not the kind I like."

Her eyebrows went up. She knew the coffee run was a ruse, but she was choosing not to say anything. She was smart to be cautious, but he needed to shake her up.

"This will give us a chance to talk," he said with a polite smile. He held his hands behind his back, doing his best not to intimidate her.

Shayla wasn't fooled by the body language. In fact, she took a step back. "Let me get dressed first."

He should let her. No, he should insist before he grabbed the edge of the towel and snapped it open. Her lack of clothes was distracting but he wanted to keep her off-balance. "We won't have that much time before Luca returns."

She watched him carefully, and he knew the alarm bells were going off in her head. "I don't have a problem with that," she said huskily.

He tilted his head and studied her. "Do you need him to watch over everything you say in front of me?"

Her expression hardened. "No."

"Then, please." He indicated for her to sit on the sofa.

Shayla marched over to the sofa and perched on the edge of the cushion. The move inched the towel high against her thighs, and Rafe swallowed hard.

Her skin looked soft and slick, and he wanted to glide his hand along the gentle curve. Shayla pressed her knees together while holding on to the towel with a death grip. Rafe wondered if that display of modesty was for his benefit.

"Once again," he said as he crossed his arms and glared down at her, "how much are you getting paid?"

She looked up at him from beneath her lashes. "Paid for what?"

"You tell me." If he was lucky, she'd slip up and give him more information. He could use a little luck since he was flying blind.

But he knew something was wrong with this setup. His brother never had any trouble getting women, but Shayla was different. Despite her appearance he sensed that she wasn't interested in someone like Luca.

Her eyelashes fluttered. "I don't understand your question."

Rafe didn't know how she did it. She distracted him with the shy lowering of her eyelashes. He knew she wasn't shy. She was playing him, and she did it well. Shayla's eyes hinted at all the sensual secrets she possessed. Any man would want to get closer and willingly be seduced.

Except for him, of course. He pulled his gaze from her eyes and stared at her lips. No, he couldn't look at her mouth. Rafe dragged his gaze to her forehead and decided to explain his position in small words.

"You haven't cashed in on your relationship with Luca yet. Most women would go for the quick and easy money. You're holding out for more. Either you're already in agreement with a tabloid—which I would have heard about—or someone hired you to seduce Luca."

Understanding dawned, followed quickly with relief. "You think that I'm some kind of a hooker?" Shayla tossed back her head and laughed, water flicking from her hair as delight filled her eyes.

Rafe liked her laugh. It was hearty and genuine, and to his surprise, it cracked the defensive wall built around him. He didn't want to like anything about her.

Maybe he wasn't as immune as he liked to think.

And why was she relieved that he thought she was a hooker? Wouldn't that offend most women? Rafe's eyes narrowed. Did she have something more nefarious in mind?

"Why would you think that?" Shayla asked, leaning back on the sofa. She acted like she was unaware of the towel inching down, exposing more of her breasts.

"You're not his usual type," he answered gruffly. He couldn't stop staring. His mouth went dry, and his lips tingled as he thought about licking a path down to her nipples.

"He has a type?" she asked, her guileless look ruined once she crossed her legs.

How could such a proper move be so provocative? His chest tightened, and as much as he tried not to look, he did. He couldn't decide if he was disappointed or relieved that she offered no tantalizing glimpses.

"Or," she continued, "does he usually select someone from your preapproved list?"

Rafe studied Shayla, wondering how she went from vulnerable and unsure to brash and confident. Didn't she know she was at a disadvantage? He knew she was up to something, but she wasn't crumbling. She fought back, wearing nothing but a sodden towel that outlined every delicious curve of her ultra-feminine body.

Rafe cleared his throat and tried to focus on his duty. He could focus on the matter at hand even if his skin was flushed and tight. "Luca knows what is expected of him and how he's supposed to conduct himself."

"He's at school," Shayla said, swaying her bare foot to a bouncing beat. "This is the time where you push your boundaries."

Rafe shook his head. "Not if you're a prince."

Shayla stretched her arm along the length of the sofa. The towel clung precariously against the tips of her breasts. He barely noticed how she leveled him with a smoldering look. "He can push all the boundaries he wants when he's with me."

Jealousy, raw and burning, flashed inside him before he could stop it. He pressed it down ruthlessly and tried to show he was unaffected by raising an arched eyebrow. "Because he's a prince?"

Her eyes glittered with anger. She leaned forward, her arms resting on her legs. "Because I have no boundaries."

The rosy areola of her breast peeked from underneath her towel. His muscles locked, his instincts primed to pounce, the blood roaring through his body as he waited for more.

What was he doing? He couldn't think about his brother's woman—a woman he didn't trust or know anything about. Shayla was his opponent, his adversary. He needed to remember that.

Rafe turned and walked toward the window. Every move hurt, but the pain cleared his head. He knew he was retreating, all because of a common girl who seemed to have an extraordinary hold on his senses.

"How did you meet Luca?" he asked as he peered out the

window. Unfortunately, there was nothing out there to distract him. Nothing could compete with the sexy siren who captured his senses and imagination.

"I met him here at school."

He cast a disbelieving look in her direction. She had to be around twenty-five years old. Or maybe her life experience gave her a more mature look. "You can't possibly be a student."

She continued to stare coldly at him. "Guess again."

He rested his back against the window frame and flicked his gaze over her. Any longer and she would clearly see the desire he was struggling to conceal. Shayla didn't flinch from his dismissing look.

"You're much older than most," he stated the obvious.

"I'm a graduate student," she said slowly, as if he were a toddler.

"So you don't share classes with Luca," he quickly pointed out. He would get her to trip up and confess her plan. "You found out who he was and sought him out, right?"

Her eyes gleamed and she pursed her lips, as if she were savoring the moment. "I'm his tutor."

"His . . ." The words blinked in his head like neon lights, but he couldn't take it in. Shayla was a *tutor*? What had this woman been teaching him?

A sly smile tugged at her lips. "In case you haven't noticed, his grades are way up this semester."

His mind clanged shut before his imagination went wild. He walked over to Shayla and towered over her. He wasn't above using his size to intimidate. "What do you want from my brother?"

She darted her tongue out and licked her lips. The move made Rafe clench his teeth, and he felt the muscle bunch in his cheek. "What does any woman want from a man?"

"Now is not a time to play games with me." Especially when every move she made had an averse effect on his breathing. "If you remove yourself from Luca's life immediately, I am willing to make it worth your while."

Her eyes went wide at the amount of money he suggested. One hundred thousand dollars sounded like a lot of money to her. She blinked and tried to recover, but it was too late. He saw her gut reaction. He was one step away from clinching the deal. This was going to be simpler than he'd thought, and he'd be back home by tomorrow night at the latest.

She let out a low whistle. "You can afford to give that much to little ol' me?" she drawled. "Just for doing nothing?"

She had done more than enough. "Do we have a deal?"

"Huh." She rubbed her chin with her fingers. He noticed they were long and elegant, and he wanted her to rub them all over *him*. "You guys are richer than I thought."

The daydream of her hands on his body fizzled. "Excuse me?" What kind of answer was that?

She coyly tilted her head and smiled sweetly. Her smile packed a punch and he held himself very still. "If I hold on longer," she said, "would you offer more?"

He felt his eyes widen until they burned. Was that how she negotiated? "This offer expires in one minute," he warned her, his voice lethally soft. "I suggest you take it."

Shayla waved off his threat with the casual swipe of her hand. "Hell, forget about being the prince's girlfriend. I'm going whole hog for the title."

A sense of impending doom swamped him. "Title?"

She jumped up from the couch. "*Princess*." The word rolled off her tongue with immense pleasure. "There's way more money in that than what you're offering."

Rafe stared at her. "Are you aware that you're speaking out loud? In front of me?"

"So?" She shrugged and made a quick grab for her towel as it became undone from the move. "Nothing you can do about it."

"I can keep my brother away from you."

"Oh, sure. Good luck on that," she said as she strutted toward the door. The roll of her hips mesmerized him. "Let's see who he's going to listen to: his big bully of a brother or the woman who rocks his world."

When she put it like that, it didn't sound good for him. He heard her unlock the door and followed her. "Where are you going? We're not finished."

"Yeah, we are." She opened the door with a flourish.

His jaw dropped as he stared at her. "You're going outside in nothing but a towel?"

"I've gone out in less," she bragged. "Like I said, Rafe, I have no boundaries."

She strolled out the door. Her towel caught on the handle, but Shayla kept going. The wet cloth slid down and revealed her graceful back and rounded ass.

Rafe grabbed the doorjamb, his knuckles whitening as his lust rolled to a full boil. He noticed Shayla didn't stumble or pause to cover herself. Clasping the towel against her chest, she gave her wet hair a good shake and kept walking.

CHAPTER FOUR

PRINCE SANTOS
West Coast of the USA

"THE ROYAL SUITE IS TO YOUR LEFT, MA'AM."

"Thank you." Kylee Dawes hid her smile as she exited the elevator. There was a definite bounce in her step as she headed for the hotel suite.

Ma'am. Kylee gave a small shake of her head. She couldn't believe the elderly and ever-so-proper elevator operator had called her that. It was official: her transformation was complete. No one recognized her in this elite Santa Barbara beach resort.

If anyone had, Mr. Jacobs would never have called her "ma'am." He would have used much more creative terms.

And with good cause, Kylee reluctantly admitted. She had been a hell-raiser. With no money and no supervision, she and her friends had found trouble everywhere they turned.

Those days were long gone. She had sworn one day she would return here as an honored guest. She hadn't quite reached that level, but she was close enough. Though Prince Santos's press office was footing her bill and the posh beach resort was not quite honored to have her there.

They would. Eventually. As an image consultant who specialized in crisis management, she was her best project. She was still amazed at how she had fallen into the industry. One moment she was helping her ex-boyfriend, who was a champion surfer in need of polishing his image. She didn't know why he listened to her since her reputation wasn't exactly spotless, but he had sensed her uncanny ability to zero in on what the sponsors and media wanted from him.

The next thing she knew, she was helping other surfers and bathing suit models. Today in a swanky Los Angeles office suite, she fielded calls from powerful Hollywood agents, frazzled record producers and the occasional royal household.

Kylee rang the bell located next to the ornate double doors. She rolled her shoulders back and tugged at the hem of her black business jacket. The nerves in her stomach fluttered wildly, and she held her briefcase in front of her legs, gripping the handle with both hands.

She wasn't sure why she felt anxious. Prince Santos's royal status didn't wow her. She didn't rub shoulders with queens and kings on a daily basis, but she had overseen media-crisis management for a few spoiled princesses. After that kind of insider look, she was so over anyone with a crown.

It must have been this assignment that made her jumpy. Transforming Prince Santos into a gentleman would be her finest achievement. She would improve his appearance, train him in how to deal with the media and teach him international protocol. If she was successful, she would become a legend in her field. She could pick and choose her assignments, name her price and live as luxuriously as her clientele.

The door swung open. Kylee blinked in surprise when she saw Prince Santos standing in front of her. She knew what he looked like, but this was the first time she got an eyeful up close. The man was tall and ripped with muscles.

Her gaze automatically focused on his bright red board

shorts—the only item of clothing he wore. They hung low, exposing his flat stomach and lean hips. She held her breath, waiting for the shorts to slip.

What was she thinking? This was her new client. Horrified as her pulse tripped and skittered, Kylee dragged her eyes back up to his impressive chest. His arms were sculpted muscle. The primitive tattoo on his deltoid snagged her attention.

She risked a glance at his face. His dark hair, streaked from the sun, fell down in waves, hitting his wide shoulders. She saw a glimmer of an earring.

Her eyes widened. How had she missed the earring? It looked like a freshwater pearl. She didn't care that it was gunmetal gray, flat and uneven—it was still an earring.

She could work with this, Kylee decided as she ignored the insistent tug deep in her belly. One problem at a time. She met the prince's curious gaze. His dark eyes twinkled and his mouth slanted into a smile.

Fake it until you make it, she reminded herself. She had always dealt with surprises and setbacks. Not any as nicely packaged as Prince Santos, but as long as she didn't let his charismatic smile distract her, she'd succeed.

"Hello, I'm Kylee Dawes," she said with a bright smile. She didn't offer her hand, and she was so glad she wasn't required to curtsy. Her shaky knees wouldn't have held up. "I'm your image consultant. May I come in?"

Not above using the element of surprise to take the upper hand in a meeting, Kylee slid past him. She tried not to touch him, but his body heat shimmered between them. She sucked in her stomach as she glided past, inhaling his scent. It was elemental and warm.

She felt herself melt a little and froze. So what if he had

smelled great and had good bones? Kylee quickly stepped away from him. His killer body would make her job easier when she stuffed him in a tux. His looks could be a blessing or a curse. It was all in how she worked it.

He was stunning, but the untamed quality of his appearance was why the paparazzi liked him just a little too much. She had read up on him before arriving at their carefully chosen meeting place, and there had been a lot to read. Most of the news items were slanted to show Santos as the royal rebel. The bad-boy prince.

But just how much was truth? Since she was his new image consultant, one of her tasks was finding that out. Then she had to hide it and spin it to make the new image work.

Of course, that required his cooperation. Rumor had it that he was not thrilled to work with her. That wasn't a surprise. Most of her clients viewed her like a monthlong stay at rehab. They realized too late that she was much tougher than any court-enforced medical treatment.

She heard Santos close the door behind her before he said, "You're not supposed to show up until this weekend."

His voice was deep and rough, with just a hint of an exotic accent. How would it sound in a whisper or making an indecent suggestion?

What was she thinking? Kylee winced and yanked herself out of her daydream, making her head spin. So what if she used to have a thing for surfers? Those days are over. This guy was a client. He was a prince.

"That's what I wanted you to think, but I've been here for a week," she said briskly. "I find it's helpful to study my assignment before we meet." And from what she saw, the man was wild and reckless.

"Like what you saw?"

His voice really had a mesmerizing effect on her. Kylee stiffened and met his hooded gaze. "Let's just say I took a lot of notes." She looked around the sitting room. It was elegant and hushed, so unlike the prince. "Where can I set up?"

He motioned at the table next to the window that overlooked a stunning view of the California beachfront. "What exactly does an image consultant do?"

"Think of me as your fairy godmother," she said as she set down her briefcase on the table and clicked open the latches. She knew she was using the briefcase as a shield, but until she got her imagination and her responses under control, it was the best she could do. "I'm the woman who has to turn you into Prince Charming."

"Prince Charming?" The term dragged out of his throat. "That wasn't the agreement."

"Check again," she said without missing a beat as she took out a stack of thick etiquette books. "By the time your embassy dinner comes around, you will be a perfect gentleman who looks like he was born to wear black tie."

"Don't be too sure about that."

"I can be, and do you know why?" She turned to him and rested her hands on her hips. "I am the best at what I do."

She was usually modest about her accomplishments, but Kylee instinctively knew that was the wrong tack when faced with a force of nature. She had to grab control from the beginning and never relinquish it.

"Uh-huh." The prince didn't sound too impressed by her claim. "Like I said, what exactly is it that you do?"

Energy buzzed through her. She was actually looking forward to this challenge. "Your Highness, my job is to tame you."

Tame me? This woman thinks she can tame me? Santos pressed his lips together to prevent himself from laughing. Kylee had no idea whom she was dealing with.

But whom was he really dealing with? Kylee was tall and had an athletic build, but she didn't look the type who would break into a sweat. Her short blond hair was tucked behind her ears, revealing big pearl earrings that matched the double strands at the base of her throat.

The mandarin-collared jacket was buttoned all the way to the top and fitted her like a glove. The skirt hugged her hips and thighs, reaching just to her knees. Her long legs were encased in silky tights.

He zoned out as Kylee gave him an overview of her plans. Santos noticed that she made such a point of covering up her body that he wondered what she was hiding. The subtle challenge of her protective layers intrigued him.

Santos watched her wide mouth and lively blue eyes as she talked. Her pale cheeks took on a hint of color. She became quite animated as she went on and on about the intense training he was going to receive.

He only agreed to do this because diplomacy was becoming a major part of survival for his island kingdom. Isla de la Perla had no armed forces but made up for it with natural resources. It was becoming increasingly important to have powerful friends. And as inviting and welcoming as his country was, diplomacy went hand in hand with rules and regulations. Something he had never been good with.

". . . like what you're wearing."

Santos caught the last of Kylee's words. He tilted his head. "What about what I'm wearing?"

"A prince should be overdressed." Her gaze went to his chest and slid down before she yanked it back to make eye contact. "It shows he respects the occasion."

"Even in bed?"

She arched an eyebrow. "Are you planning to have diplomatic exchanges in bed?"

Santos smiled slowly.

Kylee pressed her lips together, as if she was trying to hold back. "I don't think you're taking this seriously," she finally said.

"I think you're taking it seriously enough for the both of us." Santos knew what she was up to. She was trying to prove who was boss. How long was it going to take for her to realize it wasn't she?

The way he saw it, he had two choices. He could either take over right now or he could charm Kylee into getting his own way. The last time he had taken over an assignment, he managed to intimidate the project manager, and they almost failed to meet their deadline because of lack of communication. Basically the guy ran whenever he saw Santos. People normally took one look at him and assumed he was a muscle-bound threat.

Which just went to show he needed Kylee, whether he wanted her or not. But did she have to be so uptight? He gave her business suit another look. It was crisp and aggressive, just like her pointed high heels. All black, and designed to cover every inch of her.

Her outfit was beginning to bug him. "Aren't you hot?"

"No." She stood up straighter, if that were possible. The woman's posture made him feel like a slouch.

"You look hot," he decided. She needed to kick back and relax. Didn't she know this was a beach? She'd look great in a bikini, her arms stretching, those endless legs kicking as she tackled a wave.

She did a double-take. "I look . . ." Her voice trailed off. "You shouldn't make statements like that."

Was she kidding? "Says who?"

She motioned a manicured hand at the stack of books.

They looked thick and boring. He bet they had little print and lots of footnotes. "You've read all of them?"

"Of course."

"On purpose?" He grabbed the top book. It was worn and many of the pages were turned down.

"Excuse me?"

"Was it required reading?" He flipped through the pages, his eyes glazing over at the sight of the diagrams of table settings. "Some form of punishment?"

"Is this a roundabout way of asking how I got my credentials?"

"No, Kylee, I'm questioning your reading tastes." Damn, there were step-by-step pictures on how to wear a sash. What was with all the medals and ribbons? And was that a *bow*? He closed the book quickly.

"Your Highness . . ."

He had to get Kylee on his side. He'd do the white tie and the sash, but there was no way he was wearing bows. "Call me Santos."

She held her hand up to stop him. "Okay. Right there, that's two major breaches of protocol. First of all, no one but your family members should call you by your first name. And even then, behind closed doors."

"Give me a break," he muttered.

"And I did not give you permission to use my first name."

Santos gave her a look. He was never the one who asked for

permission. "You want me to call you Miss Dawes?" His voice sounded gruff.

She gave a sharp nod. "Yes, Your Highness."

"I don't think so." That would create a barrier. How was he going to sweet-talk her into his way of thinking by calling her Miss Dawes all the time?

She clasped her hands behind her back. "It's not up for discussion."

"Fine," he said with a shrug of his shoulders. He wasn't going to force the issue. Let her think she had won this round. Santos was getting the feeling that dealing with Kylee was a preliminary course in the fine art of diplomacy and negotiations.

He wasn't going to back down, though. She'd come around soon enough. He just had to keep at her like water on stone, and she'd wear down. But could he get that to happen before the embassy dinner?

Kylee seemed suspicious about his easy capitulation, but she wasn't going to push her luck. "Now about your clothes. Let's see what's in your closet." She looked around the spacious suite. "Which way is the bedroom?"

"Sorry." He put his hands on his hips. "Can't let you go in there."

Kylee blinked, temporarily distracted by his hands for some reason. "I beg your pardon?"

"Only people on a first-name basis with me are allowed in my bedroom," he teased.

She narrowed her eyes, and a cute little crease formed between her eyebrows. "Are you trying to be difficult?"

"No, it comes naturally," he said with a proud smile.

Kylee gave him a look that he thought only nannies and governesses perfected. She turned and headed in the direction of his bedroom.

"I believe this is a breach of protocol," he called after her.

She ignored him and entered his bedroom. Santos followed, more out of curiosity than concern. He walked in as she swung open his closet door. She gasped.

"Something wrong?"

She slowly turned around to face him, her eyes wide with disbelief. "You only have one jacket?"

"This is a resort. On a beach," he added, in case that point was completely lost on her. "You know, where people go on vacation."

She reached into the closet, grabbed the sleeve and clenched it in her hand. "One jacket? And it's not even for a suit."

Santos wasn't sure what the problem was. "I don't need a suit to get into the nightclubs."

She pressed her fingertips against her forehead, smoothing out the deepening crease between her eyebrows. "It's okay. I can work with this."

Her breathing grew ragged. Was she hyperventilating? "Are you feeling all right?"

Kylee didn't seem to hear him. "What am I saying? I'm not a magician." She let go of the offending jacket. "I can't work with this. We'll need to go shopping and get you more clothes."

Shopping? She was trying to break him down, wasn't she? "I have enough clothes."

"Are you kidding? I've been here for a week, and I have yet to see you fully dressed!"

He scratched his head. "You know, you're a very unusual woman."

She blew out a long breath. "Why do you say that?"

He smiled. "You're trying to add clothes onto me while most women want to take them off."

She pressed her lips together. "Your Highness, we need to go shopping." She closed his closet door with a decisive snap. "Immediately."

"There's no rush." He wanted to postpone the shopping indefinitely.

"There certainly is. Even the best tailors need time."

"Whoa. *Tailors?*"

She rolled her eyes. "I said 'tailors,'" she enunciated the word, "not 'tormentors.'"

"Same thing."

"I'll leave so you can get dressed," she offered as she looked at her tiny jeweled wristwatch. "You have five minutes."

"I'm good to go."

She gave his board shorts a sidelong glance. "You're not wearing that."

"I am." He found her bold statements and quick decisions intriguing. People were usually deferential around him. Kylee showed no signs of asking for his opinion.

"Once you're out of the resort, you need to be"—she motioned at his chest—"covered."

"Why?"

"Not only is it more appropriate—"

"I'm already hating that word." And he had a feeling he was going to hear it all the time.

"But there are photographers camped outside the gates. Every time they see you, they need another taste of your transformation. It makes the end results more believable."

Okay, she made a good point. "You're not going to pick out my outfit for me? I'm touched by your faith," he drawled.

"My only requirement is that I don't see any skin other than your face, neck and hands."

Ha. She was kidding, right? He saw the serious expression

and decided maybe not. Okay, two could play at this game. "Now, about my requirement . . ."

Her eyebrows skyrocketed. "Your requirement?"

"You can't go out looking like that." He mimicked the wave of her hand.

Her jaw shifted to one side. "There's nothing wrong with my outfit."

"It's not *appropriate* for this area." Hmm, maybe he was too hasty. It was kind of fun saying that word.

"Yes, it is."

"You don't look like you're here on vacation." In fact, she looked like she was on her way to a funeral, with all that black. He needed to fix that.

"Because I'm not," she reminded him. "This is not my idea of a vacation. I'm working."

"And if the media saw you—and they will spot you immediately if you're wearing that—they'll know that you're working on my image."

She paused and he knew he had got her on that.

"But I'm willing to negotiate," he continued magnanimously.

Her shoulders stiffened. "Negotiate?"

"For every item you take off, I'll put something on."

She scoffed at his suggestion. "I'm not agreeing to that."

He acted like he hadn't heard. "Ready, set, go."

CHAPTER FIVE

KYLEE DIDN'T MOVE. She was frozen on the spot. Did the prince expect her to strip? *In front of him?*

Her skin tingled and burned as if she had been plunged into boiling water. She made a grab for her collar and pressed it against her throat. Her clients often had unusual requests and demands, but this one took the cake. He was out of his mind if he thought she'd jump at the chance.

Hmm, maybe that wasn't a rare occurrence for someone like Prince Santos. Random women probably threw more than their clothes at him. Well, he was in for a rude awakening with her.

"No?" Prince Santos asked. He clapped his hands and gestured toward the door. "We're good to go?"

"Wait." Shoot! Where had that come from? The word popped out before she knew it.

Was she truly considering his terms? It was a bad move to give in so soon. To give in at all! Where had she lost control? Had she ever had it?

"I don't have anything to take off," she insisted.

His gaze lingered on her body, and she felt the heat coil low and tight in her belly. "I'm sure you'll think of something," he answered softly.

She tried a different tack. "You really can't go outside of the resort grounds looking like that."

"Watch me."

Her eyes narrowed at his attitude. "Then watch me standing right next to you. You know, I don't think I have enough clothes on. Maybe I should go find a coat."

"You do that. Don't forget your business cards. I'm sure the paparazzi would want those."

He had her there. She couldn't ignore that the tabloids would be much kinder to the prince's transformation if they didn't know the hard work that went behind it.

"Fine." She bit out the word as her body hummed with tension. She couldn't believe she was doing this. "A piece of clothing for a piece of clothing."

Santos leaned against the wall, his movement rippling with satisfaction. "Ladies first."

She looked down at her outfit. Each article of clothing was necessary. She had been particularly careful and restrained with her appearance today. A lot of good that had done her.

Kylee tucked her hair behind her ears and her fingers brushed against her earrings. Bingo! She quickly took them off and dropped them into her pocket.

"Your earrings? That's what you came up with?"

She wasn't going to defend her choice. "Your turn."

"Okay, what's a good exchange for earrings?" He opened the closet doors, stepped in and pulled open and closed the drawers. He was making such a racket that she stepped behind him and tried to look around to see what he was doing.

"I got it. I'll take your earrings for this."

She saw a flash of indigo blue, but didn't identify it until he covered his head with it. "A bandanna? No, no, no."

"I get to pick out my outfit, remember," he said as he tied it.

"That was before you decided to go with the pirate theme."

His smile had a rakish tilt, and it made her heart do a crazy flip. His appearance took on a dangerous edge. A woman could tell with one look that he would be an amazing adventure.

"Your turn," Santos said.

And pirates couldn't be trusted. She needed to remember that as well. They followed their own code, which could change at any given moment.

Kylee removed her double-strand pearl necklace.

Santos snatched a pair of sunglasses from a shelf and perched them on his aristocratic nose.

She struggled with the latch on her wristwatch and took it off with a flourish.

He put on a thin plastic bracelet. It was bright orange but something wasn't right about it.

She pointed at his wrist. "That is not an item of clothing."

"Yes, it is."

Kylee hooked her fingers around it, careful not to touch him, and gave it a sharp pull. It snapped back, but Santos didn't flinch.

"It's a rubber band," she said.

"That I'm *wearing*."

"C'mon!" She jutted her chin up and glared at him. She would have gone toe-to-toe with him, but she didn't trust herself. His scent alone was wreaking havoc on her senses. "You're not playing fair."

"Give me something more substantial."

"I just took off my watch!" She pointed at her bare wrist. "Believe me, that's substantial. I feel practically naked without it."

Her nipples tightened at the moment she said the word "naked." She immediately envisioned herself standing bare and proud of it in front of Prince Santos. This was a dangerous game she was playing, and she needed to pull back.

Santos was unmoved by her claims. "'Practically' being the operative word."

She took a step back. "Hey, at least I'm cooperating." She should have gotten bonus points for being a good sport.

"If you want me to wear something bigger, then you have to take off something bigger."

"You want something bigger? Then take this." Kylee unbuttoned her jacket, her moves sharp and fast. She shrugged the jacket off, revealing a white shell blouse.

"That's more like it." As she folded her jacket, Santos surveyed the clothes hanging and rubbed his hands. "I'll take your jacket and give you this."

He grabbed something cottony and white. Her throat felt tight and raw as he put it on. There was something subtly erotic about watching him get dressed.

It took her a moment to realize what he put on. "A tank top?" A *snug* tank top.

"What's wrong with it?"

She should have been happy. It was clean, and it covered most of his chest, which should have kept her distraction to a minimum. As a plus, the tank didn't have any cheesy or obscene pictures on it. Really, she should have been thrilled.

"Remember the rules?" she asked, staring at his shirt. The tank lovingly clung to every defined muscle. "No skin other than your face, neck or hands."

"Then give me something else."

"No." Everything else she wore was essential for a lady. They were her armor, and if she took off anything else, she would be vulnerable.

"Are you ready to go?" He made a move to leave.

She didn't budge, blocking his way out of the closet. "I'm not backing down on the rules."

"Then, as you Americans say, put your money where your mouth is." He did a double take and smiled widely. "Did you just growl at me, *Miss Dawes*?"

Had she? She clasped her hand on her throat. "No."

"You sure?" His eyes twinkled with amusement. "It sounded like a growl."

"Must be the air conditioner kicking on. Where were we? Oh, yes, you were going to add on another item of clothing."

Santos laughed. The deep sound gave her goose bumps. "Nice try," he said, watching her with a new appreciation. "It's your turn."

Damn, that should have worked. Okay, okay, she was going to get this guy to wear a jacket, pants and shoes. That meant she had to give up three things.

He crossed his arms. "I'm waiting."

"I'm thinking." She didn't have much more to give up. She kind of needed her shirt, skirt and shoes. "Oh, I know."

Kylee hiked up her skirt and reached underneath it. She shimmied and swayed her hips. She felt the prince's speculating gaze on her. "Almost got it," she promised.

She was stripping in front of a stranger. Her heart was lodged in her throat, her blood racing through her veins. She felt daring and scandalous. Alive.

Whoa. She didn't want to feel like this. She needed to rein

it in before it was too late. The last time she had felt this way, she lost control.

Kylee stood straight as her half slip slithered down her legs. She smiled triumphantly at Santos's confusion when the ivory silk pooled at her heels.

"No fair," he declared as she kicked her foot up and grabbed the silk.

"You didn't expect this? Are you telling me you don't know any woman who wears a slip?" Kylee asked as she laid it on top of her jacket. The moment she did that, she knew she had made a mistake. She should have placed it under her jacket. A lady wouldn't let a stranger see her slip.

He reached out and caught the delicate fabric between his finger and thumb. The sight of his big, rough hands on her lingerie did something to her. She pressed her thighs together hard, fighting off the pleasurable throb between her legs.

"Some of their evening gowns looked like this," he admitted.

"That doesn't surprise me."

He tilted his head and studied her skirt, as if he were trying to figure out what was underneath it. "How many layers do you have on?"

She swatted his hand away from her slip. "You should have asked that before you made up this stupid game. Now it's your turn to wear something."

"Fine, fine." He grabbed a chunky gray hoodie and put it on.

Kylee breathed a little easier. Santos was slowly but surely getting dressed. She was almost winning, but she was also running out of clothes.

"Done?" he asked.

She gnawed on her bottom lip. "Not quite."

She hiked up her skirt again, daring to scoot it up higher than before. Santos's rapt attention made her clumsy as she slowly dragged her panty hose down her legs.

Stepping out of her shoes, she struggled to take the panty hose off. Kylee grabbed Santos's arm before she lost her balance. Even under the thick hoodie, she could tell that he was solid and sinewy under her hand.

"Okay, your turn," she said as she stepped back into her high heels.

Santos reached for a high shelf and grabbed a shell necklace.

"Oh, please." Kylee sighed as she watched him put it around the strong column of his neck. "You were doing so well. All you need is jeans and shoes and we can go." And once he was fully covered, she could focus on the job at hand.

"I never agreed to those."

"Excuse me," she said with a touch of sarcasm. "Most people who care for their health wear shoes."

"Shoes aren't required where I'm from."

She should have thought about that. The guy lived on an island where there was nothing but sand. But that wasn't the case here. He needed to compromise.

After all, she had already made her compromise. She wasn't going to cave in again. She had to prove that she was not someone to mess with.

He put his hands on his hips. "Got anything else?"

The only things left were her bra and panties. She couldn't take those off in front of him. The pulsing intensified deep inside her. Her breath snagged in her throat. Could she? "Maybe."

"Maybe? You're maybe wearing more clothes? You don't know for sure?" He smiled. "You want me to check for you?"

She ignored that. Should she go for it? No. Taking off her underwear in front of her client on the first day was not a good idea. That was something the old Kylee would do.

Kylee smirked at the thought. The old Kylee would have taken off the panties right at the beginning. That was, if she had been wearing them. And, with little provocation, she would have stripped naked and streaked through the hotel lobby. Twice, just in case someone missed seeing her the first time around.

"Well?" the prince prompted her.

She had thought the old Kylee was long gone, but she felt the familiar naughty twinge. The need to do something outrageous flooded her veins, warming them.

Kylee briskly rubbed her bare arms, trying to get rid of the sensation. Maybe the transformation wasn't as complete as she had hoped for. She was close. Once she completed this assignment, she would have everything she had worked toward.

But first she had to bend Prince Santos to her will. If he didn't bend her first. She pursed her mouth at the thought.

"One more thing," she decided. She couldn't believe she was doing this. Kylee reached under skirt. Her hands shook as she tried to restrain herself. She was not going to whip off her clothes with a flourish. She absolutely refused.

Kylee hooked her thumbs under the waistband of her panties. Her heart pounded against her ribs as she hopped out of her panties, wishing she could have been more graceful while Santos watched.

Santos watched her tuck the scrap of ivory lace under her jacket. He made no comment, and Kylee couldn't decide if that was good or not.

She risked a glance at him. His cheeks were ruddy but his eyes were hidden behind the sunglasses. She couldn't tell what he was thinking. He was probably rethinking his strategy, not counting on her to go for it. He had no idea that she was just as surprised!

Right now she felt vulnerable. It didn't matter if anyone could see through her skirt. Her bare skin rubbed against the smooth lining. She was very aware that she wore nothing underneath. Prince Santos knew it, too.

Worse, he knew that she had done it for him! Her core felt slick and swollen. Did he know? Could he tell that she was turned on?

"Your turn." Her voice was hoarse and low.

She couldn't wait for him to get some shoes on so they could leave. She needed to get out of this closet. Out of this room, this hotel before she ripped off the clothes she had forced him to put on. She desperately needed to clear her head and keep her distance from Prince Santos.

"Right." He stepped into a flip-flop. Santos faced her and waited.

She looked at him, then at his bare foot. "Where's the other one?"

His smile was downright wicked. "I'll get it when you give me another piece of clothing."

"What?" She took a step back and bumped against the closet door. "No. That's not how it works."

Santos rested a shoulder against the shelves. "Guess again."

She thrust two fingers in front of his face. "I gave you two earrings for a bandanna."

He nodded. "And it was a bad trade on your side."

Kylee ground her molars and fought the urge to growl long and hard. "You're going to walk around with just one flip-flop?"

He lifted his foot and rolled his ankle as she studied the flip-flop. He put his foot down. "Sure, why not?"

"That's ridiculous."

"Then give me another piece of clothing."

He wanted her bra. Her breasts felt full and heavy. The fragile bra straps against her shoulders suddenly dug into her skin as her nipples puckered so tightly they stung. She felt them pressing against her bra. She wasn't going to look to see if they were visible against her blouse.

It's no big deal, she told herself. She would still wear her blouse. She had small breasts, and no one would know.

Ha. Right. A thin white blouse would reveal that she wasn't wearing a bra. She could only imagine what a photo lens from a high-powered camera would pick up.

Kylee glared at Santos. She should make him wear one shoe around town. She would love to see the captions the tabloids came up with. The way she was feeling right now, she'd volunteer to help the reporters brainstorm ideas.

She couldn't do that though. Prince Santos was her client, whether she liked it or not. She had made an agreement, and unlike pirates, she didn't change her code of honor at will.

Kylee reached back, yanking the hem of her blouse from her skirt. Maybe there was a way out of this. Perhaps she should give in and let Santos wear whatever he wanted. Just this once. Let *him* be the one walking around half naked. Not that it would bother him.

She felt Santos's eyes on her breasts. A sense of recklessness swept through her. Kylee arched her back to give him a better look. She wanted to preen under his attention.

For one brief moment she wanted to give him a show and do an impromptu striptease. Could she peel off her bra and give him a show to remember? Did she still have that in her?

Kylee's fingers brushed against the hooks at the center of her back and froze. Still have that in her? No, she had stamped that craziness out years ago. She would not give a show. She wouldn't repeat old Kylee's stunts.

Damn. Why was she feeling like her old self? She didn't know if it was being back at her old hangout or if it was Prince Santos. Neither was a good influence. The quicker she got out of there, the better.

She dropped her hands. "Forget it."

Santos shook his head, as if he were trying to clear it. "Forget what? The shoe?"

"No," she said as she hastily tucked in her blouse. "Forget the shopping."

"Seriously?" A hopeful note crept in his voice. "No new clothes?"

"I didn't say that." She wasn't going to let him have his way. "I'll call the shops and have them come around. Give me an hour, and I'll have a whole army of tailors in here."

Kylee grabbed her pile of clothes and walked away on shaky legs.

"Spoilsport," he called after her.

"Now, now, Your Highness," she chided as she left the room, "don't be a sore loser."

And if she didn't want to lose the life she fought to acquire, she needed to be very, very careful around that man.

CHAPTER SIX

PRINCE ZAIN
Deep in America's Heartland

THE LUXURY SEDAN PURRED to a stop. One of Zain's bodyguards leapt from the front passenger seat and scanned the area before he opened the rear car door. Zain tried to keep his expression blank as he reluctantly stepped onto the cracked sidewalk.

He looked around, wondering if his assistant had received the wrong directions. This was Main Street? There was no traffic. No people strolling around. He didn't expect it to be busy because it was late Sunday morning, but there should have been some sign of life.

He glanced up at the storefront where they stopped. *Renee's.* That was all it said. The sign was hand-painted and ultra bright against the dingy gray building. From the sweet yeasty aroma, he was going to guess it was a bakery.

He walked to the building, each step so slow it ached. He felt like he was heading toward the gallows. How had it all gone wrong? A trip to the middle of the cornfields was supposed to keep his bachelorhood safe. Instead, he was claiming his bride, whose name was Lauren Ballinger.

He didn't want to propose to her, but he saw no loophole that would set him free. Last night he had paced his penthouse suite at the hotel for hours before he fell asleep, exhausted. He had been furious with himself. He had known better than to tempt fate.

This morning he pushed his anger aside. Now he felt numb. If anything, he felt resigned. As a prince, he had to take action, even if it meant marrying a stranger. Personal sacrifice was not a foreign concept to royalty.

His bodyguard stepped into the bakery, and they were greeted by the high-pitched tinkling of a chime attached to the door. As the guard surveyed the small restaurant area for possible danger, Zain took the moment to breathe deeply and inhaled the scent of sugar and coffee. He noticed that the place was almost empty. Only one booth of women was crammed to capacity.

The women's laughter died down as they looked to see who had entered. Zain heard a feminine gasp. His attention was drawn to the table, his heart squeezing hard when he saw Lauren.

She looked different. Lauren was not the seductive siren who had tormented him in his dream last night. Her brown hair was pulled back in a braid, and she wore no makeup, with the exception of a swipe of lip gloss. Her long-sleeve blue blouse was buttoned all the way up to her graceful neck.

But her electric blue eyes still packed a punch. Need shot through Zain, hot and urgent. He struggled for his next breath, his chest tight, as he met her gaze.

"Can I help you?" one of the women from the booth asked.

He barely registered what the woman said or looked like. "I'm here for Lauren."

Three heads snapped and stared at Lauren, who was attempting to escape by sliding under the table.

She froze, her chin level with the chrome table. "Um, what are you doing here?" Lauren asked, her cheeks bright pink.

"Who is he?" the blonde at the table asked her.

He decided to enlighten them. "I am Prince Zain of Mataar."

"No. Way." The woman sitting next to Lauren hit her on the shoulder. "You really did meet a prince."

Lauren struggled back into her seat. "I told you I did."

"But you didn't have any proof."

"We can cross that one off the list."

Zain frowned. The women talked fast and over each other. He didn't understand what they were saying.

"Wait a second. Let's not be too hasty." The blonde held up her hands and turned to him. "What brings you here, Your Highness?"

It was bad enough he had to propose. He was not going to do it in front of an audience. "I have personal business with Miss Ballinger."

One of the other women's eyebrows went up at the word "personal." "Whatever you have to say to Lauren, you can say in front of us."

He directed a look at Lauren. She didn't look pleased as she tried to make eye contact with the woman. Or she was glaring. Either way, she didn't deny her friend's claim.

"And you are?" he asked in his haughtiest tone, but it seemed to slide right over their heads.

"We're Lauren's best friends. I'm Tanya and that is Stacy. And this is Renee, who owns the place."

"Would you like to sit down?" Renee jerked as if someone had kicked her under the table. "Can I get anything for you"— she looked around him at Zain's bodyguard—"or your friend?"

"No, thank you." He stood straight and clasped his hands behind his back. "I'm here to inform Lauren that she fulfilled a royal prophecy."

"Ooh . . ." her friends said in unison.

Lauren watched him with suspicion. "What did I do?"

As if she didn't know. "The night we met was my thirtieth birthday, and the woman who kisses the bachelor prince at midnight on his thirtieth birthday is destined to be his bride."

"His bride!" Stacy repeated in a whisper.

"Oh, my God," Renee shouted, "you hit the jackpot!"

"Damn." Tanya hit the table with her fist with such force that the cups and plates rattled. "I should have grabbed that piece of paper. I was thinking of doing it, you know."

Zain frowned at the buzzing conversation around him. Everyone but Lauren was talking. She stared at him, pale and slack-jawed.

Why was she acting surprised? Was it for his benefit or for her friends'? She must have known about the prophecy in order to have kissed him right at midnight. He had fallen for it, and now he was stuck with her.

Worse, he still wanted her. She wasn't dressed to tempt him, but he still felt the ache to taste those lips. He wanted to delve his tongue deep into her mouth. He couldn't believe that he wanted to kiss her again, when the first kiss had caught him in this mess.

Zain quickly masked the quick spurt of anger he felt and looked at his watch. "My assistant will help you with the paperwork and arrange with the move."

"Move?" That word jolted Lauren out of her stupor. "What are you talking about? Move where?"

"To my palace," he informed her, then turned so he could

leave. He had done what was required, and he wanted to escape.

"I don't think so." Her voice held an edge. "I'm not going anywhere."

He was already motioning to his bodyguard that he was ready to leave. "It's customary for a man and his wife to live together."

"I'm sure it is, but I'm not marrying you."

Had he heard her correctly? No, he couldn't have. Lauren was getting what many women would kill for. She was becoming a wealthy princess. Zain turned and frowned at her. "I beg your pardon?"

"I'm not marrying you," she repeated, enunciating every word with precision. She'd said it like she meant it.

"Yes, you are." She had to, or he would lose the only life he had ever known. "The prophecy has been fulfilled."

Lauren crossed her arms tightly across her chest, pulling his gaze to her pert breasts. He reluctantly dragged his eyes away and toward her face. She slid her chin to one side as her eyes glittered with defiance. "That doesn't mean I have to follow it."

He couldn't believe she had just said that. Didn't she understand the rules? It was useless to fight destiny. He had found that out when he tried to avoid having the prophecy fulfilled and unwittingly stepped right into it.

"I may have kissed you," she said with a shrug, "but that doesn't mean I have to marry you."

Zain blinked and stared at her. Maybe she hadn't known about the prophecy or, worse, she was changing her mind. But why would she do that when she made sure she had kissed him the very moment she needed to? "You would ignore what the stars say?"

"I do every day," she said with pride.

"But . . . but . . ." He was in trouble. He felt it descending down on him. The seers never saw this possibility. What was he supposed to do when the lucky woman said no?

Lauren's expression softened. "I'm sorry you had to come all this way to find me, but I'm not interested."

"Not interested?" Oh, she was interested. Maybe not in marriage, but she was interested in him. He felt the magnetic force of their attraction. No matter how much she tried to look away from him, she couldn't. He would almost have found it amusing if he wasn't suffering from the same need. He couldn't keep his eyes off her, and he didn't like it.

"Perhaps you don't understand," he said sharply. "I am Prince Zain of Mataar. My ancestors have ruled the desert for centuries."

"I'm aware that you're a prince."

And she didn't seem too impressed. If his status didn't mean anything, maybe his money would. "I own several multimillion-dollar companies."

"You're a millionaire?" Tanya perked up and raised her hand. "If Lauren doesn't want to get married, I'm available."

"Thanks for the offer," Zain replied gravely, "but because of the kiss, the only woman I can marry is Lauren."

"That's ridiculous," Lauren declared, appearing flustered. "If you knew about the prophecy, why did you kiss me?"

He wished he had an answer to that. "You kissed me."

She scoffed. "Well, you kissed me back."

"Enough." Stacy gave Zain a hard look. "The real question is, do you want to marry Lauren?"

Lauren found herself holding her breath as she waited for Zain's answer. She watched him closely as his eyes shuttered, showing no emotions.

Why did she care what the answer was? She was not going to marry this guy. She didn't know him, other than the fact that he was completely insane. What man offered marriage after a kiss?

But it had been quite a kiss. Lauren pressed her lips together as they tingled from the memory. She didn't believe in magic, but that kiss had almost made her a believer.

She didn't let the kiss last for long. His touch made her hungry for more. It made her want and crave—feelings she hadn't experienced in a long time.

If Prince Zain were any other guy, she would have done something about the longing that pulsed heavily inside her. She didn't have to be in love with a man to sleep with him. Hell, she didn't always wait until the third date. If she was interested in the guy, she took what was offered and enjoyed it guilt-free.

But Zain was different. She could tell right off that he was a playboy, and usually that didn't bother her. But he was a player on another level. He might have had plenty of women, but there were many, many more who had never gained his favor.

After all, the prince could have any woman he wanted, possibly more than one at the same time. Why did he have to settle for someone like her when he didn't have to?

Lauren watched Zain's face, and her gut twisted. It was obvious that he didn't want to marry her. He was blindly following a cockamamy prophecy.

"You don't have to answer that," she told Zain, trying to prevent hearing whatever doublespeak or excuse he came up with. "It doesn't matter because I'm not going to marry you."

She was kind of surprised that she didn't give his offer any consideration. After all, she didn't receive a marriage proposal from a prince every day.

And it was her rule of thumb to accept the first offer on the table—whether it was for a job or a date. She learned that there usually was nothing better out there. Hope and ambition were dangerous states of mind.

She was breaking all kinds of habits with Zain. She was suspicious of his offer, but it was more than that. She was scared of it, too.

"You don't understand," he replied. "There will be consequences if we don't follow through."

"Consequences? What is this? A prophecy or a chain letter? I don't believe in anything that threatens me with bad karma or a miserable future." Lauren scooted from the booth, deciding if he wasn't going to leave, she would. She stood up and smoothed her long, straight skirt. "I don't know why you're worried. No one knows that we kissed."

"My entourage saw us."

Well, that was a word she didn't hear very often. Lauren cast a glance at her friends. Their eyes widened as they mouthed "entourage."

"They knew about the prophecy. Everyone does, and it's written in the law. If I don't marry you, I have to renounce my place in the line of succession." He watched her, almost waiting for the comprehension to dawn. Zain failed to hide his impatience when she still didn't get it. "That means I would no longer be a prince."

"Oh. If you need to produce a bride, why don't you do a bait and switch?" Lauren offered. "Tanya would gladly step in."

"I would know."

Lauren could tell from his tone that she was stuck being the destined bride whether she liked it or not. "I'm sure you're a great guy, but I'm not interested in getting married."

"It's our destiny," he answered impatiently.

Destiny? What kind of answer was that? The guy might

have been hot and a great kisser, but he was deranged. "And that means we will automatically find happiness?"

The muscle in his cheek twitched. "I didn't say that."

Lauren felt obliged to point out the obvious. "We don't know each other." She didn't have to know his favorite color to have sex with him, but she had to know his dreams, values and expectations before she even considered marriage.

And she really had to stop thinking about having sex with him. She wasn't going near this guy. Some instinct of hers warned her that a night, a fling or even an affair wouldn't be enough. She bet Prince Zain was a tough act to follow.

Zain shrugged. "Many royal marriages have been made on less, and they have been successful."

She would really like to know what his definition of "successful" was. She read the glossy magazines and watched the celebrity television shows. Royal marriages weren't easy, and usually the princesses got the short end of the stick.

"We're obviously not compatible," she said tersely.

"I disagree. I know of at least one area where we are very compatible." His eyes gleamed as his gaze leisurely wandered from her head to her toes. Lauren felt a blush zooming up her neck and face.

"You know," Tanya said, raising her hand to butt in, "that could have been a fluke."

Zain frowned and pulled his attention away. "A fluke?" He tested the word on his tongue.

"You know, a onetime thing," Tanya explained with a flirty, hopeful smile. "You guys might have suffered instant attraction because it was predestined. Once the moment passed, all attraction fizzled."

Lauren didn't have to look at Zain to know that that wasn't true. The sexual awareness was zinging off them. She wasn't much for a guy in a suit, but it didn't matter. Her body was on full alert just by being near him.

"I don't think that's the case," she muttered to Tanya. She caught Zain's knowing smile. Great, he was going to use this to his advantage.

Usually men didn't have that kind of upper hand over her. She was in charge from the moment she decided she wanted a guy. She wouldn't say she was sexually dominant, but she never surrendered to a man in bed. Most of the time, they were underneath her, begging for more.

She'd like to see Prince Zain make a move on her. How convincing could he be? A shiver tripped down her spine. She needed to stop thinking that way. Any seductive techniques Zain used wouldn't change her mind.

"Lauren," Stacy warned as she watched them from the booth, "for all we know, Zain could have a harem of girlfriends back at home."

Lauren jerked away from Zain. Why hadn't she considered that possibility? And why did it bother her so much?

"I don't," he said tightly, as if he was not used to having his honor questioned. "I can supply"—he gave a sharp look at the women sitting down—"all of you with any references you require."

Lauren waited, but he didn't add anything to the offer. "You're not asking for mine," she prompted, then mentally kicked herself. She wasn't interested in marrying him, so why was she offering her references?

"Because he already had you fully investigated," Stacy said and shook her head, wondering why Lauren hadn't caught that.

"Already?" Lauren asked, and Zain nodded. "I see." She

looked away, feeling very vulnerable. Zain had probably read every "not working to her full potential" on her report card and every goal cut short. She had nothing to be ashamed of. She used to reach high and kept coming up short. Now she lived within her means and within her abilities.

"I realize that my proposal comes as something of a surprise," he said stiffly.

"You could say that." Lauren ignored the snorts and snickers in the booth next to her.

Zain leaned forward and murmured, "Perhaps you can tell me what is preventing you from accepting."

Lauren tried to think straight as the light scent of his cologne enveloped her. It went to her head, and she wanted more. She tried to focus on what he had said. "I'm waiting for the other shoe to drop."

Zain squinted, and the lines fanning his dark eyes deepened. "The other shoe?" He looked at his feet.

"What she means," Stacy decided to interpret, "is that your offer is too good to be true. There has to be a problem she can't see yet."

Zain kept his eyes on Lauren's. She felt pinned from his hot gaze when she knew she could walk away at any time. How could he exert this kind of power on her?

"I promise this proposal is exactly what it is," he said for her ears only.

She swallowed as her throat tightened. "So is my refusal." Why had it been difficult to say that? She meant it. She had refused him moments before. Was she weakening?

Zain took a step back and held up his hands. "Then I'm resigned to my fate."

His words startled her. "You give up?" Already? Disappointment crashed and reverberated in her chest. *Wow, way to go after a goal.*

Zain smiled, letting her know she hadn't seen anything yet. "I will stay here until you accept."

"Stay here? In town?" She shook her head when Zain nodded. She realized she had nothing to worry about. He was not going to survive a day around here.

The man's ancestry might be from the desert, but Zain was used to a cosmopolitan lifestyle. This small town didn't have a four-star hotel. They didn't have anything remotely like night life. He was not going to find the excitement or convenience he was probably used to. One day, two tops, and he would go stir-crazy. All she had to do was wait him out.

"This is great." Renee got up from her seat and put her arms around Lauren and Zain. She gave them a big squeeze that made the bodyguard flinch, but he held back. Zain appeared nonplussed by the overfriendly touch. "This will give you guys time to get to know each other."

"There's no point." Lauren disengaged herself from the group hug. "We're not getting married."

"There's no point because we will get married," Zain corrected her, "whether we know each other well enough or not."

Stacy shook her head and clucked her tongue. "Your Highness, that attitude is not the way to get to a woman's heart."

Lauren winced. Stacy might have been experienced and wise beyond her years, but she was no match for Prince Zain. With just one look at him, Lauren knew he had won and broken a trail of hearts.

"You're right," Zain admitted and looked at Lauren. She saw the sincerity in his eyes. "Miss Ballinger, if you marry me, you will be taken care of. You will have everything your heart desires."

She had to give him credit for trying again after several refusals. He was willing to try and try again. It still didn't change her answer.

It was a tempting offer. Once upon a time, she might have taken him up on it. But she was wiser now, and she had learned that if she wanted something, the only person she could rely on was herself.

"Thank you, but no," Lauren replied as she headed for the exit. "All I want is to be left alone."

CHAPTER SEVEN

ZAIN RUBBED THE SLEEP from his eyes and looked out the car window. The summer morning was bright and cheerful, but he didn't feel optimistic. His horoscope predicted that nothing would go his way today.

But he didn't have the luxury of waiting. Yesterday was a disaster and he had to regroup. If any more time elapsed, his campaign to win over his destined bride would never gain momentum.

As they passed Lauren's address, he studied the apartment buildings. They were small and nondescript. Yet his destined bride didn't jump at the opportunity to leave at the first chance and live in a palace. The more he found out about Lauren, the more she became a mystery.

His driver pulled into the back parking lot just as Lauren descended the steps, lugging a trash bag. The gentle sway of her hips and fluid movements made his cock stir. He wanted to feel her move against him and underneath him.

Her attire, however, muted the promise of sensual pleasures. Wearing khaki pants and a white polo shirt, she almost looked

RED-HOT AND ROYAL 75

like a boy. Zain frowned. Her femininity had taken his breath away and her androgynous appearance bothered him. He didn't like having her body hidden from his eyes.

When they got married, he would make sure she never wore pants—only dresses made of the most luxurious fabrics would skim her body. And no panty hose, he decided as he ached to touch her bare skin.

Lauren's pace slowed down as she watched his car pull to a stop. Her eyes narrowed with suspicion. When he stepped out, she made no attempt to hide her displeasure. She made a face and looked up at the sky, as if she were praying for patience.

Zain chose to ignore her reaction. "Good morning, Lauren."

"What are you doing here? Don't bother proposing to me again," she warned him as she walked faster to the Dumpster. "My answer is still no."

"I have no doubt," he said drily. "However, I was talking to your friends—"

She threw the bag in the Dumpster with force. Her shirt strained against her curves, offering Zain a tantalizing image of her body. His mouth went dry; his tongue felt too big for his mouth as the blood rushed from his head and pooled into his cock.

"You talked to my friends?" Lauren whirled around at him. "When was this?"

"After you walked out of the bakery. Didn't you find it odd that I didn't follow?"

"No, I found it a relief. Just because you're a prince doesn't mean you get diplomatic immunity from annoying me."

What had he done in his past life to deserve this? Were the fates having a good time at his expense by giving him a soul mate who didn't want to be anywhere near him?

He'd never had to work this hard to spend time with a lady. He usually had to employ tactics to get away from them. Women had been known to break trespassing laws, backstab sisters, and even cancel their own wedding to spend time with him.

Not that he would tell Lauren that. He got the feeling that his playboy image was one thing holding her back. He didn't blame her. He had no proof that he would make a good husband.

She looked at her watch. "I have to get to work, so whatever you have to say, say it fast."

Zain suppressed the wave of irritation that crashed through him. Usually people paused long enough to hear what he had to say. Lauren acted as if it was a waste of her time.

"Why don't I take you to work?" He gestured at his chauffeur-driven car. This way they could have uninterrupted time and talk in privacy.

She didn't look at his car. "No, thanks."

"I don't understand this," he admitted in a harsh tone. He was making all of the compromises, and he didn't like it one bit. "I offer you marriage, you refuse. I tell you I'm a prince and my net worth, and you don't care. You won't even take a ride."

"And you haven't caught on yet?" she asked as she headed for her white compact automobile.

But he knew she was not totally unaffected by him. "I remember how you kissed me. You got carried away."

Lauren looked over her shoulder. "I wasn't the only one," she said with a twinkle in her eye.

"You're morally opposed to my wealth?" He'd met a few women who'd said they were, until he showered them with gifts.

Lauren rested her arms on the top of her car. "Hey, don't get me wrong. I'm all for the good life. But I'm not accepting anything—not even a ride—from you. The last time I did, I had a royal prophecy thrown in my face."

He stood on the other side of her car. "That's what we need to talk about."

She shook her head as she unlocked her car. "I can't. I'm late."

"It's important."

The tone in his voice made her hesitate. Her mouth tugged to one side as she made a choice. "Then hop in."

He took a step back. "Your car?"

"That's right." She opened her door.

"You're driving?" Women didn't drive him around. They didn't take control of any part of their relationship. He always decided what they were going to do, and the women followed. This was unprecedented, and he didn't like it.

Lauren was about to sit down but stopped. "Do you have a problem with that?" she asked, an eyebrow rising in challenge.

It was probably best not to answer. "Let me inform my chauffeur about the change." He headed back to his car, realizing he had to compromise to ultimately win his bride. Compromise. He hadn't done that for a while, and it didn't sit well with him.

He returned to Lauren's car and wrestled with the door handle before it flew open. He sat down, and his knees went to his chin. Zain found the lever to the seat and slammed it all the way back. Now his knees were level to his chest.

"Nice car," he deadpanned, noticing the collection of CDs and discarded scratch-off lottery tickets.

"Thank you." She flashed a dazzling smile and he forgot to breathe. "It took me forever to scrape up the money but it's all mine."

He heard the pride in her voice. It was more than the car; it was how she had got it. Achieving something by hard work was very important to her. He needed to remember that.

She swerved out of the parking lot, narrowly missing the Dumpster. "Okay, Zain, why are you so determined to marry?"

"I'm not," he admitted. Telling the truth was probably not the best strategy, but Lauren needed to know that they both weren't eager to marry. "I came here to escape the prophecy."

"You went halfway around the world so you could remain single?" She shook her head and floored the gas pedal. "If I had only known . . ."

"Are you sure you didn't know about it?" Zain asked, secretly checking the restraint of his seat belt.

"You're accusing me of setting this up?"

"It seems too coincidental." He pointed at the red octagon whizzing by. "Uh, stop sign."

"What happened to your 'it's destiny' argument?"

He winced when she took her hands off the steering wheel to make air quotes. He wanted to grab the wheel and take over. "Some women make a point of being at the right place at the right time."

"Zain, in case you have forgotten, I refused your proposal."

"This time." Zain flinched and stamped his foot on the floor as if he had a brake pedal. "C-car! Car!"

"I see it."

But was she going to do anything about it? He exhaled shakily as she passed the car. "You know that you are the only one who can be my wife. Now you choose to make me chase you. What are you holding out for?"

"I don't believe this." Her voice rose. "That is not why I kissed you."

He leaned back on the headrest and studied her. "Why did you kiss me? Did you know who I was?"

"Well, yes." Her cheeks turned red and gave him an apologetic look. "I really am sorry that I kissed you."

"No, you're not." He glanced out the front window and decided he had looked too soon. He squeezed his eyes shut. "And can you keep your eyes on the road?"

"What's that supposed to mean?"

"So you can see the road and stay between the white lines."

"I meant about the kiss."

He gradually opened his eyes and studied her profile. He found her beauty exotic and stunning. "You liked it and you'd do it again," he said softly.

"What's your point?"

Her frank honesty aroused him quicker than any of the bedroom games he'd played in the past. What would it be like to take her to bed? Would she be this bold and forthright? Or would she make love the same way she drove a car—wild and out of control?

Zain swallowed a groan as his cock pressed against the confines of his clothes. He tried to remember his point. "You haven't tried again, and you're not the type to wait for me to make the first move."

She smiled. "True."

"But you haven't touched me. You were brazen on my birthday."

Lauren rolled her eyes and floored the gas pedal again. "That was different. And who knows what I'll be pledged to if I touch you again?"

"You are already pledged to me." He didn't try to mask the

warning in his voice. He didn't want her to get any other ideas. "There's no more need for the stars to interfere."

She gave him a sidelong look and made an abrupt turn onto a one-lane road nearly hidden by foliage. "I have not pledged myself to you."

"Yet." He closed his eyes and gripped the armrests as he heard the leaves and branches slap the car. "How much farther?"

"About five more minutes," she said with a shrug. "Let me ask you something. Why do you believe in what the stars say?"

"If you visited Mataar, you would understand. It's part of our heritage, our laws, and our daily life. Everything we do is based on superstition. The jewelry we wear wards off evil spirits. The food we eat or the way we build our houses will give us good fortune. Everyone from the beggars to the king consults with astrologers."

"Are they always right?"

"You don't believe in astrology or predicting the future. I get it. You're not the first person I've met who questions it."

"I used to be a very superstitious person," she admitted. "I was always reading my tarot cards, and I carried around a lucky rabbit's foot. Whenever I had the money, I had my fortune read."

"A rabbit's foot?" Disgusting. Then again, he'd worn some strange talismans to ward off the evil eye.

"While my friends in school would check their horoscopes for love and fashion, I wanted to know about my future career. I was going to be a dancer, but not just any dancer," she said with a touch of bitterness. "A prima ballerina."

Zain could see her in that role. She had the toned, lithe body. When she danced, she had been a mix of restraint and passion. He wanted her to dance like that with him, but naked, skin to skin. She would move against him, straining underneath him, driving them both to the edge of heaven and back. He longed for her brand of passion in his bed, and he would welcome it in their marriage and life.

"I had my first class when I was three years old, and there was no stopping me after that." She stamped on the brakes, and the car juddered to a stop at a traffic light. "I worked hard to become a dancer. If I wasn't in school, I was at the dance studio. I didn't have any social life. I didn't care about school. I was driven."

He knew she wasn't a dancer now, and she didn't do anything in the dance industry. According to the investigators, Lauren worked in a cubicle for an agricultural corporation. "Did they tell you to give up dancing?"

"No, the fortune-tellers told me what I wanted to hear: that my dancing was going to take me places"—her voice hitched but her expression was blank—"and put me on the world's stage."

"So what happened?" he asked quietly.

"Everything was going great until my senior year in high school when I got injured. While I was recuperating, I found out that I didn't get in the troupe I had my heart set on. It was a shock, because I was so sure I was going to get it."

"A minor setback."

"So I thought." She made a tight turn into an office parking lot, the tires squealing against the pavement. "Then I went to plan B. Then plan C. Long story short, I went through the alphabet, and the only place that wanted me was my dance studio. But they didn't want to pay me," she said with a humorless laugh. "They would give me a price cut on my tuition if I taught dancing."

"So you stopped?"

"No, I kept going, kept hoping, kept believing. I really thought that if I worked harder, my luck would change." She tapped the brakes and shoved the car into reverse. She threw an arm over his seat and looked in the rear window as she tried to squeeze her car into a tiny parking space. "Money was becoming a bigger problem, and then finally, when everything started to look promising, I reinjured my knee. That was that."

"And you gave up dancing for good?"

She turned her head and met his gaze. Her electric blue eyes dimmed with remembered pain. "Dancing gave up on me a long time before that. The surgery was the final blow."

"I see why you're against marrying because of a prophecy." She wasn't interested in marrying, and telling her it was foretold just made it worse.

"Glad to hear it." She shoved her car into PARK and ripped the keys from the ignition.

"Would you have kept dancing if all the fortune-telling told you to?"

She didn't look at him as she unlatched her seat belt. "Would you be proposing if some prophecy told you not to?"

No, he wouldn't, but he was reluctant to say it out loud, even though Lauren acted like she knew the answer. "That doesn't answer my question."

"I would have kept up with the dancing, as stupid as it sounds." She grabbed her purse and threw her door open. "I loved it, but I wouldn't have sacrificed so much. I really thought my destiny was calling and that I couldn't fail."

"I know what you mean." He didn't think he would have any problems acquiring his bride. It should have been a done deal.

"And that's why I didn't kiss you to become your bride," she told him as he cautiously unfolded from his seat and got out of the car. "If I had known, I would have run the other way."

"No, you wouldn't have."

"Okay," she said with a smile, "I would have waited for another time. You know, had you kept quiet about the proph-

ecy and given me a whirlwind courtship, I wouldn't have suspected a thing."

"Now you tell me." She would have trusted a whirlwind
courtship more. It certainly would have been more enjoyable.
If only he could go back and start again. Then again, why
couldn't he start now?

"So no hard feelings?" she asked as she locked her car and
walked around the hood.

"For what?"

She exhaled slowly and put her hands on her hips. "Zain,
haven't you been listening? I just explained why I can't marry you."

"No, you explained why you wouldn't accept my proposal."
He straightened his shirt cuffs and smoothed his silk tie. "Does
that mean you can't go on a date with me?"

She hesitated. Zain felt as if his heart were lodged in his
throat as the seconds ticked by.

"I shouldn't. I don't want to lead you on."

"You won't," he lied. Everything she did—the way she
moved, the way she looked at him, even the way she didn't look
at him—made him believe it was only a matter of time before
he won her over.

"A date? Nothing else?"

"We'll do whatever you want." He knew she wanted him;
he had felt it the moment they met. Was the feeling strong
enough for her to be with him, even though she knew he
wanted more? Or was he making a mistake, believing her interest was just as painfully strong and distracting as his.

"I might be able to," she said slowly, "as long as it doesn't
require any visits to the justice of the peace."

He almost pumped his fist in victory. He didn't make any
blatant moves, but he was certain his eyes blazed with triumph.

"It won't." He was going to be a courting gentleman even if it killed him. Zain reached for her hand, and his skin tingled the moment he touched her. He slowly raised her hand to his mouth and brushed his lips against her fingers.

Lauren pulled away just when he was going to gather her closer. She was able to read his body language before it had registered in his brain. It took a moment for him to gain his composure.

"I'll pick you up tonight," he said gruffly. No way was he getting into the car with her behind the steering wheel.

"Tonight?"

"And wear a dress," he said as he walked to his car, which was idling a few spaces away. If he was going to plan a whirl-wind courtship, it needed to be fast and fabulous and to knock her off her feet. By this time next week, she'd have his wedding ring on her finger.

CHAPTER EIGHT

CROWN PRINCE RAFAEL
East Coast of the USA

SHAYLA JUMPED WHEN her office door flew open and crashed against the wall. Luca stormed in, tension pinching his face. His eyes were wide, and his hair looked like it had been pulled in many directions.

He slapped his hands on her desk and leaned forward. "What did you say to my brother?"

She'd been waiting for this conversation since yesterday. She had to downplay what went wrong, or Luca would go ballistic. Shayla shrugged. "Not much," she said as casually as possible. "Just that I'm going to marry you."

Luca paled. "What?"

"And then I sort of"—she winced at the memory, her face flushing hot—"flashed him."

"Oh." He reached for a chair. "My." He sat down hard. "God."

Okay, her mistake was as bad as she thought. She was going to have to abandon any Scarlett O'Hara inspiration for being the "other woman." Anyway, Scarlett might lie, cheat, steal, or kill, but she would have drawn the line at walking home in a towel.

"The flashing was an accident," she insisted. She had wanted to make a quick grab for the towel and cover every inch of herself, so why hadn't she?

It wasn't because she was trying to stay in character. It was because she had felt Rafael's hot gaze on her. She had his full attention, and she wanted to revel in it.

For once, she hadn't been invisible or cast to the sidelines. She usually didn't care that she wasn't center stage. Only this time, the man she wanted was aware of her.

It had felt like her heart was going to pump right out of her ribs, and she didn't try to control it. Her hips had sashayed as she glided down the hall. Her skin had stung with awareness. She knew Rafe had watched her every move, and she had been half hoping that he would follow.

Luckily, he hadn't. She didn't know what she would have done. She'd like to think that she would have met the challenge in his eyes and rendered him senseless with her innate sensuality. Chances are she would have made a run for it and hidden until the coast was clear.

How was she going to act when she saw him next? She knew she had to get one thing out of the way. "I need to apologize to him."

"Why?" Luca asked, his voice buzzing with excitement. "It's going great. Now I can slide Cathy in, and he's going to think she's one hundred times better than you."

She didn't like that idea. It had been the plan, but that was before she met Rafael. She didn't know why she wished they had met differently. The prince wouldn't have noticed her otherwise.

"No offense," Luca quickly said when Shayla remained quiet, "but that's what we were hoping for. Wow, when you go after a goal, you just do it."

"No, Luca. I went too far." She leaned back in her chair and looked out the window, but the summer day was a blur. "If anything, he's really going to question your judgment in women."

"What do you mean?"

"It's like in those romances when the widower wants to find a mother for his children. Those guys always manage to pick a horrible woman. Someone who is high and mighty, rotten to the core and plans to throw the kids in the dungeon once she gets the wedding ring on."

"Okay, you've lost me. As usual."

Shayla turned to him. "And who cares if he comes to his senses just in time to realize that he really does love the homely but kind governess or maid? The guy can't be that great to make a mistake in the first place."

Luca gave her a blank look.

Shayla released an impatient breath. "Let me put it to you this way. If you've fallen for a blatant gold digger, they aren't going to trust your opinion about any woman. Your brother is going to yank you out of here so fast that you won't even have time to say good-bye to Cathy."

Luca bolted from his seat and tossed his hands up in the air. "Why didn't you say that in the first place? You've got to do something!"

"I'll do it right now." She reluctantly rose from her chair. "Where's your brother?"

"This morning he's getting the grand tour of Wolfskill from the chancellor."

"Poor Rafe," Shayla muttered. The head of the university liked meeting VIPs. His office walls were covered with pictures of him with visiting dignitaries. Since Wolfskill focused on international studies and was close to the nation's capital, the chancellor's walls were packed with photos.

"He should be almost finished by now," Luca predicted. "This place isn't that big."

Shayla smiled wryly at that statement. She had grown up around here, and the university was the biggest place she'd visited. It probably did seem tiny to a man who had traveled everywhere. The castle he lived in was probably bigger than the entire campus. "I'll go wait for him at the office."

"Dressed like that?"

She glanced down. Her purple T-shirt was faded and the college emblem was flaking off. Her cutoff jean shorts were snug but soft. "He's seen me half naked. I don't think it matters anymore."

She said good-bye to Luca before she walked to the administration office building. She waved at a few students sprawled on the manicured lawns, hiding from the heat of the day under shady trees. She'd been at this college for almost seven years and knew everyone.

She liked being from a small world. It was comfortable and she lived by its rhythm. Shayla knew she was different from her peers. While she studied about the world, the other students had seen it. Once they got their degrees, her classmates planned to go to far-flung places and put their knowledge into action. She wanted to stay here.

Shayla climbed the steps to the administration building and waited for Rafael by the door. A tall, lanky boy and a petite girl walked out of the building. They walked hand in hand, unaware of their surroundings. Shayla smiled, remembering she had just given advice to the girl on how to get her man.

She watched the couple cross the campus. Their walk was in sync, and the way they touched each other signaled a deepening intimacy. Shayla felt a pang in her chest and turned away.

What was wrong with her? She was glad her advice had worked. It was yet another sign that she should use her powers for good, not evil. Or maybe she should work in the background and let others take the risks.

Shayla heard Rafe's voice before he strode out of the building. Her mouth went dry at the sight of him. He wore a pearl gray suit that emphasized his dark complexion. She couldn't stop staring.

He was exotic and beautiful. And dangerous. His presence disrupted her quiet life. Rafael was like no man she had ever met before, but he'd had millions of women like her.

She forced her legs to move, and she approached him. Shayla wanted to be near him and, at the same time, stay far away. She hated the sensations boomeranging inside her.

"Shayla!" the chancellor's voice boomed. Shayla jerked to attention, her gaze whipping toward the older portly man. She hadn't even seen him. What was wrong with her?

"Sir." Her voice came out in a croak. She clasped her hands behind her back.

"Have you met the crown prince?" Before Shayla could answer, the head of the university made the introductions. "Shayla is Luca's tutor," he added.

Rafael held her gaze. "So I've heard."

Shayla was aware of the ice in his voice and fought the urge to hunch her shoulders.

"Shayla is doing a terrific job," the chancellor bragged. "She's one of our most brilliant students. She makes Wolfskill University proud."

Rafael's eyebrow rose in disbelief. "Does she?"

Her mouth twisted. Rafael wasn't prepared to believe anything good of her. She wasn't used to that and couldn't shake off the feeling. She'd been around the university long enough that she didn't have to prove herself. If someone accused her of gold digging, the students and faculty would fall down laughing.

"Did you know that her thesis is about Tiazza?" the older man continued. "She has quite a few ideas that might interest you."

Shayla winced. She wished the man hadn't mentioned that. That tidbit of information was like throwing gasoline on some flames.

Rafe's gaze grew speculative. "Is that right? I'm sure we have a lot to talk about. If you will excuse us . . . ?"

"It was good to see you, Your Highness," the chancellor said as he pumped Rafael's hand a few more times. "Please drop by my office anytime."

Rafe and Shayla waited silently until the chancellor stepped back into the building. Shayla found it difficult to look Rafe in the eye. She settled her gaze on his mouth.

"You're doing a thesis on my country?" he asked.

"It's not completed." She didn't want to discuss it with Rafe, and she definitely didn't want him to look at it.

Anyway, he wouldn't be able to. She was still polishing it. Over and over again. She was reluctant to turn it in, but she wasn't going to tell Rafael that!

"I can't imagine that's a coincidence," he drawled and folded his arms across his chest. "How long have you had your sights on my brother?"

She tried to drag her attention away from his mouth, but

found it impossible. It was as if she were hypnotized. "Your brother and I met because I had some questions during my research. When he needed a tutor, he requested me."

"I'm sure he did." She felt his gaze skimming down her body and her skin flushed.

Temper. She must control her temper. She darted her lips across her lips. "Your Highness," she began.

"'Your Highness'? What happened with 'honey'?"

Shayla gritted her teeth. "Which would you prefer?"

His mouth quirked. "Call me Rafael."

"Rafael . . ." She suddenly felt hot and frazzled, and rushed to finish what she had to say. "I'm sorry about what I said yesterday."

"Really?"

The way he said it made it clear he didn't believe a word. "None of it was true, but I said it in the heat of anger." She slowly dragged her gaze to meet his eyes. "I'm sorry."

"The money offer is no longer on the table."

She frowned, confused, until she remembered his offer. "I'm not interested in the money."

His eyes narrowed with suspicion. "What is it that you want?"

She wasn't sure where she wanted this to go, but she was willing to start small. "A truce."

His eyes were now slits. "Why?"

Because she was driven by a need for him to see the real her. But that would ruin everything. Rafe would immediately lose interest in the real her, and Luca needed a woman who was anything but the real her.

She bit her lower lip as she tried to come up with a reasonable explanation. "Because it's important to Luca."

Understanding dawned in Rafe's eyes, and Shayla's ribs clenched. Was she that transparent?

"You want to make it look like you can get along with his family," he said, "fit in."

She exhaled raggedly as the tension in her chest waned. "Do you ever get tired of being suspicious of everyone?"

"No. It has saved so much time."

"I said I was sorry. If you don't want to accept it, that's not my problem."

He tilted his head and studied her for a brief moment. "I believe we need to start over."

Was he accepting her offer? She couldn't believe it. "I agree. Clean slate."

"I invite you to dinner."

"Dinner?" Her eyes went wide. She suddenly had a vision of candlelight and roses . . .

"With Luca, of course."

The vision went haywire and her cheeks turned red. "Of course," she mumbled.

"And one or two other guests."

The capitulation seemed too sudden. Was he going to test her to see if she knew which fork to use? "I'll have to ask Luca if he's free," she said as she took a step away.

"You don't know?"

Damn, she had stepped into that one. She wasn't used to thinking like a girlfriend. She needed to leave now before she revealed too much. "I don't keep him on a leash," she said breezily as she started to walk away.

"I'm glad to hear it. But someone should keep you on one."

It was turning to dusk when Shayla arrived at the restaurant. She stood very still, trying to calm the butterflies in her stomach. She was supposed to fail spectacularly, so why was she so nervous? What could possibly go wrong?

Luca gave the keys to the car valet and stood beside her. He looked at the restaurant and sighed. "Cathy is going to be furious when she finds out we went here. It's her favorite."

"Oh, enough about Cathy." Shayla tugged at her floral-print dress. The hem was supposed to hit just above the knee, but maybe the designer's idea of "just above" was a lot different from hers.

"You don't understand," Luca said as he held the door open for Shayla. He leaned down and whispered in her ear. "I had to break our date for this."

"Believe me, I would switch places with her in a heartbeat," Shayla said with a forced smile. Her high heels were already hurting her feet.

"She's mad at me," he insisted as they walked through the elegant lobby. "She thinks I'm hiding her from my family."

"You are."

"No, I'm not." Hurt and something close to uncertainty tinged his voice. "I'm protecting her. I'm strategizing her introduction."

Shayla gave her skirt another firm tug. "I'm sure if you thrust her into the spotlight, Cathy would do just fine."

Luca looked at Shayla like she was talking crazy. "But that will destroy everything we've worked for."

"I don't care."

"Okay, what's with the attitude?"

One of the spaghetti straps slid over her shoulder. Shayla sighed and hoisted it back up again. "I hate this dress."

"It's . . . uh . . ."

She looked down and wished she hadn't. Her breasts pressed against the silk fabric, threatening to spill over. The dress was supposed to skim her body, but it hugged her hips. She had to hike the skirt up high if she wanted to sit down.

She didn't remember the dress feeling like this when she had bought it a couple years ago. Unfortunately, she hadn't worn it since, waiting for the perfect opportunity.

This night was not it.

She clenched her evening bag in her hands so she didn't pull at her dress again. "It's too tight," she muttered.

"Yeah," he said flatly, staring at her cleavage, "I noticed that."

She hit his arm with her purse. "Shut up. You aren't doing anything for my confidence."

"You're going to be great," Luca assured her, placing her hand on his arm as he escorted her to the restaurant. "Rafe will burst a blood vessel when he sees you."

She didn't want that. Yes, she wanted Rafe to keel over, but with lust, not horror.

"So how are we going to play this?" he asked softly.

Shayla decided to tell him the truth. "I don't know."

He jerked his head. "You don't know?"

She shrugged and froze, realizing this was not the kind of dress to move her shoulders in. "I was thinking Julia Roberts in *Pretty Woman*. You know, the scene where the escargot flies in the air."

"Yeah, I saw that movie."

"I bet your brother has, too." She couldn't do anything that reminded him of a popular film. That would make him very suspicious. "So I think I'm going to have to wing it."

Luca's arm stiffened under her hand. "Wing it?"

"Shayla. Luca." Rafael suddenly stood in front of them. "I'm glad to see you. I wasn't sure if you would make it."

"Sorry we're late, Rafe," Luca said.

"My fault." Shayla quickly took the blame as she snuggled closer to Luca. Luca almost flinched, but Rafe didn't seem to notice. His eyes were focused on her.

"We're just about to start dinner." Rafe's voice was rough and low, but he showed no expression as he guided them to the private dining room.

Shayla stepped across the threshold and stumbled to a halt. Hadn't Rafael said one or two guests? Try *nine* other guests. Dread spiraled deep inside her when she recognized the men and women seated at the table. Wealthy and influential, they featured regularly in newsmagazines.

She risked a glance at Rafael and found him watching her. His arrogant smile triggered something inside her. It was hot and angry.

She should have known. He had not accepted the truce, and this was no friendly dinner. He was throwing her into the lion's den. His goal was to show Luca how inappropriate she was for his station in life.

Shayla glared at him. Rafael had no idea who he was dealing with. She wasn't just going to survive this dinner; she was going to have every one of these guests eating out of her hands.

"Miss Pendley?"

Shayla snapped out of her thoughts as she heard Rafael's voice. She realized one of the waiters was behind her, prepared to seat her. The chair was close to Rafael and on the other end of the table from Luca.

She met Rafael's eyes. They glittered with a challenge and she smiled in return. *Bring it on.*

CHAPTER NINE

PRINCE SANTOS
West Coast of the USA

"HEY, KYLEE."

Kylee rubbed the crease between her eyebrows. Kylee, again. Why did he insist on calling her by her first name? She suspected it was to drive her crazy. He was doing a pretty good job of it.

She noticed he didn't call anyone else by their first name. He spoke to the hotel staff with respect. Friendly but never overfamiliar. And he always used their full names.

"Yo, Miz Dawes," he said louder.

Good enough. Even if he gave a wicked flip to her name that went straight to her knees. "Yes, Your Highness?" she asked, not looking up from her papers.

"You know what we should do?"

She tensed at the question and stopped sorting through her papers. She had no idea what he was going to say, but she knew she would probably have to shoot it down.

Prince Santos was an exhausting student. He was smart, but easily bored. It was difficult to keep him on topic, and he prowled around the suite like a wild animal.

"What is that?" Kylee braced herself before turning to face him. Santos was pacing around the suite like a caged animal. He tried not to complain, but she could tell he hated being indoors.

Her gaze zeroed in on his chest. Every muscle, every rib was clearly delineated in his sun-bronzed chest. Her hands tingled as she imagined running them along every hard plane and compact muscle. She bunched her fist and accidentally crumpled the paper in her hand.

Kylee winced and smoothed out the paper. She wished he would button up his shirt. She complained about his inattentiveness, but she was just as distracted. She'd had male clients who were considered much more handsome than Santos, but they hadn't made her pulse skyrocket every time she looked at them.

Santos was sinfully sexy, from his wicked smile to his casual attitude. He always looked like he had just rolled out of bed, and a part of her wouldn't mind dragging him back there.

Kylee snuck a look at him. At least he was learning how to dress fully. If faded, distressed jeans, an unbuttoned shirt and no shoes were considered full attire.

It was a step in the right direction, she decided. A baby step, when she needed to make giant leaps. And from what she knew of Santos, he would wander off the path at the first opportunity.

Santos strode toward her and was suddenly in her personal space, crowding her. Kylee fought the urge to step back. She needed to stand her ground. Appear immovable.

"We should head to the beach," Santos announced.

She found herself staring at his chest. She looked up, inhaling his scent. It made her think of hot summer, and it went straight to her head. "You were already at the beach early this morning."

"So? Let's take the lessons out there." Santos cupped her elbow and faced her toward the door. "I think much better outside."

She dug her heels into the thick carpet. She had thought giving him an outlet for all that energy would tire him out. No such luck. "That's going to be helpful when you're at a garden party, but most events will be held indoors."

"Come on, Kylee." He gave her elbow a squeeze. "You can't like being cooped up."

"I'm fine," she said as she shrugged off his touch. The guy was very touchy-feely without being aware of it. "In fact, I prefer it."

Santos rubbed his unshaven jaw. The sound of his hand against the stubble gave her a peculiar quiver in her stomach. She could imagine how it would feel if his chin grazed against her cheek . . . her neck . . . her breasts . . .

"You know," he said, dispelling her thoughts, "it's strange. I don't think I've seen you outside the whole time we've been here."

"I sunburn easily." The lie rolled off her tongue.

Santos's gaze leisurely took in her pale complexion. Heat flashed through her. He couldn't see much underneath her mannish white shirt and black pencil skirt, but the way he was looking at her made her feel exposed.

"We'll go when the sun sets," he offered.

She shook her head as the beginning of panic bubbled inside her. "I don't like the beach."

Santos's mouth dropped as his eyes widened. For once, he was speechless, and she was going to make the most of this rare moment.

"Now can we get back to these military titles?" She waved the papers under his nose. "You need to memorize them."

"You don't like the beach?" The words came out slowly, as if he had difficulty comprehending the idea.

"That's what I said."

He splayed his arms out wide. "How can anyone not like the beach?"

"It happens."

Santos shook his head. "We need to take care of this."

Kylee almost rolled her eyes. "You make it sound like a mental disorder. Believe it or not, Your Highness, I have been living quite well without setting foot on sand."

The truth was that she was hesitant to return to her old haunts. The only way she had managed a complete transformation was by avoiding beaches, pools and oceans. She no longer swam, even for exercise.

She didn't miss the sand and surf anymore. There were moments when she felt stressed or crowded and envisioned lying on the beach, but she wasn't going to act on it.

Santos's face darkened. "Are you expecting me to give up the beach?" he asked coldly.

"Of course not."

"Sure about that?" He folded his arms across his chest. "I'm spending less and less time in the ocean."

"You're undergoing an intensive training course."

His eyes narrowed. "Most of my board shorts are missing. So are my flip-flops."

Damn, she was kind of hoping he hadn't caught on. She struggled to keep an innocent expression. "If you had a valet . . ."

"I'm not kidding, Kylee." His voice held a hint of steel. "If this image consulting means giving up who I am, we can call it quits right now."

Kylee gulped. She had never seen him this serious. He

wasn't smiling, and she saw the storm brewing in his brown eyes.

Worse, he had every reason to be suspicious. She was using the same techniques she had used on herself. The only way she had become a refined lady was by turning her back on everything that made her a beach bunny.

She was going to have to change tactics with Santos. Gradually, so he didn't realize what her original plan had been. She might even have to—dare she think it?—adapt.

She could do this. Kylee rubbed the crease between her eyes again. It meant just concentrating on the basics. It went against her need for total immersion and her pursuit of excellence, but there was no way she would lose this primo assignment.

"If you felt closed in," Kylee said, "you should have said so when I gave you the schedule."

"You gave me a schedule?"

She rubbed her forehead harder. "I'll tell you what. Here's the test I made on political and military titles. If you ace this, you can go to the beach right now."

Santos snatched the paper and slapped it on the table. He grabbed a nearby pen. Hunched over, he scrawled his answers in bold, decisive strokes. Within minutes he dropped the pen and handed the test back to her.

Kylee glanced at the answers and blinked. She studied them more closely. He had got every one of the answers right. And all this time she thought that he hadn't been listening, that her explanations had been going in one ear and out the other.

She looked at him, but he wasn't waiting to hear if he passed or not. He knew he did. "You're coming, too."

Alarm tripped through her veins. "I didn't agree to that." She saw the determination in his face, but he was going to have to get used to it. She knew she was risking her most prestigious job all because she had an aversion to sand. It didn't make sense, but her transformation had been slow and painful. She wasn't going to test it.

"Kylee," he said with a smile, pouring on the charm, "how are you going to understand me if you don't see me in my element?"

"No one else is going to see you in that element at the embassy dinner."

"Okay, okay." He held up his hands. "Let's negotiate."

"Forget it."

He braced his legs and folded his arms across his chest. "Why?"

"I don't trust you."

He didn't seem concerned by that. In fact, his eyes twinkled. "I'm not the one sneaking around stealing flip-flops."

She wasn't going to get sidetracked. "I'm not going to the beach."

"You know you want to," he cajoled.

"No, I don't," she said with force.

The crinkles fanning the edge of his eyes deepened with concern. "The ocean scares you?"

"No." The ocean had been her playground. But even if she lied, she didn't think it would have gotten her out of the excursion. She could read Santos's body language. He would protect her, be with her every step of the way. It was kind of sweet in a way.

"Can you swim?"

"Yes." Like a fish. Or she used to. She didn't know how much she had lost or forgotten. She didn't want to find out.

He tossed his hands up. "Then what are you afraid of?"

"Nothing." Except of what might happen to her. Would she discard her clothes and everything she worked for to plunge into the water warmed by the sun? Or would she stand on the sand, feeling foreign and uncomfortable over a stretch of beach she had once ruled?

"Oh, I get it." He playfully slapped his palm on the side of his head. "You don't have the appropriate outfit."

Her lips twitched as she hid a smile. She couldn't show any signs of softening. "As a matter of fact, I don't."

"That doesn't surprise me."

"I don't even own a swimsuit," she added.

"Whoa. Now that's just crazy talk. We need to work on that right away." He placed his hand on the small of her back and escorted her to the door.

"We're too busy working on you," she said in a soft voice, all too aware of his large hand inches away from her bottom.

"All you need is a sarong. How long could that take?"

A sarong? She stumbled. He wanted her to wear a skimpy sarong on the beach? He was really pushing it. And somehow she could picture it. Standing in front of the water, the waves lapping at her bare feet. The tropical breeze rolling over her as the sun kissed her skin. A pang hit her hard. She really missed those simple pleasures.

"Let's go visit the boutique," Santos said as he opened the door leading to the hallway. "I get to pick."

Kylee flattened her hand on the door and pushed it closed. "I'll tell you what. I'll buy the sarong after you visit the barber."

"Barber?"

"You get your hair cut. And I'm talking short, not a trim," she clarified, "and I'll meet you on the beach in a sarong."

"I'm not getting my hair cut."

"It's on the schedule."

He speared his fingers in the soft black waves of his hair, as indecision flitted in his eyes. "You go on the beach and I'll go to the barber."

She shook her head. "Nice try. I've learned my lesson from you with the flip-flop."

"Which I still can't find."

She ignored that and opened the door. "If you want me on the beach, you know what to do."

"Throw you over my shoulder and run to the waves?"

Her breath snagged in her throat. He wouldn't . . . would he? The look in his eyes suggested he'd considered it.

And, really, how hard would she fight? Not very. He could never know that. "Have fun at the beach," she said with feigned breeziness as she stepped into the hallway.

Santos leaned against the door. "You don't know what you're missing."

Kylee looked away abruptly. "Yes, I do."

Santos frowned at his reflection in the mirror. The barbershop in the resort was as quiet as a morgue and probably just as sterile. He couldn't believe that he was there, or that he had given up a chance to catch some waves to do this.

He glared at the plastic burgundy cape that surrounded him. Kylee would be so thrilled to see him fully covered.

"How short do you want it? This short?" the barber asked. The elderly man had stooped shoulders and smelled of antiseptic. The lenses in his eyeglasses were so thick, Santos wondered about the man's vision and accuracy.

"Shorter." He wasn't going to let Kylee wiggle out of this deal.

"This short?" The barber held his hand up higher. Santos noticed a visible tremor in the man's hand.

He should ask the barber to shave it all off. Santos smiled, imagining Kylee's reaction. Maybe he should get a Mohawk, or have a design shaved in his hair. It was tempting, but he was going to play by the rules. He wanted to see Kylee on the beach, and he wasn't going to squander this opportunity.

"Are you sure, Your Highness?"

He nodded and watched the barber take the electric razor to his hair. He felt nothing—no anxiety or loss when the first hank fell to the ground. He used to be very defiant about his hair, probably because his mother had always clucked over the length. Rafe and Zain teased him about it all the time. It was no big deal. It should grow out fast.

And he would get to see Kylee in nothing but an itsy-bitsy piece of cloth. Santos cast a quick look at the boutique bag he had brought in. His gut clenched with anticipation, knowing he had picked the perfect sarong for Kylee.

How had that woman gotten under his skin so fast? She was not his type. She was too uptight and proper. Didn't like to get messy or ruffled. She didn't like the beach!

So why did he like her so much? It was more than the fact that he found her a challenge. Santos smiled as the hair fell around him. He wanted her out of those clothes. She might want to tame him, but he wanted to untame her. He was sure he could reach his goal first.

He was not usually this competitive. But when he was around Kylee, he was pushing the limits. Constantly trying to gain her attention, distract her and make her smile.

He had never worked so hard for a smile, but every time she did, he felt the same when he tackled the elements. Powerful. Conquering. Alive.

"There you go, Your Highness."

Santos blinked. The buzz cut was a shock, but it was just what he asked for. Short. Kylee can't back out now. "Perfect."

He stood up from the chair and paused when he saw all the

hair around the chair. It was as if a lion had been shorn of his mane. Santos rubbed his bare neck with his hand.

Was he being tamed? The question invaded his wandering thoughts as he generously tipped the barber. He was making changes at the speed of light, Santos admitted as he headed to the lobby. Becoming the Prince Charming of Kylee's imagination.

And Prince Charming was a wuss.

Santos frowned. He should have gone with throwing her over his shoulder and heading toward the beach. He could have done it easily, but he wanted Kylee to come to him. She would surrender, as long as he didn't run out of time.

Santos stepped into the open-air lobby and looked around. He saw Kylee by one of the exits that overlooked the beach, as if she expected him to emerge from the ocean. She tapped her toe impatiently and looked at her watch. Obviously, she didn't appreciate his cryptic message to meet her there.

Santos retrieved the fire-engine red sarong from the plastic bag and walked behind her. He dangled the bold material in front of her. "Here's your sarong," he said as she jumped in surprise.

"Your Highness, I am not—" She whirled around and stopped. Her eyes widened.

"A deal is a deal," he reminded her.

"Your hair." She reached out to touch his skull. Her fingers brushed against the bristly hair before she yanked them back.

"You don't like it?" He ducked his head and scratched the back of his neck. He should have gone for the Mohawk.

"You look . . . great." She dropped her hand and stared at him. "No, really. You look wonderful."

"And so will you." He waved the red fabric in front of her.

Kylee clenched her teeth and exhaled sharply. "Fine." She snatched the sarong from his fingers. "But you realize this is a onetime deal."

Not if he could help it. "After an afternoon on the beach, you won't be able to stay away."

"Don't bet on it."

CHAPTER TEN

CROWN PRINCE RAFAEL
East Coast of the USA

RAFAEL STOOD IN the doorway of Shayla's office and watched her tutor his brother. She patiently summarized a book, but her lilting voice made him hang on to her every word. Rafe ground his teeth to ward off the heat rushing through him. Shayla Pendley was more dangerous than he gave her credit for.

He knew that after the dinner. It had gone against his grain to make her uncomfortable, but he had to protect his brother. Rafe had expected her to be very, very careful. He thought she would trip up. It should have shown her what she could expect if she were in a relationship with a prince.

But Rafael hadn't expected that she would shine in this situation. That she could employ diplomacy and a hint of glamour, or that she could gain the support of everyone at the table. It had been a triumph, and there had been nothing he could do about it but stand back and watch in awe.

He knew he had to learn everything he could about Shayla. As much as he wanted to say it was for his brother's protection, Rafe reluctantly admitted to himself that Shayla intrigued him. She was no ordinary woman. He couldn't figure her out, and he needed to. Fast.

He had his assistants digging up what they could, but he'd rather watch her in action. Although she didn't have to move for him to take notice. She could lie on the couch, sprawled as if she had no energy, and lob one pointed question after another to his brother.

She was giving Luca quite an inquisition. There was no tenderness, no intimate gestures or loving glances. In fact, they sat far away with no awareness shimmering between them.

"Come on, Shayla." Luca's familiar whine grated on Rafe's nerves. "I'm sick of this. Let's move on."

Strange. Rafe's eyebrows went up. If he hadn't seen Shayla in Luca's apartment, he wouldn't have thought they were lovers. They didn't sound like a couple. When it came to education, Shayla was all business. And his brother was doing his best to get out of it.

"Fine," Shayla told Luca. "Let's move onto intellectual history. The great minds of the twentieth century."

Luca made a face. "On second thought . . ."

What was she doing with his brother? All week Rafe kept coming back to that question. None of it made sense.

Rafe understood why his brother found Shayla fascinating. She was an older, more experienced woman. She was funny, forthright and demanding. Sexy as hell, too. Shayla only had to smile at him and he got hard. He had been aroused to the edge of pain when she had worn that tight dress to dinner.

He barely controlled his body's response, and he hated the hold Shayla had on him. She belonged to his brother, and he shouldn't look at her. Think or dream of her . . .

But why was Shayla with Luca? Rafe studied her profile, his chest tightening, but he couldn't come up with a satisfying answer. It had to be more than Luca's royal status. She could have anyone she wanted. Why pick Luca? He was not her equal. She was far more superior when it came to discipline, responsibility and intelligence.

Rafe was surprised by the disloyal thought. His brother was his primary concern. But Luca was in way over his head when it came to Shayla.

Rafe, on the other hand, wouldn't mind testing his luck with her. It was too bad his brother had found her first.

"Rafael."

He gave a start when he heard Shayla's voice. How did she know he was there? She wasn't even looking in his direction.

"Yes?" His voice sounded rough, and he cleared his throat.

"Don't you have something better to do? Like look after a country?"

He stepped into the office. "I thought I would drop by and watch the tutoring in session."

She raised her head and looked at him. "Not quite what you expected, huh?"

"Less intimate"—he emphasized the last word and watched her frown—"and more strenuous than I imagined."

Her eyes narrowed. "I don't think I want to know what you imagined."

Luca tilted his head and looked past Rafael and into the hallway. He jumped up from his chair. "I'll be right back."

"Don't worry," Shayla called after him. "We won't continue without you." She looked up when Rafe stood in front of the couch. "He's always finding a way out of tutoring."

It sounded like Luca. "And you have no way of luring him back in?"

She pursed her mouth and thought better of whatever she was going to say. "You can go after him if you want," she offered.

"No, thanks." Rafe studied her. Shayla wore no makeup,

and her hair fanned around her head. His heart gave a sudden sharp twist.

"What?" She brushed her hand against her nose. "Do I have something on my face?"

"I've read your work."

That got a reaction out of her. She propped herself up on her elbows. "What work?"

He had planned to keep it secret. He didn't want her to know how far he had gone to check up on her. "Your entrance essays. Your term papers."

She scrunched up her nose. "Fascinating stuff, I'm sure."

"Your thesis," he added.

"What!" She sat up abruptly. "It's not finished. That's just a rough draft."

"So you keep saying."

She rose from the couch, standing toe-to-toe with him. "How did you get your hands on it?"

He smiled. "I asked."

Her mouth fell open. "And they just gave it to you?"

"Your professors are very proud of the excerpts they had." And they had every reason to be. Shayla was one surprise after another. "And since it has to do with my country—"

"I don't believe this."

"It's good, actually."

She made a face. "Which means you agree with it."

He smiled. "Most of it." Shayla viewed the world the same way he did. That should have given him pause, but in a strange way, it comforted him.

"I am going to have a talk with my professors," Shayla said, shaking her head. "They can't let random people read my stuff."

That was a new one. He'd never been accused of being random. "I find it strange that you've done all this research about Tiazza, but haven't visited."

"There's nothing strange about that. It deals with two different schools of thought," Shayla explained. "One believes that a person must be fully immersed in the subject matter to understand it completely. The other school of thought believes a person must stay apart from the subject matter for the sake of impartiality."

"So you have no personal interest in my country or culture?"

Shayla paused as if she sensed a trap. "My research is academic," she answered slowly. "My relationship with your brother is personal. Anything else?"

"What got you interested in Tiazza in the first place?" She had to be passionate about the topic if she was going to spend that much time and energy to research it.

"Oh." She couldn't hide her surprise by his question. She shrugged and looked away. "I don't remember."

"Now, Shayla, I'm sure you do."

She snapped her fingers. "Oh, yeah. I was flipping through a teen magazine and saw this really *cute* picture of you guys." She fanned herself and gave a high-pitched sigh. "I tore it out and taped it to my bedroom wall. I swore that I was going to hook up with one of you."

"Right." Her exaggerated look of adoration was playing havoc on his senses. It made him feel strong and invincible. And she was just playing around. How would he feel if she looked at him like that for real?

"I don't have the picture anymore." She pouted. "All those lipstick kisses messed it up."

He silently waited for the truth. He didn't move or look away. His gaze rested on her lips. He wondered if they were as soft as they looked.

She looked up at him. "Cross my heart."

He slid his hands in his pockets and rocked back on his feet. "I can wait a long time for the real reason."

She sighed. Her reluctance really piqued his interest. For a moment he thought she wouldn't answer.

"I liked the fairy tales," she muttered.

"Excuse me? Did you say the fairy tales?" Was she telling the truth or was this another diversion?

"I found them at a very impressionable age." She wrapped her arms around her waist. "I liked them. The women took action. They had power."

"They got the prince," he was compelled to point out.

Shayla rolled her eyes. "You need a refresher course, Rafael. The *prince* got *her*. Those women were smart, resourceful and always saved the day."

"So?"

"They weren't considered worthy because they were pretty," she answered softly. "Their skills didn't rely on being feminine and having the inclination to break into song."

He tilted his head and studied her expression. She really meant what she said. "Every time I think I know what makes you tick, you manage to prove me wrong."

"That's not surprising. I have a tendency to drive men crazy." She suddenly looked away and a wild blush scorched her cheeks. "Give up while you're ahead."

"Why?" he asked softly. "It might be worth the ride."

He was close enough to kiss her. All he had to do was dip his head and brush her mouth with his. He wanted to get closer.

The need ripped through him. He couldn't remember a time when he had burned so hot and so fast for a woman.

What was he doing? He took a step back. This was his brother's woman.

"Well . . ." Shayla brushed her hair back, her moves lacking her usual grace. She took a nervous breath. "It looks like Luca has escaped again. If you see him on your way out, let him know he's in big trouble."

Luca? Rafe had almost kissed her and she thought of Luca? "Are you trying to get rid of me?"

"Yes."

"Don't worry. I'll be gone soon." He needed to before he lost control and claimed Luca's woman as his own.

"How long are you staying?"

"As long as necessary." He watched her eyes widen. Had she taken his answer as a threat or a challenge? He wasn't sure anymore.

Rafe strode out of the office, his steps measured and careful. What was he doing? He was not going to figure her out by getting closer. He should follow her example. Understand the subject matter by staying away as far as possible.

He took the stairs two steps at a time. Luca was on the ground floor talking to a pretty young girl. The way he leaned in on the woman, with his hands flattened against the wall, trapping her in, it looked like Luca was flirting.

"Luca"—Rafe's voice was almost a bark—"Shayla is waiting for you."

Luca jumped away guiltily from the girl. "Oh. Right. Okay."

His brother's reaction made him pause. Was there more than flirting going on here? Anger sparked inside him. What was Luca doing trying his luck with another woman when he had Shayla?

"Gotta go," he told the girl. "I'll see you around."

A look of hurt flitted across the young woman's face. Rafe felt there was an unspoken exchange between the two.

"Aren't you going to introduce me?" Rafe asked. He didn't know why he was pushing it. His instinct flared at the underlying sense of trouble.

"Oh, uh, yeah." Luca gestured toward the woman. "This is . . . this is . . ."

"Cathy," the woman said, with more than a hint of defiance. She gave Rafe a firm handshake. "And I know who you are. Luca speaks about you all the time."

"Is that right?" Rafe slid a look at Luca, who had not mentioned Cathy at all. Now that Rafe thought about it, he had not seen Cathy around for a week, yet Luca spoke to her *all the time*.

"Well, I hate to rush . . ." Luca took a few steps back, ready to dash away.

"Luca, I want to talk to you," Rafe said.

Luca froze. Cathy even seemed to sense the serious nature of the upcoming discussion. "I should go, too," she said as she hugged her books close to her chest. "It was great to finally meet you."

Rafe inclined his head and noticed yet another unspoken exchange between Luca and Cathy. He refrained from saying anything until the woman left.

"Can this wait?" Luca pleaded. "I have to see Shayla."

"It's about Shayla."

Luca thrust his chin out. "What about her? I know she doesn't have the same background—"

Rafe decided to cut right to the chase. "I was wrong about her."

"Wrong?" Luca blinked. He squeezed his eyes tight and opened them wide. "About Shayla?"

"Not entirely," Rafe was quick to add. "She needs work with decorum and dress, but she's proving to be a good asset for you."

God, it hurt to say that. It was true, but his instinct was to challenge Luca for Shayla. Reason won over. Barely. Luca would never forgive him if he stole her away.

"What are you saying?" Luca asked.

"I didn't approve of her in the beginning. After all, first impressions count."

"Absolutely." Luca nodded his head vigorously.

"But I'm warming up to the idea of her."

Luca stopped in midnod. "You are?"

"Of course, I haven't done a background check," he admitted. He desperately wished there was some secret that Luca couldn't handle, leaving Shayla free and clear. "And she will need some training before you can introduce her to our parents."

"Our parents?" Luca's voice cracked. "You're already talking about meeting the parents?"

"There's no need to worry. Shayla will charm them." Rafe heard the clock chime and glanced at his watch. "I need to go for a teleconference. We'll discuss this later."

"Yeah," Luca said, his voice trailing off. "Can't wait."

"What have you done?" Luca asked the moment he entered Shayla's office.

"Me?" Shayla frowned at him. "I'm not the one running out on you every time your brother shows up."

Luca put his hands together as if in prayer and pleaded. "Just tell me, word for word, what you said to him."

"Forget it." She sat down on the couch. "Why? What did he say?"

"He likes you."

"Likes me?" Hope fizzed in her veins. "Likes me how?"

"He hasn't given you his stamp of approval, but he wants you to start some sort of training before you meet my parents."

"Oh . . . what?" Shayla felt off-balance and fuzzy. She curled her legs tightly against her. She hadn't expected this. "Is this some kind of joke?"

Luca scoffed at the possibility. "Rafe doesn't joke about the parents."

"Right." She stared at Luca. "This is bad."

Okay, not necessarily bad. How could it be bad that the guy she wanted approved of her? That he was interested to read her thesis, let alone liked it? That he wanted her to meet his parents?

For his *brother*. The hope fizzled. She couldn't forget that detail. *For his brother.*

"He met Cathy."

Shayla perked up at that bit of news. It meant her role in this game would be over soon. "That's great."

"Not really." His shoulders sagged. "It was hardly a meeting. More of an encounter. Rafe's first impression of Cathy should have blown him away. That didn't happen. He barely saw her, because he was waiting for her to leave so he could tell me how much he approved of you."

"We can salvage this."

"How?" For a moment Luca appeared defeated. "You were supposed to make Cathy look good. Now she's nonexistent."

"Not for long," Shayla promised. "I need to slide down the approval rating. Let's brainstorm." She leaned forward and spoke in a confidential tone. "I need to do something fast that will give me permanent disapproval. What can I do?"

"Commit a crime."

This was the first thing off the top of his head? "I'd rather not have a record, thank you."

"Go into rehab."

"No."

His eyes lit up. "Naked photos of yourself splashed on the Internet."

"Never going to happen." And she was beginning to worry at how Luca's mind worked.

"You could always have another lover."

"That has possibilities." She juggled the pros and cons of the idea and couldn't see any great risk. "Where can I find one on this short notice? He would have to be convincing."

"Does it really matter?"

"Of course! I'm risking the slam dunk of catching a prince. He has to be a better catch in a gold digger's eyes. Who can I get to pretend?" She tried to remember who was enrolled during the summer program. "There aren't that many guys here."

"And we need someone fast," Luca reminded her.

"Is there anyone ranked higher than a prince? What's better than a prince?"

"A crown prince."

That was a level up the royalty food chain. "Know of any?"

"Yeah." Luca straightened his spine. "My brother."

Rafael? She gasped at the idea, her skin going hot and cold as her stomach did flips. Luca was suggesting she make a move on Rafael? Shayla waved her hands, warding off that idea. "Forget it."

"No, think about it." His eyes glowed with eagerness. "We won't even have to manufacture and plant proof."

"I—I . . ." She paused and tried again. "I can't. He's not going to be seduced. Not by someone like me."

"He doesn't have to be seduced," Luca said. "He wouldn't let it go that far. Rafe won't touch you because he thinks you're my girlfriend."

She wasn't sure if she liked that idea. She wanted Rafael, but she knew she couldn't control him. Except in this circumstance.

A hot sensation swirled inside her chest. She could be seductive and tease him, driving him wild and calling all the shots. "So I can throw myself at him and he won't catch me." Shayla smiled. "Now that I can do."

CHAPTER ELEVEN

PRINCE SANTOS
West Coast of the USA

SANTOS SCANNED THE BEACH, reining in his impatience. He squinted in the fading sunlight and gave up waiting for Kylee. It was time to hunt her down and carry her to the beach. A deal was a deal, after all.

He shouldn't have let Kylee go back to her hotel room. That had been his first mistake. So what if she wanted privacy to change? He had put on his black board shorts and been waiting for almost a half hour. Obviously it had given her enough opportunity to hide.

Santos sighed as he trudged through the sand, heading back to the hotel. He didn't know why he was pushing this. Some of it was because he wanted her to understand where he was coming from. The island life defined him, and she was wasting her time trying to change it.

What he really wanted was for her to decide there was no need to change or hide his real nature. Sure, he wasn't as sophisticated as his friends, but that didn't mean he was a barbarian.

Except when he was around Kylee. The more she tried to restrain him, the more he wanted to break free. He couldn't help it. Didn't want to.

Santos veered toward the sidewalk, ignoring the appreciative glances and comments from the bikini-clad women trying to catch some sun, not to mention his attention. The only woman he was interested in seeing was Kylee.

He frowned when he thought he saw Kylee's face pop around the small man-made grotto that separated the hotel structure with the beach. She disappeared before he could call her over.

He ran over to where he had spotted her and found her by the small waterfall. Her head was bent, and she was muttering to herself as she fiddled with her huge sunglasses.

He skidded to a halt. The red sarong was expertly tied high on her hips, exposing her long, slender legs. The fabric covered just enough to flare his imagination. What did she have on underneath? Would he get close enough to find out?

She had paired the sarong with a white cotton camisole. It made him think of those shipwreck adventure stories he used to read as a boy. Kylee reminded him of someone who desperately clung to her civilized exterior as the savageness of the island slowly peeled away the layers of decorum.

Santos's gaze lingered on her navel, which was peeking out from the camisole. Heat flooded his body as he licked his lips. He wouldn't mind getting deserted on an island with her.

What was he thinking? She'd vote him off the first chance she got. Santos cleared his throat. "It's about time."

She jerked her head up. "Sorry. It took me a while to come up with a shirt." She tugged at one of the straps on her camisole.

"Why are you hanging around here? The sand is this way." He thumbed in the direction of the beach.

She still seemed hesitant and was about to turn in the other direction. He couldn't see what she was thinking, thanks to the sunglasses. He needed to stop her before she came up with an excuse.

"Come on." He grabbed her hand, and was surprised when she didn't resist. He liked the feel of her small hand in his. It was solid and comfortable, but his veins were popping and fizzing with some undefined emotion.

Santos guided her onto the beach and heard Kylee hiss between her teeth. She rose on her tiptoes as they walked on the hot sand. "You aren't wearing shoes? Ms. Dawes," he said mockingly, "that is so inappropriate."

"I don't have any shoes for the beach."

"You need flip-flops."

"I don't think so," she said as she hopped from one foot to the other. "If they aren't proper for a visit to the White House, they aren't in my closet."

"Riiight. And how many times have you been invited there?"

She tilted her chin up. "It's never too early to be prepared."

He swung her up in his arms, and she shrieked. Kylee kicked her legs as he held her close. She clawed his shoulders as he strode across the beach.

She glared at him. "Do not drop me in the ocean."

"I wouldn't dream of it." He tried not to laugh, but only Kylee would take an authoritative stand when he could easily dangle her over the waves.

His gaze drifted to her white camisole, and he wondered how she would look drenched. The shirt would be transparent and plastered to her skin. His cock leapt as he imagined it.

"Here you go." And not a moment too soon. He slowly let her down, her stomach and breasts sliding against his chest. He felt her tense when her hip bumped against his cock.

She hurriedly looked at the large beach umbrella anchored in the sand. Two canvas chairs were tucked under the shade it offered, as well as a stack of fluffy towels.

Kylee grabbed the top towel and threw it on the sand. She stood on it and gave a sigh of relief. "That's better."

"The sand isn't that hot," he insisted. But maybe it was unbearable for someone who only walked on carpeting and sidewalks. He grabbed a bottle of sunblock nestled next to one of the chairs.

She shoved her sunglasses on top of her head. "Oh, I don't need that."

"Yes, you do." He had never seen pale skin like hers. Sometimes he could see blue veins just underneath the surface. It would show any mark from the sun or, say, his mouth instantly.

He stared at the curve of her neck, imagining how sweet it would taste. He shook the bottle with more vigor than he intended and squirted a big blob of cream in his hands.

She reached for the bottle. "I can do it."

"I'm sure you can." He held on to her wrist and slathered the cream on her arm. "But I can do it better."

He stroked his hand up and down her arm. Her skin was silky smooth against his rough palm. His hand looked dark and huge against her pale arm. Santos found the contrast of their skin mesmerizing.

He glided the lotion over her shoulder, narrowly missing the strap. He rubbed the cream in small concentric circles until it disappeared, all the while wishing for the strap to sag and fall.

Santos silently squirted more sunblock in his hand and smoothed it along her collarbone. His hand stilled when he felt her pulse jump frantically against her skin. He rubbed his fingertip harder against the spot, the throb as strong and primitive as the one in his chest.

Kylee turned and stepped slightly away from his touch. Santos cupped her nape, and she dipped her head, blocking him.

He dropped the bottle onto the sand between them and reached for the back of her head. Threading his fingers through her short blond hair, he tilted her face back, exposing her neck for his touch.

He met her wide-eyed gaze as he stroked her neck. His hand, coated with lotion, slid over every long line and slope. She felt her breath snagging in her throat as he continued his exploration.

His hands went past her collarbone. Kylee's chest rose and fell quickly. His heart started to pound hard against his ribs as he edged along the top of her camisole. He rubbed small circles, over and over, until his fingers tingled.

"Hey, Santos!"

The shout startled Kylee, and she jumped. Santos continued to grip her hair, and she remained still. She watched him silently, but he knew the moment was gone. Santos reluctantly let go.

He took a deep breath and glared at the intruder. He saw a few of his beach buddies standing nearby, tossing around a volleyball. "What?" he said in a low growl.

"Are you in?" one of them called out.

"Go ahead," Kylee said hoarsely. "I'll sit here and watch."

"You don't want to join in?" Was she too much of a lady to sweat? Or was she trying to gain some distance?

She gave the volleyball net a long look. "I don't play."

"That doesn't stop me."

"Nothing stops you," she muttered as she picked up the sunblock bottle and sat down on one of the canvas chairs.

He clucked his tongue and walked toward his friends. "Kylee, you say that like it's a bad thing."

Kylee watch Santos join his friends and flopped back on her chair. What was wrong with her? Her heart was banging like a drum and her legs felt as heavy as lead.

Just because a nearly naked man had held her close? His broad chest and massive shoulders were made for holding on to tight and never letting go. Watching his retreating figure made her a little weak in the knees.

She dragged her gaze away from Santos and turned her attention to the ocean. It wasn't as painful or bittersweet as she had expected. The moment she had walked down to the beach and inhaled the briny scent of the water, she had been hit with nostalgia. It came to her in splashes of color, like photos from an old camera. Friends. Parties. A collage of her swimsuits, each getting tinier as she got bigger—and wilder and wilder.

Kylee grimaced at the memories and viciously pushed them aside. She had been all about maximizing the fun, but she had gone overboard. That wouldn't happen again. She would not revert to the old Kylee because she was sitting on a beach.

She purposely kept her feet on the towel and hastily rubbed sunblock on her legs. If she didn't actually touch the sand, she might survive this afternoon. She wouldn't go wild and crazy, throwing caution to the wind.

Probably not, she admitted as she bit her lip. Within minutes she had almost accepted the invitation to join in the beach volleyball. That didn't concern her as much as her reaction to Santos.

Kylee turned her attention back to the game just in time to see Santos leaping into the air and smashing the ball over the net. His muscles rippled as sweat glistened off his bronzed body. The sun rays glowed around his head like a crown.

She shook her head. *Show-off.*

Santos crouched, and he looked like a predator ready to

leap. She wanted to rub away the naughty flip in her stomach. Santos slid a look at her before diving for the volleyball.

Realization punched her in the chest, and she forgot to breathe. Santos was showing off for *her* benefit.

She looked around, just to make sure there wasn't some blond bombshell or sexy, practically nude sunbather. There wasn't, and she still couldn't believe it.

It was like in the wild, where the male species showed his prime physical prowess to the female. But that was for an animal looking for a mate.

He was trying to impress her. Her heartbeat fluttered. A man as primitive as Santos would adhere to the biological need of sexual selection. If he met her approval—and why wouldn't he?—would she allow him in her bed?

Absolutely not. He was a *client. A prince.*

And a fine specimen of a man. He only had to wear shorts and her adrenaline started pumping. She was going to melt in a puddle when she saw him in a tuxedo.

Or maybe not. She studied his new haircut. As much as she preferred the sophisticated look, she missed the flowing black waves. He looked gorgeous, but the untamed hair was the Santos she knew and loved.

Loved? She sat up straight in her seat. No. She liked him. Definitely liked. He made her laugh and think. He drove her crazy, but he also fascinated her. Even when he was at his worst, it never stopped her growing affection.

Her gaze collided with his. She wasn't quick enough to shutter her feelings. Time stood still. The motion of the ocean froze as the noise faded. The heat evaporated, and she shivered.

The volleyball hit Santos on the head.

"Come on, Santos." His teammate clapped his hand on Santos's back. "Eye on the game."

Kylee looked the other way. She briskly rubbed her arms. Taking a deep breath, she closed her eyes and allowed the tropical breeze to waft over her, cooling her overheated skin.

Her mind was playing tricks. This was what happened when she got on the beach. She couldn't help but look for trouble. She was tempted by a gorgeous man, but she could restrain herself when she was in his hotel room.

"Watch out!"

Kylee looked up just as Santos was flying in her direction, straining to hit the ball. She heard the ball hit the umbrella, sensed it whiz next to her, but she never saw it. She didn't have time to block or curl up before he fell on her. Her chair rocked back and threatened to collapse.

The man was solid muscle. Thick, hard and sweaty.

"Ow," she said slowly. She wasn't hurt, but she didn't dare move a muscle. Not when she was tempted to widen her legs and allow him to sink into her.

"Sorry." He looked up and smiled. "Are you okay?"

She looked down, his chin resting on her stomach, his broad shoulders pinning her down. A coil of heat warmed deep in her pelvis at the sight of his body between her legs.

"Comfy?" Her attempt for sarcasm was ruined by her high, tight voice.

His smile widened. "Oh, yeah."

"You're squashing me." It wasn't entirely true, but she felt trapped and overwhelmed.

He untangled himself from her. She stiffened as his hands slid down her legs while he slowly got to his feet.

"If I didn't know any better," she said, trying to give her words some bite, "I would think you had done that on purpose."

"And lose a point in the game? Never." He looked around. "Where's the ball?"

She looked around the shadows her beach umbrella offered. "I don't see it." She took the excuse to get up from her seat, wishing her legs weren't so shaky.

She found the ball behind her chair and grabbed it. It felt familiar and good against her manicured hands.

"Toss it here," Santos ordered.

"It's not your turn," she reminded him. She tossed the ball high in the air. Without thinking, Kylee jumped up and slammed an overhead serve. The ball sailed to the opposing team.

She shouldn't have done that. She knew it the moment her palm slapped the ball. It was as if her body had gone on autopilot.

Kylee was ready to crawl back into the shadows but a hard, sweaty chest stood in her way. She looked up and saw Santos's speculative gaze.

"And you don't play?"

She sidestepped him. "That's right." She didn't. Not anymore.

"Kylee," he said, trotting backward to the game, "I'm going to figure out what's lurking underneath that proper exterior."

Panic gripped her chest. There was no wild child inside her. No inner vixen waiting to be unleashed. She was a lady, damn it. "What you see is what you get."

A slow smile played on his lips. "Promise?"

CHAPTER TWELVE

PRINCE ZAIN
Deep in America's Heartland

SHE HAD FOLLOWED HIS request and worn a dress.

Not just any dress, Zain admitted as they walked out of the nightclub, the music still pulsing in his ears. He guided Lauren to the car, placing his hand at the small of her back, muffling a groan when he touched her warm, soft skin.

Lauren had chosen to wear a backless red dress that hugged every curve. The halter top plunged between her breasts, and the skirt stopped mere inches past her hips. Her bare legs went on endlessly, and her bright red heels were feminine and daring.

Her outfit gave the illusion that she wore nothing underneath. All night he had wondered if she had on anything else. He was beginning to think she didn't. The dress was designed to tempt, and he had a strong feeling that she wore it to drive him crazy because he had told her what to wear.

Zain allowed his fingertips to dip beneath the scooped cut of her dress. His heart pounded as he fought the urge to explore. He reluctantly pulled away, clenching his fingers into a fist. He was going to be on his best behavior, even if it killed him.

As Lauren climbed into the car, the hem of her dress rose precariously. His breath snagged in his raw throat as silky red fabric stretched tautly against her hip.

Zain got in the car after her and sat far on the other end of the backseat. It was the least he could do. He had been tortured all night. His restraint had slipped the moment he saw her in the red dress. It took a serious tumble during the intimate candlelight dinner. He couldn't sit too close to her without touching her, but sitting too far away was agony.

Taking her to the nightclub where they had first met was his downfall. His body still hummed with need as images of their tangled bodies flickered in his memory. Why had he taken her dancing? Was he a glutton for punishment? He had been unable to keep his eyes and hands off her. Lauren had bewitched him with her sensuous moves and the promise in her eyes.

"Thanks for the evening," she said, her voice husky, as the car pulled away from the nightclub. "I had fun."

"My pleasure." And it had been, minus the constant ache to claim her. Zain flexed his hands and kept them firmly at his sides. His skin was hot and tight. His cock was rock-hard.

He gritted his teeth as she pushed her hair back. Lauren arched her back slightly, and her stiff nipples thrust against the thin fabric of her halter. The move was simple and innocent, but it stoked his desire.

They watched each other silently. Did she know that he was fighting every primitive instinct to pounce? He didn't think he was going to get through this long drive without touching her. He had to refrain, because once he touched her, he wouldn't stop. It was best to stay at arm's length.

The car turned away from the bright lights and sped down the long, isolated road. Only headlights pierced the darkness. He felt the tension swirling between them, and it wouldn't take much to break it. Zain glanced at the privacy window that separated him from the chauffeur and bodyguard in front. For a moment he was tempted to open it.

The idea fizzled the moment Lauren slid closer to him. Zain's chest clamped tight. He couldn't see her expression in the shadows, but there was intent in the way she moved.

He braced himself as she leaned forward. He inhaled her light scent just before she placed a gentle kiss on his startled mouth.

It went against every instinct not to capture her mouth with his. Zain dug his fingertips into his palms, refusing to move. He was trying to court her, and he was pretty sure that meant no sex on the first date.

"What was that for?" he asked, bemused by his weak voice.

"Adding to my thanks," she whispered and placed another feathery kiss on the corner of his mouth. The light touch teased him when he wanted so much more.

"And that?" He felt her slow smile against his lips.

"Because I like kissing you." She outlined his lips with soft kisses as heat streaked though his body.

He went rigid when she swiped the tip of her tongue between his lips. Zain tilted his head back. "And that?"

"Because you like it, too."

Driving need pulled at them. He could understand why she had run away the first time they kissed. Whatever was going on between them was ferocious and hungry underneath the surface. A gentle kiss could easily turn into something wild.

He was tempted to be swept away. It was like being under a spell. A part of him wanted to break it, to show he was more powerful; but another part of him wanted to go deeper and get caught up in the storm.

What was it about her that made him get this hot and hard? Did it have something to do with the prophecy, or was it natural attraction? Whatever it was, he had to fight it, or he was going to take her in the most animalistic way.

"I promised myself not to claim you tonight." He couldn't remember why it had been so important to be on his best behavior. It was part of his strategy, which he was very close to abandoning.

"Then you're in luck," Lauren said while nuzzling the sensitive spot under his ear. "I didn't make that kind of promise."

He squeezed his eyes shut. "I mean it, Lauren. I'm not touching you."

"That's okay." She nipped his earlobe. "I'll do all the touching."

Anticipation quivered low in her belly. He was hers for the taking. Now if only she could trust this hunger pounding through her veins. She knew it could consume her.

In a way, she hated feeling like this. Kissing and touching wasn't going to be enough to get Prince Zain out of her system. She couldn't remember the last time she had felt this hungry for anything. Or anyone.

Lauren knew she was playing with fire. Once she had sex with Zain, she would never be the same. But if she didn't go for it, she would regret it. He would always be the one who got away. And once he had given up on her and left, she could never go after him again.

She had to go for it. Take advantage of his undivided attention and forget about the real reason he was there. She didn't have to marry him to have sex. She was going to savor this night without regrets.

Placing her hand on his chest, she felt the heat radiating beneath his tailored shirt. His heart thudded against her palm, but what surprised her was the tension shimmering off his body. He was holding back. She needed to be in full command before she unleashed this intensity.

Lauren pressed her thighs together as the coil of desire twisted deep in her pelvis. Zain's fingertips brushed against her bare leg, and she shivered. He continued to stroke her, as if he couldn't deny himself the skin-on-skin contact.

She leaned into him, enjoying the feel of his hard, strong body as she claimed his mouth with hers. She kissed him deeply, feeding her growing hunger. She delved her tongue past his lips. He tasted of the forbidden.

She playfully explored his mouth, wrestling for complete surrender. He wasn't going to let her have it. Lauren mewed as he drew her deeper into his mouth, and she clenched her hands into his soft, dark hair.

Her breasts were pressed against his solid chest, but it wasn't close enough. She straddled his legs, her dress riding high. She broke off the kiss when she felt his erection between her legs. His hard cock pressed against her wet heat, and his pants were the only barrier.

She was going too fast, she realized as she gasped for air. It was kind of embarrassing. She never acted like this with a guy. She liked sex, probably more than she should, but with Zain she was almost out of control.

Lauren darted her tongue along her reddened lips. She watched Zain's gaze follow her movement. He might not touch her, but that didn't mean he wasn't going to reciprocate. He was with her every step of the way.

His skin was drawn tight against his cheekbones. The shadows gave his face a dangerous edge. His eyes glittered with frank need.

"We need . . . to stop this." He had trouble forming the sentence.

She knew he was right. It didn't matter that she liked him or that she liked being with him. She didn't care that he wanted more than a one-night stand and that he had marriage on his mind. It was too much, too soon.

She knew that, but it wasn't enough to stop her.

"Why?" she asked as she rubbed her hands over his chest. Her fingers glided over his shirt. She wanted a peek at what was underneath. Were his muscles as lean and sculpted as she imagined?

Zain's mouth opened and shut. "Because . . ."

Lauren leaned in for another slow, wet kiss. "Because . . . ?" she prompted him as she began to unbutton his shirt.

He grabbed her wrists. She was dimly aware of how fast he had moved. Trepidation trickled down her spine. Just how much was she in charge here? He was letting her tease him, but he could take over within a split second.

"Our first time should be in bed," Zain said through clenched teeth.

"Absolutely." She was all for having enough room. If he was spread-eagled on her bed, she could have her way with him. If he didn't pin her down first, that was. Right now, in this car, she could do the claiming.

She moved to unbutton his shirt, but Zain held on to her wrists. Lauren smiled and bent her head, unbuttoning the first button with her teeth.

Zain's fingers tightened, and he groaned with surrender. He dropped his hold and splayed his hands on her naked back. Lauren arched her spine, evading his touch.

"Ah, ah, ah," Lauren chided playfully as she quickly unbuttoned his shirt. "You don't want to break your promise, right?"

He reluctantly pulled his hands away. "You're killing me," he muttered as he stretched his arms along the back of the seat.

She yanked open his shirt and took in the sight before her. Zain was stretched out, his head lolled back. He watched her with hooded eyes as his naked chest rose and fell with each deep, careful breath.

Lauren rubbed her hands along his chest, enjoying the contrasting texture of hot, smooth skin and rough hair. Her hands tingled as she discovered every plane and dip.

His cock pressed insistently against her. Lauren bit her lip, holding back a moan as she rocked against him. She reached for his belt and unhooked it before he could protest. When she unzipped his pants, Zain placed his hands over hers.

"Going too fast for you?" she asked.

She watched the shadows play on his throat as he swallowed roughly. "No, not at all." He had difficulty talking.

"I just want to touch you," she confessed, as her sex pulsed with urgency. "Taste you."

His cock lurched violently at her words. Zain groaned and clasped his hands at the back of her head. He tugged her forward, grinding her mouth with a kiss. She felt Zain's struggle for self-control.

Lauren pulled away, breathless, as she tugged his pants over his hips. She sensed Zain was going to make his move and take over. She quickly slid off his lap and settled between his legs.

Her core clenched at the sight of his cock. He was thick and large. She clasped him with both hands. Zain groaned and tilted his head back.

Lauren squeezed him gently. He felt smooth, hot and powerful beneath her hands. She bent down and wrapped her lips around the wet tip. She liked how he shuddered the moment her tongue darted against him. She pumped him at the base while she swirled her tongue along the crown.

She continued licking and darting her tongue along his length until Zain started to pant. She began to suck him deep in her mouth. Hard, fast pulls that made him buck from his seat.

"Lauren," he said between gasps, sinking his hands in her hair. He guided her closer, silently showing her what he liked.

Lauren removed her hands from the base of his cock and cupped his heavy balls. She fondled the tight sacs as she took most of his cock into her mouth. Bobbing up and down, she heard the prince's long, guttural moans. She was stripping his sophisticated veneer, layer by layer, exposing the elemental, primitive man that he was.

She felt his body tighten and his struggle to prevent the inevitable. Lauren sucked hard and long, giving his testicles a sharp squeeze. He came violently, his body lurching as he pulsed hotly in her mouth.

Zain slumped against his seat. His hands shook as he stroked her hair. She slowly withdrew, and he hissed between his teeth when she moved away from him.

A streetlight illuminated the car. She glanced up and smiled at Zain's magnificent body. He was sprawled against the backseat, a picture of a satisfied male.

She rose from her position, her sex throbbing. Her knees were shaky as she made her way to the other side of the backseat. She tried to smooth her hair down and catch her breath.

"Why are you over there?" Zain asked as he reached for her.

He cradled her at his side, gathering her tight, as if he couldn't bear to be away.

"Streetlights," she murmured with a hint of regret. She pressed her hand against his hot chest. "We're back in town."

"This night isn't over," he growled in her ear.

Anticipation raced through her blood. "I should hope not."

CHAPTER THIRTEEN

LAUREN'S HEART THUMPED against her chest as she opened the door to her apartment. Zain was right behind her. He wasn't crowding her, but she felt surrounded by his presence. He didn't touch her, but she knew he wanted to. He was holding back. Just.

She stepped inside her home and flipped on the light switch. Zain grasped her wrist and pressed his mouth against it. She cupped her hand against his cheek, and he slid his mouth against the center of her palm.

"I thought you weren't going to touch me tonight," she teased as his gentle kiss made her pulse skip a beat. "Are you going to break your promise?"

"I can't stop myself," he admitted in a raw tone.

Lauren's stomach did a tiny jump at his confession. He found her that irresistible? It was impossible, but the way he looked at her made her feel like she was the sexiest woman.

When he flicked his tongue against the spot, Lauren felt it go straight to her core. Her shaky legs buckled, and she leaned against him for support.

"Undress me," he murmured as he closed the door behind him.

She usually didn't take orders from a lover. She was always the one who was in charge and determining the next move. But the rules were different when it came to Zain. She surprised herself when she reached for his jacket and pulled it off his shoulders, hearing it fall onto the carpet.

He gathered her close as he kicked off his shoes. She walked backward, guiding him to her bedroom in the back of the apartment.

She didn't want any more barriers. Lauren was desperate to get him naked. She quickly unbuttoned his shirt and yanked the fabric off his broad shoulders and down his sculpted arms. The sleeves stopped at his wrists. She tugged at the shirt, but it didn't budge.

"Cuff links," Zain muttered, jerking at the uncooperative sleeve.

She had forgotten about the cuff links. It wasn't her fault—she had never known a man to wear them. But she liked how Zain's movements were limited. She took the opportunity to rub her hands over his chest and abs. She enjoyed feeling the rumble of pleasure when she tweaked his nipples, and smiled at the growl of warning when she lightly brushed her fingertips against a ticklish spot above his ribs.

Zain wrestled with his sleeves in earnest, and Lauren knew she didn't have much time left to play. She slid his belt buckle free and unzipped his pants, shucking the rest of his clothes past his powerful thighs before Zain struggled out of his shirt. She cupped his cock with the palm of her hand, tightening her hold as he kicked his clothes to the side.

By the time they reached the bedroom, Zain stood naked

before her, proud and strong. He was beautiful, and for tonight, he was all hers.

She took his hand and drew him into her bedroom. Her bed, which dominated the tiny room, suddenly seemed incredibly small. There was no way the two of them would fit on there. There was not enough room to do all the things she wanted to do to him.

Zain's hands gripped her shoulders and slowly stroked her arm as if he couldn't get enough of her. "Sit on the bed," he told her.

Sit? Lauren hesitated but decided to follow his lead. Just this once. He probably realized they had more room in the back of his car. She was eager to see how he was going to improvise.

She lowered herself on the bed, perched on the corner, when Zain crouched in front of her. Her stomach did a crazy flip, and she found it difficult to breathe.

How could a man look so powerful when he was naked and kneeling before her? The intense look on his face was a little bit intimidating, actually. Was he going to jump her and take her in one swoop? She hoped so.

To her surprise, he reached for her foot. Lauren set her hands on the mattress, not sure what he planned. She watched silently as he slid her shoe off and lovingly held her heel.

Lauren curled her toes, wishing she could hide them. Why did he have to go for the feet first? They were riddled with scars and looked a hundred years old. She never went barefoot around other people because her feet were so ugly.

Zain didn't seem to think so. He caressed her foot before he dug his thumbs against the sensitive arch. Lauren gasped and pressed her lips together. It didn't diminish the ribbons of pleasure dancing up her legs and streaking along her pelvis.

His sensual massage was the sweetest form of torture. His touch could be soft or strong, as light as a feather or as unyielding as stone. Each touch was unexpected, and her body reacted in ways she couldn't control. She was on the edge of surrendering, and he hadn't even started.

The smallest pressure on her foot, and she could feel it straight in the hot center of her sex. When he pressed down, a tremor rippled through her. She refrained from whimpering as he set her foot down and went to the other one.

She felt boneless by the time he glided his hands along the length of her bare legs. She struggled to remain still as he explored. The back of her knees tingled as he kissed the faint incision mark, faded by time.

Lauren lay back and parted her legs as he trailed kisses along her thigh. Her breaths were choppy and shallow as he bunched her dress up. Zain stopped, his tension soaring, when he saw she wore nothing underneath her dress.

She knew her dress had driven him crazy. He had been wondering if and wishing that she wore nothing underneath it. And that she had done it for him. She had seen it all in his eyes.

Lauren tried to catch her breath, ready for him to devour her relentlessly. The waiting was too much to bear. She flinched when he tenderly brushed his mouth against her hip bone.

He gently kissed and licked her inner thighs, holding her down as her hips undulated. He trailed kisses along her pelvic bone, and she could smell the scent of her wet heat. He circled closer and closer to the throbbing center of her sex. Just when she was about to sigh with relief, his hot breath against her core, he retreated and started all over again.

Lauren dug her hands into the bedspread. She was going to scream for sure. His teasing was too much. She needed him to plunge and bite. His touch had to be stronger. Harder. Faster.

She grabbed for him, prepared to take over, but he anticipated her move and dodged out of the way.

Chuckling, Zain rose and helped her back on her feet. She was shaky, hot and then cold. She felt incredibly small without her high heels.

Zain reached behind her and untied her halter top. Her red dress slithered off her body. She kicked it to the side and stood boldly naked in front of him. She placed her hands on her hips, thrusting her breasts, silently begging him to touch her.

Beg? What was happening to her? She never begged. Never waited. She always made the next move, and this time shouldn't be any different. She was going to take, grab and squeeze every opportunity of this moment.

"Lie down," she told him.

Zain arched an eyebrow.

"Please?" she added and pulled him onto the bed. Splaying her hands on his sculpted shoulders, she eased him back to the center of the mattress.

Lauren straddled his hips, running her hands over his body before she stroked his hard, erect cock. She leaned over to her bedside table and opened the drawer. Pushing aside her vibrator, she quickly found a box of condoms.

She grabbed a condom, opened the package and looked down at Zain. Her pulse skittered with excitement. She couldn't believe this gorgeous, powerful man was between her legs. She felt his strength and heat, and now she was going to harness them for her own pleasure.

Zain stroked her legs and waist, finding a ticklish spot right above her waist. His fingers went over that spot again and again. He smiled as she gasped and twisted out of his way while sheathing him with a condom.

Lauren rose to her knees and grasped his cock with both

hands. She felt the thick tip pressing against her and bore down. Zain clamped his hands on to her hips, his fingers digging in, as he slowly lowered her onto him. Even when she was on top, Zain couldn't relinquish control.

Heat flashed through her body as he slowly filled her. Lauren slid her hands over her stomach and breasts, and the prickly sensations burned her skin. She cupped her breasts and heard Zain's guttural encouragement. She played with her nipples, pinching and squeezing them, moaning as the sensual pleasure rushed deep into her belly.

Zain moved her hips forcefully, and he filled her completely. She arched her throat and groaned, swiveling her hips. She tentatively rocked and swayed, enjoying the feel of him. Soon she picked up her pace. Wild sensations swirled inside her, going faster and faster, tighter and tighter.

Lauren rode him hard, and Zain's hands fell away. He clenched the sheets beneath him. He bucked against her, his face tight as he held back. She placed her hands on his chest, felt the thundering of his heart against her palm, as she ground her hips into him.

White-hot pleasure stormed through her, rising from her hips and streaking through her body. She cried out as her world exploded in a kaleidoscope of swirling colors that flared brilliantly before fading into darkness.

Lauren wobbled and gulped for air. Zain sat up and cradled her against his chest. She leaned her head on his sweat-slick shoulder.

"Hold on tight," he suggested, as he rolled her underneath him, his cock firmly embedded into her. "Now it's my turn to be on top."

Zain wrapped a towel around his waist and exited Lauren's small bathroom. He saw the first rays of dawn filtering through the blinds and lighting the apartment. Padding barefoot in the living area, he picked up the trail of clothes. He spotted his jacket at the door, grabbed it, and retrieved his cell phone.

Hitting the speed dial, he waited impatiently for his assistant to answer.

"Yes, Your Highness?" Ali greeted, his voice groggy with sleep.

"Ali, I need you to contact the royal astrologer. Find out the most auspicious day for Lauren and me to marry."

For the first time since his birthday, he didn't cringe at the word "marry." In fact, he was looking forward to it. Maybe not that far. More like cautiously optimistic.

There was a pause on Ali's side. "Miss Ballinger finally agreed?"

"Not in so many words." But then, he hadn't asked again. It would be a mere formality. After all, a woman did not surrender her body the way she did over and over to just any man.

"Then I won't prepare any press releases at this time."

"It won't be long now." Zain disconnected and watched the sun rise. The new day always made him feel that it was full of promises. Things were finally going his way.

"Who was that?"

Zain turned around and found Lauren standing in the doorway to the bedroom. His chest tightened at the sight of the bedsheet wrapped around her body. Her hair was tangled and he could see marks from his whiskers on her pale skin.

"I was speaking to Ali, my assistant," he said as he felt a kick in his pulse. He switched off the phone, preventing any interruptions.

She brushed her hair from her eyes and yawned. "Is there a problem?"

"Not at all," Zain said as he strode toward her. He could

easily imagine taking the end of the bedsheet and spinning her out of it. "I asked him to find out the most auspicious day from the royal astrologer."

She blinked the sleep away from her eyes. "The most auspicious day for what?"

He plucked the edge of the sheet between his fingers. "To get married."

Those three words woke her up with a start. "We're not getting married! I told you that I would go on a date with you, not pick a date."

"But that was before—"

"Before I slept with you?" She rolled her eyes. "If I married every guy I took to bed . . ."

Zain went very still. He clenched his jaw so hard he thought it would shatter, but he refused to react to the mention of other men in her bed.

Her mouth pursed as she realized what she had just said. She winced and looked away. "Never mind."

"Lauren, last night proved that we are good together. You can't deny that. Now imagine enjoying that every night as man and wife."

"Imagine doing that without having to get married." She turned and walked back into the bedroom.

"I don't believe this." He didn't know which surprised him more: that she still refused or that she walked away from him during a conversation. No one turned her back on him.

"Neither do I."

"That's it." His low voice made Lauren pause. "I'm giving you an ultimatum."

She scoffed at the idea. "You have got to be kidding me. You've only been chasing me for three days, and you've had enough."

"Is that what you want: for me to chase you, work hard for your favors and earn your hand in marriage?" He felt like he was trying as hard as he could with no results.

"I didn't say that." Her words lacked conviction.

"And while I court you, you choose to take advantage of me." It bothered him saying the words out loud. No one took advantage of him, yet he had allowed Lauren to do so.

She wrapped the sheet tighter against her body. "That's not true."

"You'll let me chase and bed you, while you dangle the promise that you have no intention of fulfilling." Zain frowned and tilted his head. Had those words actually come out of his mouth? The same complaint he had heard from women in his past?

She pulled the bedsheet higher, clasping it to her chest. "I did not ask you to chase me."

"But you didn't keep me out of your bed." He motioned at the bed behind her. "Is that all you want from me, the sex?"

She exhaled long and hard. "No."

"Good." Zain smiled and crossed his arms against his chest. "Because you're not getting any from me until you say yes."

Her jaw dropped. "I'm sorry. It's really early in the morning, so I must have misunderstood. Did you say that you are withholding sex from me?"

"That's right." He placed his hands on his hips. "You can't accept one part of me and push away everything I have to offer."

She shook her head as if trying to clear her mind. "Let me see if I'm getting this straight. You're dumping me because I want sex?"

"No, I'm not giving up, but I'm not giving in to your demands, either."

"Zain, your ultimatum is not going to affect me," she boasted. "In fact, you will cave before I do."

"Don't be too sure." And yet he had a feeling she was right. It didn't take much for him to lose control around her.

"You're going to deprive yourself of sex?" Lauren dropped her hands and allowed the sheet to fall from her breasts and drape against her hips. "Deny yourself this?"

He grasped the bedsheet and saw the tremor in his hand. All it would take was one yank, and they would tumble into bed. It was tempting, but he couldn't give in. "I'm willing to make the sacrifice for my cause." He tugged the sheet to her chin. "Are you?"

CHAPTER FOURTEEN

CROWN PRINCE RAFAEL
East Coast of the USA

SHAYLA FELT THE THUNDER under her feet. She slammed her back against the wall and reached out for Rafael. Her hand spanned across his rock-hard stomach as she pressed him against the wall.

"What—?"

Four guys raced past them, red-faced and chanting. They knocked over chairs and bumped into a couple making out, but nothing stopped them as they ran for the stairs to the second floor.

"You learn to move fast at one of these parties," she said. She flexed her fingers against his abdomen, enjoying how his body heat warmed her hand.

This was the first time she'd seen him without a jacket. The white buttoned shirt emphasized his wide shoulders and flat stomach. He had rolled up the sleeves, revealing strong arms.

Her gazed dragged down to his jeans again. She couldn't stop looking. His legs were long, lean and powerful. The faded denim caressed the compact muscles. Her hands twitched, wanting to cup his ass and squeeze.

Shayla looked away from his jeans. Was it getting hot in there? She pulled at the square neckline of her cotton dress.

Rafe took a sip of beer from his plastic cup and grimaced. "This is what you do every weekend?"

"There's always a frat house or sorority having a party. Even in the summer." It didn't quite answer Rafael's question. When she had been a freshman, she'd attended every party she could, eager to experience everything. These days she didn't have much use for them. She loved her cozy little world, but she felt restless. Cooped in.

"And you like this music?"

She had no idea who the group was, and she could care less. "Absolutely." Her smile froze as the guitar riff on the stereo screeched. She felt it go straight to her molars.

A smile tugged at his mouth. "Are you saying that because Luca likes it?"

"Oh, please. In case you haven't noticed, I'm not attached to him at the hip." She realized her tactical error. She didn't want to point out that Luca had abandoned them once they'd stepped into the fraternity house. "Let's dance."

"To this?"

She grabbed his cup and set it down. She held his hands and walked backward to where everyone was dancing. "Come on, Rafael. You're not *that* old."

She knew he was only twenty-eight, but it was like waving a red cape in front of a bull. A challenging glint entered his dark eyes. "I'll try to keep up," he said drily.

She drew him into the room reserved for dancing. It was dark and crowded. She weaved her way into the center of the room. The other dancers swayed to the beat of the loud, primitive music.

Rafael wrapped his arm around her waist and drew her up against him. Her heart hammered against her ribs as she inhaled his scent. She was surrounded by him, and she didn't want to break free.

Her hands instinctively flattened against his chest. He was all heat and muscle. Nerves fluttered low in her belly as she slid her hands up to his shoulders and linked her hands behind his neck, creating an intimate haven from the loud, crazy world around them.

She immediately realized that Rafe knew how to dance. He wasn't stiff or showy, but his sinuous moves took her breath away. They were pressed hip to hip, chest to breast, and she couldn't anticipate his moves, but simply followed his lead.

Her heart was pounding. He held her close, every move, every hard muscle of his awakening her body. She felt the sparks popping just under her skin.

Would they be like this in bed? They would never make it that far, she reminded herself sternly. Rafael wouldn't allow it, and she didn't think she would have the nerve to see through this seduction.

Now would be the best time to make her move on Rafael. She could be bold, knowing there would be no consequence. He would reject her.

He had better reject her. She wouldn't know how to handle him. Yet, secretly, she wanted him to accept her dare. Did she have the power to break through his restraint? And once she proved irresistible, she would want Rafe to take over. Take her.

He slid his leg between her thighs. Before she could make a move, he held her by her hips and glided her up and down. The sensation made her wet. Shayla rode along his leg, grinding down and bucking. She licked her lips as the delicious pressure promised gratification.

"Where'd you learn how to dance like this?" she asked breathlessly, trying to appear unaffected. "Cotillion lessons?"

He did a move, and her heart violently skipped a beat. "I'm making it up as I go along," he said with a smile.

His hand brushed along her bare leg, and his fingers hitched her dress up. Shayla closed her eyes and rested her forehead on his shoulder. She wanted him to continue and seek what was underneath her dress.

She was disappointed when he didn't. He clasped her hips, his fingers digging in as he fought the urge to delve underneath her dress.

She was supposed to be making the first move. Make him think she was after him. And she was, to a certain extent.

Why was she hesitating? She was free to have sex with whomever she wanted. And she really, really wanted Rafael. She winced at the sharp twist in her stomach. Even if it was the life-changing moment she suspected.

His hands slid along her rib cage and just under her breasts. Shayla pressed her lips before the whimper escape. Why didn't he keep going? Her nipples tightened until they stung. She found it difficult to breathe.

Shayla looked into Rafael's eyes and saw his desire. It sharpened his face. She wanted to experience it. She wanted to get as close to this man as she possibly could. She hadn't felt like this about a guy in a long, long time.

She hadn't felt like this about anyone.

This was not the flirty, feel-good joy she wanted in a relationship. This was hot, sticky and sweaty. It was going to be fierce, fast and out of control.

She wasn't going to wait another minute. Shayla cupped his head and pressed her lips against his. His mouth slanted over hers, delving his tongue past her lips. Her knees buckled as he conquered her. Raw, hot energy bloomed in her chest, rushing through her blood and pressing against her skin.

She rubbed her body against his, subconsciously going with the beat of the music. His hard cock pressed against her soft belly. She clung to him, weak with the need throbbing inside her, coiling tighter and tighter. There was only one way that the tension was going to break free.

Rafael's mouth stilled against hers. He wrenched away. "What the hell are you doing?"

"Excuse me? Wrong pronoun. What are 'we' doing?"

He stepped away, reluctantly breaking contact. She felt the loss of his body heat, her body aching as she watched him thrust his hands in his hair.

The sight of his hand shaking made her feel very powerful. She had just made this man lose control and forget his surroundings. Maybe, just maybe, he wanted her as much as she wanted him.

Rafe looked flustered, rumpled and thoroughly kissed. She really shouldn't be proud.

He pointed an accusing finger at her. "You kissed me."

"Yes, I did." Shayla put her hands on her hips. It was either that or grab him for another kiss.

"That was a mistake."

"No, it wasn't." Couldn't he say he wanted to kiss her? Or that he needed to? That he wanted to claim her body and soul?

"You're dating my brother."

She guessed not. The denial was on the tip of her tongue, but she had promised Luca she would see this through. "What's your point?"

His mouth tightened as his eyes grew hard and cold. She noticed his lips were reddened by her kiss. What could she say? She gave as good as she got.

"Luca is very serious about you."

She took a deep breath. "And I am very serious about him."

"Then what was this?" He motioned between them.

She wasn't sure what to say. "Fun?"

"Fun? Fun?" A muscle bunched in his clenched jaw. "This was . . . wrong."

She made a face as her heart still pumped furiously. "I suppose you're going to run and tell your brother?"

"I have to." But it was clear that he didn't want to.

She shrugged and wished she hadn't. Her breasts felt full and heavy, sensitive to every move and touch. "He's not going to believe you." She held up her hand. "I have him wrapped around my little finger."

"Is that right?" He didn't believe her. "What do you do to him with that finger?"

She wished she could come up with something shocking and audacious, but her imagination was not on the same level as Rafe's expertise. "You'll never find out," she said as she lowered her hand, watching Rafe's expression darken. "Luca's not going to believe you, so don't even bother trying."

"I'll take my chances."

"It's too bad you stopped," she said as she sashayed around him. "No telling where this might have led."

He grabbed her arm and met her gaze. "This was going nowhere."

"For now."

"For good."

"Sure." She dragged the word out and purposefully removed his hand from her arm.

"Where are you going?"

"Where I belong. To my boyfriend's side. See you around." And she strutted away. She hoped her movements came across as unconcerned and flippant. It was difficult to strut when her legs shook.

She kept strutting, or tried to, as she walked through the fraternity house, trying to locate Luca. She found him outside on the wraparound porch, a little too close to and cozy with Cathy.

"What do you think you're doing?" Shayla asked Luca, tapping him hard on his shoulder. "You're supposed to be my devoted boyfriend. Sorry, Cathy."

"I appreciate what you're doing, but I can hold my own," Cathy said with weary impatience. "I don't need this kind of protection."

"I agree," Shayla said as she wedged herself between them. "But I think it's sweet that Luca wants to shield you."

"Thank you," Luca said. He looked around the porch. "Where is Rafe?"

"I think he left."

"So your seduction plan . . . ?"

"I didn't get as far as I would have liked." She winced the moment the words came out. "You know what I mean."

He laughed. "It's okay. It was a long shot anyway."

Yeah, Shayla thought with a wry smile. A prince like Rafe could have any woman he wanted. Why would he want a girl like her? Those kinds of odds only happened in fairy tales.

CHAPTER FIFTEEN

RAFAEL GLARED AT the numbers on the door to Shayla's apartment. He didn't want to be there and definitely didn't want to see her again. Rafe gave a fierce knock on the wood and waited. He felt something close to relief when he didn't hear any sounds on the other side.

Relief? That couldn't be good. He wasn't going to be scared off by a two-timing woman. A woman who was forbidden to him and, if he could help it, off-limits to his brother.

He understood why she had such a hold on Luca, but Rafael knew he could resist better than his brother. He wasn't going to fall for her special brand of temptation.

Rafe pounded on the door again before folding his arms across his chest. He braced his legs, ready for another meeting with Shayla. As long as it required no touching. The less interaction with her, the better.

He should never have kissed her. His first mistake had been dancing with her. Now he knew to stay arm's length away. The moment he touched her, he would be in trouble.

"Who is it?" Shayla's voice was loud and clear from the other side of the door.

His heart lurched and Rafe gritted his teeth. "Rafael."

There was a pause, and he felt the tension arc between them through the heavy wooden door. Rafe frowned, wondering if she was going to ignore him in the hallway. He finally heard her unbolt the lock. The door opened as far as the chain allowed.

His gaze zeroed in on her face. She looked sweet and innocent with no makeup. Her black hair was loosely piled up on her head, and he knew it wouldn't take much for it to fall down in waves.

His eyes drifted down and found she was swathed in a fuzzy pink bathrobe. The thick terry cloth overwhelmed her slight build and covered every inch of her body, but it piqued his interest more than the hot little number she had worn to the dinner. And that dress had made him break into a sweat.

He really wanted to know what she was wearing underneath the robe. He suspected she wore nothing at all. Her neck and hands were wet, and he easily imagined rivulets of water trailing down her curves.

"What can I do for you, Rafael?"

He could think of a few requests. Most of them required her shedding the bathrobe. "You can let me in."

Wariness entered her eyes. "I don't think that's a good idea."

Did she think he wanted to repeat his biggest mistake? "I'm looking for Luca."

"He's not here."

"I don't believe you."

Her eyes widened. "Why would I lie?"

"The possibilities are endless."

She made a face and slammed the door. He heard the scratch of the chain, and she swung the door open. "See for yourself," she offered as she arched her arm in a flourish.

He stepped inside and realized it was a small studio apartment. Bookshelves lined the walls. Many of the shelves were yawning under the weight of textbooks, romance novels and chick flicks.

An old desk rested by the window, separating the kitchen from the rest of the living area. Rafe pivoted on his heel, deciding that his closets were bigger than this apartment.

He saw the small brass bed and the big pillows cast down on the floor in a haphazard pile. It was unmade, the yellow floral top sheet twisted and abandoned at the bottom of the mattress. Had Luca and Shayla shared that bed last night? Jealousy pierced Rafe, and he found it difficult to breathe.

"As you can see," Shayla said, never leaving her spot by the door, "he's not here."

Had Rafe just missed his brother? He dragged his gaze away from the bed and stepped into the bathroom. The shower curtain was drawn to the side, revealing the tiniest bathtub he'd ever seen.

Mountains of bubbles crackled inside the bathtub. The room was humid and thick with the floral scent he recognized as Shayla's. He hurried out, stepping on a discarded novel on the wet rug.

"Where is he?" he asked as he walked toward Shayla.

She shrugged. "Ask his bodyguards."

"They only give that information in case of an emergency." He put his hands on his hips and watched for any reaction in her face. "He skipped an important meeting, and I can't find him. Where do you think he is?"

"I don't know."

"I think you do."

"I can't help you." She watched Rafe carefully and slowly closed the door. "What kind of meeting was it?"

"That is none of your business."

Shayla leaned against the door. "You were going to tell him about me, weren't you?"

He clenched his jaw and felt a muscle bunch in his cheek.

A sly smile played on her mouth. "What's taken you so long?"

He wasn't trying to delay the uncomfortable discussion. "I can't find him. He's not even answering his cell phone."

She propped one of her feet against the door. Her bathrobe fell away from her bare leg. Her skin glistened with water. "He probably knows you're going to try and warn him off me."

Rafe watched a drop of water slide down her thigh. "He will drop you once he hears about you."

"I'm not concerned."

He looked up and met her confident gaze. "You don't have that much power over him."

"But I don't think you're trying to protect your brother," she said as she casually reached for her loose bun. "I think you want to make it clear for you to go after me."

"That's not true," Rafe said hoarsely as he watched her hair tumble past her shoulders.

"What you don't seem to understand," Shayla said as she untied the sash to her bathrobe, "is that I'm available now."

He grabbed the ends of her sash and held them in his fists. He didn't know if he was preventing her bathrobe from falling away or if he wanted to rip it off her.

He could take her right now. Throw her onto the bed and sink into her. His hands shook as his restraint slipped. The only thing that stood in his way was his brother's claim on her.

If it had been any other man, he would have disregarded the claim. Nothing would stop him from making Shayla his.

"Having second thoughts?" she whispered with a knowing smile. "Why am I not surprised?"

He really wanted her. He couldn't contain the need erupting inside him, threatening to overflow.

"You should leave." Shayla stepped away from the door. "You've managed to interrupt my bubble bath. Unless you'd like to join me . . ."

His mouth crashed against hers. Shayla gasped in surprise but didn't turn away. She tasted sweet and juicy, but her lips were wicked. She grasped his head with both hands and drew him closer.

He pressed her against the door. Rafe wanted to fall into her. His knees started to sag, but first he slid his hands underneath her bathrobe. She was naked, her skin slick and fragrant.

Rafe yanked the bathrobe off her shoulders, but it fell to her elbows, dangling behind her. He dragged his mouth away from hers. Her mouth was red and swollen from his kiss, he noted with satisfaction.

His chest squeezed tight when he saw that Shayla was naked and open for him. His cock ached at the sight.

He cupped her breasts and groaned as her curves filled his hands. Rafe squeezed and kneaded her flesh, pinching her nipples until they reddened. He watched Shayla as she weakly closed her eyes, panting and twisting in his hold.

He lifted her up, and Shayla surprised him by wrapping her legs tight around his waist. Her hot, wet core pressed against his cock. He couldn't stop stroking her wet skin. His hands roamed over her breasts, waist and hips.

He dipped his head and laved his tongue against her nipple before he bit down gently. Shayla arched back, gasping, her fingers digging into his hair as she pushed him closer, offering more.

He stroked her breasts, sucking her nipples until they were rosy and tight. The beat of his heart thundered in his head as he slid his hand down to her sex. She was drenched, and he could smell her arousal. Rafe slipped his thumb between the slippery folds and pressed against her swollen clit.

Shayla stiffened, her skin flushing as she struggled for her next breath. She wiggled against him, aroused and out of control. He knew how she felt. His cock was rock-hard and he fought against the lust kicking in his veins.

He tapped his thumb against her clit, hard and fast. He bent down and took her nipple between his teeth. It sent her over the edge. Her choppy, high cries went straight to his cock. She bucked wildly, pulsing against his hand.

His heart twisted as she looked at him in dazed wonder. She had finally surrendered to him. He needed to take her to bed right now and convince her he was the only man for her.

Oh, God. Dread slammed down on his shoulders. He had done it again. He had touched her and fallen for her trap.

He couldn't take much more of this. He wanted to take her to the bed more than he wanted to take his next breath, but he wouldn't. He wouldn't touch her again. Not until he was the only man in her life.

He gently unhooked her legs from his waist and set her down on the floor. Shayla hastily looked away and fumbled with the sash to her bathrobe. Rafe struggled with the urge to pull the sash free and keep her naked for his eyes only.

"Did you come here to find your brother," she asked coldly as she brushed the hair from her eyes, "or to continue what we started?"

"To find Luca. I didn't expect you to be so accommodating."

Her eyes glittered with anger, but she didn't throw the fault squarely on him. Instead she stepped away and opened the door. "I don't know where he would be."

Even if she did, she wouldn't be helpful. Rafe gave a nod and silently stepped out of her apartment. He was reluctant to walk away without looking back.

Shayla stalled him. "Are you going to tell Luca about this, too?"

He looked over his shoulder. "Let me make something very clear. I will never let you near my brother again."

He heard the slam of the door and slowly walked away. If he had anything to say about it, he'd keep her away from every man and have her all to himself.

Rafe splashed cold water on his face and gripped the porcelain edge of the sink. He glanced up at the mirror and unflinchingly looked at his reflection.

He would tell Luca. There was no question. It was simply a matter of when.

It would destroy his relationship with his sibling, and Rafe would lose more than his brother's respect, but he would accept the consequences for his actions.

He needed to tell Luca right away, Rafe decided as he slicked back his dark hair. But was that the smartest thing to do? He was being called away to Washington and wouldn't get back for at least a week. Shayla might choose to fight back with every seductive technique she knew. But if he didn't tell Luca right away, Shayla could cause even more trouble.

Of course, he was assuming that Luca would dump Shayla after finding out the truth, Rafael realized as he strode out of the men's restroom and headed for the unmarked door in the administration building.

What if Luca didn't want to leave Shayla? If Luca chose to

stay with her, Rafe didn't know what his strategy would be. It would be all-out war. His brother was going to wind up empty-handed because Shayla would be his.

He knocked on the door, and it immediately opened. A stocky older man stood before him. His fading red hair was clipped close to his head, and he wore a gray suit. "Your Highness."

"Mr. Holt," Rafael replied as he stepped into the room. He immediately saw a maze of cubicles. Overhead were video surveillance sets showing familiar spots throughout campus.

"My parents asked that I check on the security measures." It wasn't completely true, but he hoped the surveillance team might slip up and give him Luca's location.

"As we have told the queen, we are not a babysitting service." There was no emotion in the older man's voice. "If there's a concern, we will inform the palace."

"I'm sure that went over well."

Holt didn't crack a smile.

There was no chance Rafe would find out Luca's whereabouts. "The university promised to be accommodating. Is that the case?"

"Yes. This place is well-equipped."

Which was why his family allowed Luca to attend. Wolfskill University was driving distance from the nation's capital. There were many students who came from important political families, and the risk of a kidnapping was part of life.

Rafael gave a quick look at one of the video screens, but he didn't see his brother. "Has Luca been cooperative?"

"He's tried to dodge his bodyguard from time to time, but I don't think he realizes that some of our men are undercover as students and staff."

"Why has he been ducking?" If Luca ever went missing,

even for a half an hour, the palace would yank him out of the
school so fast his head would spin.

"He's been serious about one particular lady."

"Right. I got it now." He wanted privacy so he could spend
uninterrupted hours with Shayla. Rafe took a slow breath as the
spurt of jealousy burned like acid.

"But they haven't ventured far off the mountain," Mr. Holt
assured him.

"I wonder how Shayla feels about that," he murmured.

"Cathy, Your Highness," Mr. Holt corrected him.

A low buzzing filled his ears. "Pardon?"

"I believe you mean Cathy." The security specialist showed
no expression. "Cathy McGill is the name of Luca's girlfriend."

"Cathy?" The buzzing intensified.

"The two of you met earlier this week after Luca's tutoring
session."

"Right." He remembered seeing Luca with her. There had
been something about their body language that bothered him.
"How long have they been together?"

"Since after winter break."

"Now I remember," Rafe lied. *Cathy* was the girlfriend.
Luca had given him the switch. Why? What was wrong with
Cathy that his brother would dangle someone as sexy as Shayla
in front of him?

He didn't know whether to strangle Luca or kill him slowly.
He'd deal with his brother later. He needed to know more
about Shayla's role.

Why would Shayla get involved with this? It didn't make
sense. "Shayla is the tutor, right? What are your thoughts on
her? She seems more involved than the average tutor."

"That's Shayla," the older man said with a hint of affection. "The other students come to her for help on their love life."

"Is that right?" Rafe watched, stupefied, as Mr. Holt's expression softened. He had never seen the older man go soft about anyone.

"She plays matchmaker a lot." His mouth tugged in a smile and Rafe wondered if Mr. Holt had firsthand knowledge of Shayla's expertise. "She will go beyond the call of duty to help love conquer all."

"Who has she dated on campus?" He needed to know how much competition he had.

"She rarely dates."

Rafe found that impossible. The woman was too passionate, too sensual, to be without a lover. "I thought she was the expert."

Mr. Holt's eyes gleamed. "She's something of an expert on romance novels and chick flicks."

"And fairy tales," Rafe murmured.

"Sorry, Your Highness?" Mr. Holt tilted his head. "I didn't catch that."

Rafe waved his hand, dismissing the words. "It was nothing. Thanks."

He stepped out of the office and stood in the middle of the hallway, his mind buzzing with the new information.

Shayla wasn't dating Luca. She wasn't dating anyone. She was pretending to pull one over on Rafe. Why was she doing that?

To help love conquer all, of course. Or in this case, to help Luca and Cathy. But how? By playing some warped role of good cop, bad cop?

He bet Luca had come up with that scenario. And it had

almost worked, Rafe realized grimly. He would have been thrilled if Luca had found any other woman if it meant he had given up Shayla.

Shayla was good at her job. She was an expert at tormenting Rafe. Was that part of the role? Or was that something she couldn't help? He didn't know, but he was going to find out.

The next time Shayla Pendley made a move on him, Rafe wasn't going to stop her. He would find out how far she was prepared to go for love to conquer all.

Chapter Sixteen

Prince Santos
West Coast of the USA

"Miss Dawes," Santos greeted Kylee the next morning as she stepped into his suite, the hem of her flirty dress swishing against her legs. "You are looking very . . . tropical today."

He wanted to say "casual," but bit the word back just in time. That word would have had her turning around and returning to her room to change. He closed the door before she came to that conclusion on her own and left.

Kylee was in a dress. A dress with color. Okay, the shade was a pastel. It probably had a fruity name like peach or apricot or melon. He didn't care. It was a huge improvement from her neutrals.

He turned and found her at the table, flipping open her briefcase. She acted the same, all business, but that would soon change. He was making bold strides in the transformation of Kylee Dawes.

The dress was pure Kylee. Proper but not dowdy. It didn't turn heads but she wasn't invisible, either. The lines of the dress hinted at her feminine curves, and his only complaint was that the style didn't offer a lot of cleavage. He would have to work on that next.

He glanced down and noticed her legs were bare. Now that was a major change. Satisfaction permeated his chest. He had caused this change. He was making her aware of her body.

He was so going to meet his goal. Kylee would turn into a hedonist and wear a bikini before she got him into a tux. "Don't mess with me, Your Highness." She closed her briefcase with a sharp snap. "I'm in no mood for your fun and games today."

"You know what you need? A walk on the beach." He grabbed the door handle. "Let's go down before it gets crowded."

She crossed her arms against her chest. "Forget it."

"You don't even have to change."

"Your Highness, the reason I'm dressed like this is because I had too much sun." She turned her back on him. "I am burned to a crisp."

Santos hissed at the bright pink skin. He hurried over to her and inspected the damage. "How did that happen? I covered you in sunblock."

"Yes, you did." She turned and flashed him a tight smile. "The front of me. My back didn't receive any of your special attention."

Santos winced. Kylee had been out in the sun, unprotected from the rays. He had remembered her adding another coat—had watched, mesmerized, as her hands glided over her oiled skin. She hadn't let him help, and she definitely hadn't asked for assistance to do her back.

"Here, sit down." He pulled a chair out from the table. "I'm going to run down to the hotel lobby and get some medicine for you."

She didn't accept the seat. "Thanks, but I already got some. I'm only uncomfortable if something brushes against my skin."

He dipped his head, his mouth close to her ear. "Today, I'm going to lather every inch of you," he promised.

She took a step back. "Not today, you aren't."

Santos bit his tongue before he responded. He had expected her to say something along the lines of when hell froze over. It sounded as if she could be persuaded to go to the beach again. *Interesting. Very, very interesting.*

"Are you sure it's the sunburn that prompted the casual wear?" he asked. "Maybe this place is getting to you."

She straightened her spine. "Absolutely not."

"Huh." He rubbed his hand against his chin. "Because it looked like you were having too much fun yesterday. Relaxing. Doing nothing."

"Unfortunately, the afternoon doing nothing put a dent in our schedule," she said primly. "We have to get back up to speed."

"We're doing fine. I'm practically house-trained. Which reminds me"—he snapped his fingers as something jogged his memory—"we're invited to a party."

Her eyebrows rose. "We are?"

"Yeah, next week." He waved his hand dismissively. "Some billionaire has a house nearby, and I have to go visit him."

Horror flickered across her face. "When is it? Which billionaire? Who is going to be there?" She grabbed his T-shirt. "What kind of party?"

"Relax. It's just a party." He gently removed her clenched fingers from his shirt before it ripped.

"You are no help," she announced. "I'll find out the details myself."

"Look at it this way: it's a great dress rehearsal for the embassy dinner."

She rubbed the crease in her forehead so fast he wouldn't

have been surprise if she'd rubbed a hole clear through. "I can do this. . . . I can do this . . ." she muttered.

"I have no doubt. Of course, I have no idea what exactly you're trying to do . . ."

Kylee held her hands up. "We have a lot of ground to cover. That means working late at night."

He narrowed his eyes. Was she trying to get out of their earlier deal? "Fine, but I'm still going to the beach."

"Your Highness . . ." she pleaded.

"You promised. A lady never goes back on her word." But the waver in her voice almost did him in. He almost backed down. He hoped she would never know how powerful that technique was against him.

She closed her eyes. Whether to control her temper or because she was about to do something she'd regret, he couldn't say for sure.

"Fine," she finally agreed. "We'll do *some* of the work on the beach."

He smiled. "I knew you couldn't stay away from there."

She ignored him. "Let's assess where we are. You still need to learn . . . You know, let's not think about that right now."

"Why not?" He rested against the table. "You've been cramming place settings in my head all this time."

Her eyes widened. "That's all you remember?"

"What else have we worked on?" he teased.

"I'm going to pretend that I didn't hear that. Let's consider the external transformation." She studied him with an intensity that gave him a buzz. "Your hair looks great, the clothes are improving . . . all that's left is the earring."

Heat tingled in his ear. "Earring?"

She nodded. "That's the last thing that has to go."

He cupped his hand over his ear. "Forget it."

Kylee sighed. "Your Highness."

He dropped his hands and folded his arms across his chest. "Not. Going. To. Happen."

"We are trying to convey a certain image. The earring doesn't go with it."

"Then change the image."

"That's not possible," she said very calmly. "Now I'm sure the earring has sentimental value. . . ."

She was choosing her words very carefully, but she wasn't going to win this argument.

"No, it has cultural significance," Santos informed her as he stood to his full height. "In Isla de la Perla, every boy on the island gets his ear pierced on his thirteenth birthday. It shows that he's considered a man in the eyes of our clan."

"I see."

She wasn't being aggressive, but he saw the determination in her eyes. A change of strategy wasn't going to work in her favor. "The earring stays."

"You never take it off?"

"I'm not taking it off," he clarified for her.

"I get that the earring is important to you. Do you understand that wearing it hurts our objective?"

"*Your* objective."

Frustration clouded her eyes, just for a moment before she changed tactics. "In fact, to demonstrate how important I think it is, I'm willing to let you set the terms."

"What are you talking about?"

"A sarong for a haircut, an item of clothing for an item of clothing. What's it going to be this time? You want me to get a stud in the cartilage in my ear?" She pinched the curve of her ear and wiggled it.

"You still don't get it." Disappointment crashed inside him.

He'd thought she would respect his wishes. He'd thought she would get what he was about.

"Belly-button ring?" she offered brightly.

He could take off the earring if he wanted to. He didn't want to remove it because of her reasons. He wasn't going to hide who he was or where he was from.

She wrinkled her nose. "Nose ring?"

How would Kylee like it if he pressed his cultural ideas on her? What if he demanded she had to get a tattoo? She'd shriek so high, the chandeliers would break.

"Pierced tongue?" she asked weakly.

How would she like it if he told her she had to go topless at the beach like the women on Isla de la Perla? Would she follow local customs? He didn't think so.

His eyes lit up at the idea. Maybe it was time to give her a taste of her own medicine.

Uh-oh. Kylee cringed as Santos's eyes lit up. He could not possibly want her to pierce her tongue. She instinctively pressed her tongue against the roof of her mouth, as if she could protect it from unimaginable pain.

"I was kidding about that last one," she said.

"I had a feeling you were."

There was something different about Santos. He studied her as if she were a puzzle and he was just about ready to put all the pieces together. He was not going to have an easy time, she assured herself, but the tension pinched her stiff shoulders.

"You want me to look more like your American gentlemen, right?"

"That's why we're here." If his appearance made those around him comfortable, made people think he was one of them, then his true goals would be easier to accomplish.

"Then I want you to act like the women on my island."

Kylee took a slow, deep breath. Why were her clients so difficult? And why was she always in a position to cater to their demands? She wanted them to feel safe while they reinvented themselves, but sometimes they asked for too much.

Although, she had to admit, Santos's request sounded reasonable. Too reasonable. There had to be a catch.

"I'm assuming that means casual dresses and sandals?" She could probably find some really cute open-toe heels and get away with it. And the casual dress was no hardship. She liked what she was wearing, and much to her surprise, it felt comfortable.

"They also spend most of their day on the beach," Santos said, gesturing to the panoramic view of the golden sand.

"Of course." She rolled her eyes. Had this been his ulterior motive? He wanted more beach time? "I'll be right out there with you, *working.*"

Although she had no idea how she was going to do that. As an image consultant, she was working on Santos's appearance and media training, and brushing him up on cultural sensitivities. How was she going to do that lying on a beach?

"And swimming."

Swimming. Kylee closed her eyes as the word echoed in her head. She had been doing so well to avoid the water. Had she really thought she could stay at this resort for a month and not dip her toes in the ocean?

It should be fine. It had been years since she swam and it wasn't going to change her fundamentally if she splashed around. Her hard-won image wasn't going to disintegrate the moment she returned to her childhood playground. It wasn't like she was going to turn into a mermaid once she hit the waves.

Her biggest problem would be once she left the ocean.

Would she want to go back? Again and again until nothing mattered anymore? As it was, she was secretly pleased she could spend more time on the beach.

"Okay, fine. I'll go swimming," she said as casually as she could. She didn't want him to know how big a sacrifice this was for her. "But that's it, okay?"

A slow smile spread along Santos's mouth. "So when you go swimming like the island women, I'll take off the earring. Agreed?"

"Agreed." She felt a spurt of pride that she accomplished the necessary changes for Santos's appearance. And not a moment too soon! "Now I have to go shopping for a swimsuit. You have no idea what kind of torture that will be."

"That won't be necessary." His smile widened. "The women on Isla de la Perla swim in the nude."

"What?" Her heart jumped as her body went hot, then cold. "They do not!"

"It's natural."

"No, it isn't. I don't believe you. I'm checking this out." She wasn't going to take his word on it! Kylee marched over to her laptop and got online. Her hands shook as she typed key words into the search engine.

Four words flashed in her mind as she scanned the results. "swim in the nude." Santos wanted her to swim—in the nude! Kylee pressed her hand against her hot cheek.

Santos sat on the edge of the table. "We have some of the best nude beaches in the world."

"But not all of the beaches are like that." She clicked on the tourism page and straightened. "Aha! See this?" She pointed at a picture taken on Santos's beloved island. "These women are wearing something."

But not much, she admitted. All of the women were topless, as if it was the most common thing to do. The bikini briefs and thongs were so tiny they were practically nonexistent.

Kylee hunched her shoulders. Her breasts suddenly felt large and heavy. "I am not going skinny-dipping."

"Then I'm keeping the earring."

"I'm not going topless, either." She needed to make that point very clear in case he started negotiating. "There's this thing called indecent exposure. I'll get arrested." She knew that from experience.

"We'll go at night," he offered.

"Nice try, but people will still see me." Not that the possibility had bothered her in the past. She had been an exhibitionist without a modest bone in her body.

"Look." He pointed at the far end of the beach. "There's a private spot behind those big rocks. No one will see us there."

Us? What was this *us* he was talking about? "You're going skinny-dipping, too?"

He shrugged. "Sure."

Ooooh, boy. Heat spread through her until her skin tingled. No, she wasn't looking forward to that. That was just asking for trouble.

Santos must have been crazy if he thought she was going to jump at this chance. Kylee suddenly turned and looked at him. He was watching her closely.

She realized his plan. Santos had made this outrageous bargain because he knew she wouldn't do it. After all, what well-brought-up lady would, right?

That had been his first mistake, Kylee decided as she looked out the window at the rocks he pointed to. She hadn't been brought up in a strict, caring or comfortable home. She wasn't really a lady.

But she was good at pretending. She had managed to fool

a prince. She had kept her prim-and-proper persona when facing worse adversaries.

Could she do it while going topless? In front of Santos? She inhaled sharply as her skin tingled.

She wasn't going to talk herself out of this. The longer she delayed, the more difficult it would be. It was time to use a motto the old Kylee have would used: *Don't think about it.*

"Okay, Your Highness," Kylee said, enjoying the look of shock on his face, "we'll do it at midnight."

CHAPTER SEVENTEEN

IT HAD JUST STRUCK MIDNIGHT.

Kylee stared at the softly illuminated numbers on her wrist-watch. Her heart gave a little flip. She couldn't believe she was doing this. She had sworn years ago that she wouldn't repeat her mistakes.

So why was she doing this? she wondered as she gave a nervous tug to the sarong wrapped around her chest. The flimsy garment barely reached her knees. Was it all to get an earring? To show a man who was boss? If so, she was compounding one mistake on top of another.

Santos wasn't just any man, Kylee decided as she watched the ocean in the dark, the resort lights barely reaching this spot on the beach. It wasn't because he was built like a god or had been born as a prince. Santos managed to break through her defenses with relative ease.

He made her yearn for the wild days of her youth. She hadn't thought that would ever happen. She hadn't looked at her past with anything but embarrassment, and now the need to break free was building inside her. Hadn't she learned from her mistakes?

But it was more than that. She wanted to get wild with him. While her head was suggesting she indulge in a romantic escapade, her body called for something hot, sweaty and dirty.

It was unladylike. Inappropriate. Crazy.

She couldn't wait.

Nerves fluttered in her stomach. Kylee closed her eyes and took a deep, calming breath. Of course, she was jumping ahead. She hadn't even kissed the man yet. But she would. Tonight.

Now that she thought about it, Santos was the best man to have a lighthearted affair with. He might not have been debonair but he was discreet. They could be with each other during this intensive course—after hours—and then part without worrying if he would destroy her reputation.

She heard a sound and looked toward the resort just in time to see Santos striding to her. Her mouth went dry at the sight of him. He wore a dark pair of board shorts and nothing else. Dragging her eyes away from his impressive physique and his exotic tattoo, she tried to keep her attention above his chin. "You're late."

She cringed at her words. What was she doing? She wanted to act natural and be seductive. She knew complaining to him was not the way to set the mood, but keeping the attitude was her only defense. If she wanted to get closer to him, she had to let her guard down.

Kylee shivered at the thought. She wasn't sure if she was ready for that.

"I thought I'd give you a chance to get into the water before I showed up," Santos said. "I was being a gentleman—couldn't you tell?"

"I'm not ready," she declared as she took off her watch and set it on top of her purse. She was stalling and she knew it. "Why don't you go in first?"

"If you insist." He stripped off his shorts without a care in the world and tossed them next to her purse.

Kylee did her best not to stare, but she couldn't help it. A naughty thrill rushed through her. It heated her blood before coiling tight in her belly.

Maybe the shadows were playing tricks on her eyes. She clenched her thighs at the sight of his cock. It was thick and huge—a clear reminder that Prince Santos was a primitive, uncivilized male.

Kylee silently watched Santos stride into the ocean. She watched the play of muscles on his back and buttocks. She wanted to follow him. She wanted to touch him.

"The water's great," he said over his shoulder.

She knew it would be. The hot sun warmed the water during the day. She stepped along the edge and allowed the water to slap against her feet. She closed her eyes and tears pricked beneath the lids. He was right; the water felt good.

"Kylee?" Santos said in a teasing tone. "Are you backing out?"

"No." Her voice came out thin and reedy. She looked at him, hoping the darkness could mask the indecision in her face. Santos stood a few feet away, the water just reaching his hip bone. Had he done that on purpose? Was he trying to tease her senses? If so, he was doing a damn good job at it.

She knew that if she wanted him, she would have to embrace the water and the sand. It was time to face facts, and she wished she didn't have to. She didn't want to believe that the old Kylee was still with her. She had never got rid of that side of her personality. She had only suppressed it.

She needed to accept that the old Kylee was still inside her. Rather than ignore that part of herself, she had to admit that it was okay to let her come out and play. *On occasion,* she quickly amended. *Very rarely.* It might only mean being wild exclusively with Santos.

"C'mon, Kylee." He curled his finger, motioning her over. "Or I'm coming to get you."

Santos's threat made her tremble, but not in the way he'd probably intended. She imagined him powering through the waves and running toward her before he tore off her sarong and clasped her against his wet, naked body.

She exhaled shakily. She wasn't against that idea, either. It was tempting. Very tempting. But if she was going to go back into the ocean, she was going on her own.

Kylee reached for the knot nestled between her breasts. One pull and she would be bare. No business suit to convey an image. No pearls to hide behind or high heels to make her feel tall and powerful.

She stared at the water lapping at her feet. She knew Santos was watching her. Waiting. Anticipating.

She wasn't going to do what he expected. No asking him to look the other way. No hiding or anything like that. She would admit to herself that this was something she wanted to do, but it had taken some goading for her to take that first step.

She removed the sarong, desperately trying not to go too fast or too slow. Kylee stood tall and proud, and possibly a bit defiant, as she captured Santos's gaze. She discarded the scrap of fabric, allowing it to drift onto the sand.

The tropical breeze wafted over her. Her skin tingled as her nipples puckered. She kept her hands firmly down at her sides and walked slowly into the small waves. Her eyes were locked with Santos's as she steadily advanced, but her heart was racing.

She smiled at Santos's expression. He liked what he saw, and made no attempt to hide his interest. But it was much more than that. It was as if he had always known what she looked like under her business suits.

She waded toward him, enjoying the silky water rolling off her skin as much as the natural sway of her bare breasts. The water reached high at her waist by the time she approached him.

Kylee held out her hand with her palm up. "I met my end of the deal. Now hand over your earring."

Santos ignored her hand. "I didn't say I would give you my earring."

She curled her fingers into a fist. "Your Highness."

"But you can get it." His eyes glittered with the challenge. "If you dare."

If *she* dared? Prince Santos did not know who he was dealing with. Kylee took a step closer, and then another, until the tips of her breasts brushed against his warm, solid chest. She pressed her lips together, fighting the urge to sink into him.

She felt the heaviness of his cock rest against the soft swell of her belly. She almost forgot her mission until she saw the gleam of the pearl. Kylee reached for his earring.

He ducked and went under the water. Kylee couldn't see him, but she felt him move away. She put her hands on her hips and waited patiently for him to resurface. He had to come up for air some time, and she wasn't going to chase him.

There weren't any telltale ripples in the water. "Your Highness?"

Nothing.

She looked around her, but the dark water revealed nothing. She tentatively dragged her hands in the water, hoping to bump into him. "Your Highness?"

Santos sprang from behind her in one giant splash. Kylee jumped as Santos wrapped his arm around her waist. His fingers splayed possessively against her stomach.

He held her flush against him. His cock prodded between her buttocks. Her breath snagged in her throat as he pressed his mouth against her ear.

"Don't you think you should drop the 'Your Highness' by now?"

"No." Her voice was high and breathless.

"Kylee." His hands drifted up and stopped tantalizingly close to the undersides of her breasts. Her nipples stung with anticipation. "I'm going to get you to say my name by the end of the night."

She wasn't going to bet against that. Kylee had a feeling that she was going to mindlessly chant his name or scream it. If she was lucky, it would be both.

Santos gently cupped her breasts. Kylee's knees buckled, and she thought they would give out from under her. Water trickled down her curves, and she was tempted to lean into him. She felt the groan rumble in his chest as he caressed her.

Kylee turned and faced him, her breasts aching for his hands again. But first she had to get the earring. She linked her arms along his shoulders and tilted her face up.

Santos dipped his head. He brushed his mouth against hers. He tasted of salt and elemental power. She could tell he was holding back, letting her set the pace.

As much as she appreciated the kid-glove treatment, she didn't want it when it came to sex. And she definitely didn't want it from Santos.

Kylee reached up and made another grab for the uneven pearl in his ear, but Santos reared back.

"You're sneaky," he accused with a smile. He dodged another attempt.

He was now more than an arm's length away. She tried again, this time lunging for him. The splashing of water sounded incredibly loud to her ears. She stopped abruptly, not wanting anyone to hear them and investigate.

She looked around the beach to make sure they were unnoticed. "You promised," she said in a fierce whisper.

"And you believed me?" He shook his head. "What were you thinking?"

She wasn't going to be a poor sport. She wasn't going to chase him around the ocean, either. All she needed to do was change tactics. She needed to distract him until he couldn't think straight.

She would distract him the same way he was distracting her. The idea was bold and naughty. She was surprised she had even thought of it. She'd been so out of practice at making a scene and calling attention to herself.

"Fine." She shrugged. "I should have known you were setting me up. Never mind, Your Highness."

She took a step back and hesitated. She lay on her back and floated on the water. It was almost impossible to keep her eyes on the starry night and not on Santos.

Kylee felt like all the light suddenly gathered on her naked form. The water lapped along the edges of her body, and she couldn't relax. She felt Santos's gaze travel over her and sensed the tension forming inside him.

"What are you doing?" he asked gruffly.

"Nothing."

Santos didn't say anything for a moment. "You're going to give up just like that?"

He sounded closer, but she couldn't be sure, with her blood pounding in her ears. This position made her very vulnerable. Lying down, arms outstretched. She couldn't bend her knees or position her legs in any attempt of modesty. She was exposed.

Worse, she knew he wanted to pounce, but he didn't touch

her. She realized her back float was the wrong tactic. Santos was the kind of man who preferred a moving target.

She stood up and gave a vigorous shake of her head. Water sprayed from her short hair. She reached up and slicked it back, knowing that Santos tracked every move she made.

"I'm sorry," she said, smoothing her hands down her neck and chest, as if she were trying to wipe off the excess moisture. "Did you say something?"

"No." His voice was strangled as his head moved in tandem with the sweeping of her hands.

Kylee couldn't hide her knowing smile. He was going to make his move, but she wasn't going to make it easy for him. She turned away and dove into the waves, giving a strong kick. She hoped she splashed Santos, waking him from his stupor.

She hadn't felt this good in years. Alive and excited. Was it the water? Was it Santos? Maybe it was a little of both. She missed letting loose, but she was scared. In the past, she hadn't cared about the consequences. Now she knew better.

What if she went too far again? Kylee slowed down and headed back to the surface. Santos wasn't the kind of guy who could protect her reputation. He was the royal rebel, and she was the tamer.

She bobbed up in the water, taking a deep breath of air. She treaded water and looked around. Santos was nowhere to be found, but she knew he was close.

She muffled a scream when she felt his hand close around her ankle. She had just enough time to fill her lungs before he tugged her beneath the surface.

She couldn't see anything. She kicked out of his hold and headed for shore. Santos easily caught up with her. No matter how much she twisted and turned, he found her, his hands all over her body, drawing her closer.

Their legs started to tangle; their hips bumped and slid against each other. His hands cupped her back and the base of her skull before the two of them churned and spiraled in the waves.

Kylee grabbed on to his solid shoulders and held on tight. She wasn't going to break away or fight his hold. She was ready for the wild ride Santos offered.

He must have sensed her moment of surrender. Santos stopped and slowly stood up. The water was at his waist, and Kylee clung to him as she gulped for air.

She looked at his face, and his smile was different. She expected him to be triumphant or have a daredevil grin, but instead his smile was hopeful and uncertain.

Her heart took a tumble. Kylee wanted to get even closer. She pulled herself up and curled her legs around his hips. Crossing her feet at the small of his back, she fitted snugly against him.

She cupped his face, and her finger brushed his earring. She flicked his earlobe and moved on. She didn't want to focus on the pearl. She wanted to focus on Santos only.

CHAPTER EIGHTEEN

KYLEE PRESSED HER MOUTH against his. She sighed with pleasure as she kissed him slowly. Santos was holding back, desperately trying not to dive and grab, his muscles humming with restraint.

She wanted to make this last, refusing to be rushed as her tongue darted between his lips. She explored his mouth, the excitement quivering inside her. Her fingers dug into his wet hair as she tried to get closer.

Santos broke the kiss, slicking his mouth along her arched throat as he glided his hands along her spine. She felt the edge of his teeth as he suckled her skin. Kylee reacted by playfully biting his ear. He still didn't give up, determined to brand her, until she darted her tongue in his ear.

He stopped and held her legs, his fingers digging into the back of her thighs. Arching her back, Kylee grabbed on to his arms, thinking she was gong to fall back into the water. Santos clasped her tightly as he kissed a path down to her breasts.

Kylee's grip tightened when Santos reached up and caressed

her breast. She rocked her hips against him, heat flowing through her, filling her with longing.

Santos started walking, and Kylee linked her arms around his shoulders. She burrowed her head against his neck as he headed for the beach. The moment he stepped away from the water, they tumbled onto the sand. Santos was suddenly underneath her, his hands protecting her head and back as Kylee and he rolled.

She captured his mouth with hers. Their kisses were fierce and urgent. Need washed over her as she roamed her hands over him, unable to get enough.

He rolled over, and Kylee's back hit her sarong. It was damp and scratchy against her skin. Santos hovered above her, blocking out the starry night. He filled her senses. Nothing existed beyond him.

His mouth and hands were everywhere. Seeking and demanding. He was insatiable, and she was with him every step of the way.

When Santos cupped her sex, her world stopped. He dipped his fingers between her wet, plump folds. Kylee dug her heels in the sand and bucked against him.

His mouth was on her stomach, licking and nibbling. Kylee grabbed his head, wanting him to go down farther between her legs. She felt his smile against her wet skin as he made a leisurely journey.

She held her breath, her heart pounding against her chest as he glided his tongue against the folds of her sex. Her eyes rolled back, a groan ripping from her throat as he tasted her.

She couldn't stay still. She twisted and bucked against his mouth as he teased her swollen clit with his tongue. Shivers racked her body with each lick. Her breath came out in little pants. Heat, thick and wet, coiled tighter and tighter in her pelvis as he played with her clit. When he sucked it gently, the coil sprung wild, lashing her with sizzling, biting heat as she shattered.

Dark spots danced in front of her eyes and faded along the edges. "I need you in me," Kylee confessed as her sex pulsed. She should be satisfied, but she was desperate for more.

He lifted his head. " 'I need you in me' . . . what?"

Oh, my God. This was not a time for a lesson in manners. "Please," she said in a groan.

He laughed, his breath dancing along her sensitive flesh. "No. Say 'Santos.' "

She ignored his order. "There's a condom in my purse." She reached out and blindly grabbed for it. Her fingers only touched sand. She knew her purse was somewhere around there.

Santos dipped his tongue in her navel and then up her stomach. "Were you planning this?"

"Hoping," she admitted. She was momentarily distracted as he kissed her ribs. "Do you know you're going in the wrong direction?"

"You haven't called me Santos," he reminded her.

She knew it wasn't an unreasonable request, but the moment she called him that, it was the point of no return.

Her fingers brushed against the purse. "Found it." She forced it open, her fingers shaking as Santos kissed the trail between her breasts.

She frantically searched and almost cried with relief when her fingers clasped the foil packet. She held it in front of Santos's face.

"Do you need help putting it on?" she asked sweetly as her body pulsed, begging for satisfaction.

Santos didn't reach for the condom. He braced his forearms

on both sides of her shoulders and looked deep into her eyes. "Do you need help pronouncing my name?"

She abruptly sat up and got on her knees. "I'll help you." She tore the packet open, and he stopped her.

"I'll do it." He took the condom. His face was rigid, a muscle bunching near his clenched jaw. A tremor swept through him as he sheathed himself. She realized why he wouldn't let her. One touch and he wouldn't have been able to hold back. It would be like unleashing a wild beast.

She gently stroked his jaw and gave him a kiss on his stubbled cheek. Santos moved fast. She was suddenly flat on her back, and he knelt between her legs. The tip of his cock probed the entrance of her wet core.

He slowly entered her, his muscles shaking as he reined in his urgent, ferocious need. Wild sensations crashed inside her. "Santos," she said in whisper.

She felt the tension inside him arc and shimmer before he hurled forward, slamming into her. She gasped as he filled her completely. She rolled her hips, her breathing shallow, as the heat rippled through her body.

Santos roughly grabbed her hips and tilted her so he could drive in deeper. His cock tapped a spot that lit her on fire. Kylee tossed her head from side to side, the intense pleasure so sharp she almost couldn't stand it.

A flush swept across her skin like a wave as Santos pumped inside her. Every thrust threatened to send her over the edge. Her flesh gripped him, refusing to let him retreat.

His movements grew uneven and uncontrolled. He tossed his head back, the tendons of his neck straining, his teeth clenched. He was holding on, trying to make it last as her muscles squeezed his cock.

He was a glorious sight. Santos was blatantly primal and

dominant. His tattoo was pronounced against his wet chest. The pearl glimmered in his ear. He looked uncivilized, naked and he symbolized raw masculinity. And she wouldn't have him any other way.

The next morning, Kylee hurriedly pressed the elevator button and looked at her watch. She was late.

She was never late, and she couldn't start the bad habit now. Kylee smoothed down an errant tuft of hair and watched it spring back. She didn't feel as calm and controlled as she usually did, either.

Today had to be business as usual, she decided as she stared at the lit floor numbers, willing the elevator to go faster. She needed to show Santos, and herself, that she could enjoy a red-hot affair and still be professional.

The elevator chimed and the door swept open. "Good morning, Mr. Jacobs," she greeted the elevator operator with a polite smile. "The royal suite, please."

"Good morning, Miss Dawes." The door slid shut with a whisper. "I see you are up to your old tricks."

A cold shiver went down her spine. She gave a quick glance at the older man, who kept his eyes directly ahead. Perhaps she misunderstood him. Maybe her imagination was running wild.

"I beg your pardon?"

"I admit I didn't recognize you," he said, never looking at her. "It must have been the clothes. Or the fact that you had some on."

Dread twisted in her stomach. She could act like he had got the wrong girl, or she could ignore him. What did it matter what the man thought of her?

But she wanted him to know that those days were over. She

wasn't going to let an outdated reputation hurt her now. "Those days are over," she answered coldly.

"The pictures say otherwise."

Pictures? The dread twisted so sharply she felt the bitter acid rise in her throat. "What pictures?"

The elevator door slid open. She hadn't heard the chime. She wanted to hurry out, but she needed to know what he was talking about.

Mr. Jacobs turned to her, his smirk grating on her nerves. "The ones with you and Prince Santos frolicking in the sand," he told her. "Try the celebrity sites on the Internet, and you'll see them."

It felt as if someone had punched her in the stomach. Someone had taken pictures of her last night. Oh, God. What had they seen? What did the pictures show? She wobbled off the elevator. They couldn't be that bad, right?

"I don't know why they added strategically placed stars," Mr. Jacobs continued, suddenly chatty. "It's not like we haven't seen it all before."

Kylee stood frozen at the elevator. *Strategically placed stars?* She bolted to the royal suite, pounding on the door and pushing the doorbell.

The door swung open. Santos stood in front of her, wearing torn jeans, an ancient T-shirt and a wide smile.

"Wow, you're eager to see me." He rested his hand on the doorjamb, blocking her entrance. "I told you that you would regret going to your own bed last night."

She ducked under his arm. "Out of the way. I need the computer." She ran to the laptop on the table. Her fingers shook as she got online and typed in a popular celebrity site.

"What's going on?"

Her heart stopped when she saw a picture of Santos and

herself on the home page. She clapped her hands over her
mouth, holding back a torrent of words she didn't remember
knowing.

The picture was from the night before. Fortunately it was
one where they had clothes on and were heading back to the
hotel. But those were the only good things.

They were wet and sandy, and if their body language didn't
indicate what they had just been doing, the intimate smiles
slammed the truth home.

Santos had held her close against him. She had quickly
wrapped the sarong around her breast, and it had slipped. The
bright orange stars and the ever-so-helpful "Oops!" from the
reporter made it all seem worse. She couldn't look at the cap-
tion. She didn't feel strong enough.

"What the hell?" Santos asked, coming up from behind her.

"I just heard these were on the Internet." She looked away,
but the sickening feeling didn't disappear. "I thought this was a
no-zone for paparazzi."

"It is." He leaned closer to look at the picture, putting his
hand on her shoulder. For some reason, his touch gave her
comfort. "It looks like it's from a cell phone. Another guest or
one of the staff could have taken it."

This was bad. Very bad. Not just for Santos, who was in the
midst of transforming his bad-boy reputation, but her proper-
lady image was blown to smithereens.

Stop panicking, she warned herself as she started to pace. She
was a media-crisis expert. She had dealt with worse. She needed
to stop taking this personally and spin it.

"Okay." She held her hands out as if she could stop the
world from spinning. "This is what we're going to say. You saw
me swimming alone and saved me from drowning."

He looked up from the computer. "I did what?"

"This is perfect." Hope bubbled inside her chest. "That makes you a hero and me a victim of aggressive reporting. I'll demand a retraction and an apology."

"No one is going to believe it," Santos replied, "especially if any other pictures surface."

Kylee felt the blood rush from her face. She felt cold all over. The possibility of more incriminating evidence was all too real. "This is bad. This is really, really bad."

"Why is it bad? I say we don't have any comment other than telling them to leave us alone."

"That might work for you. No one is going to do anything to you other than give you a few knowing winks." She walked to the sliding door leading to the balcony and opened it. The walls were closing in on her, and she needed to breathe. "I'll get the brunt of it. I already am."

"Who?" Santos followed her onto the balcony. "What did they say?"

"Nothing that hasn't been said to me before." She wrapped her arms around her waist and held herself tight. "You probably should know. I grew up on this beach. My dad worked for this hotel."

Surprise flickered across his face. "This is your home?"

She gave a humorless chuckle and looked out onto the pristine beach. "No, this place was forbidden for the likes of me. But that didn't stop me. I was the wild child. A terror. And as I got older, I got more out of control. There wasn't a public-disturbance or indecent-exposure law I wasn't intimately acquainted with."

The corners of his mouth kicked up with a smile. "I find that hard to believe."

"I am my best client. I was fed up with the way people treated me, even when I wasn't causing trouble. I swore the next time I stepped foot in this resort, I was going to be treated like a queen." She exhaled sharply. "So much for that."

"So one indiscreet moment and you think people are going to mistreat you?"

"You don't know what it's like," she explained wearily. "You're a prince. You could pull a stunt, and people are still going to show you some respect."

"I'm not going to let anyone mistreat you, Kylee."

Tears stung her eyes. She couldn't remember a time that someone was protective over her or her reputation. She wouldn't mind leaning on him, finding strength and acceptance, but she was too afraid to give in to the impulse.

She knew he meant what he said. His voice was steely and he seemed bigger, taller than she remembered. But he didn't know what he was getting into. He wasn't going to see every snub and slight, but she appreciated the sentiment. "Thank you, Your Highness."

Santos raised an eyebrow. "Your Highness? We're back to that?"

She looked away. "It's probably for the best. It won't be long before they discover that I'm your image consultant."

"You are much more than that," he said softly. He reached for her but she pulled back.

"That could be a problem. Your transformation—or lack of one—is going to reflect on my career."

She didn't want to think about it. How many future clients would scurry away, knowing she had got caught in a compromising position with her most famous client?

Santos looked out onto the water, deep in thought. He stood straight, as if he had come to a decision. "If my image is going to make or break your career, then we better get busy. We have a lot to cover."

She did a double-take and stared at Santos. "Excuse me? Did you say you're ready to get to work?"

"I did." He reached up and removed his earring. "Here. Hold on to this."

He placed the earring into her hand. Kylee's mouth dropped open. She felt like crying for real now. "Are you sure?" she asked.

"I wouldn't ask anyone else."

And she knew he wouldn't have removed it for anyone else, either. She closed her fingers around the uneven pearl and held it against her heart. "I'll keep it safe," she promised.

CHAPTER NINETEEN

PRINCE ZAIN
Deep in America's Heartland

"SIR?" ALI POPPED his head around the door.

"What?" Zain barked out and immediately regretted it. He closed his eyes and rubbed his forehead. "I'm sorry, Ali. Please continue."

He wished he had never uttered that damn ultimatum. What had he been thinking? That Lauren would get on her knees and beg for more? And he would demand marriage before he gave in?

Yeah, that was about it. Zain wanted to roll his eyes at his incredible stupidity. It was obvious that Lauren was not as desperate for him as he was for her. She was perfectly content with the no-sex policy.

And why wouldn't she be? He was attentive and generous. His days revolved around her. He would drop everything he was doing just to spend a few moments with her.

If any of his ex-lovers saw him, they would have been stunned. He knew Santos and Rafael would take one look at him and suggest an intervention. Somehow Zain had gone from a playboy to a boy toy, without the benefits of mind-blowing sex.

And it had only been a week since he gave the ultimatum.

Zain wanted to groan at the realization. Bang his head on the desk a couple times for good measure. Take yet another cold shower until his skin became pruney.

He couldn't take much more. It had gotten to the point that his hands shook if he touched her. His thoughts and dreams were filled with Lauren. How bad was he going to be once they got married?

"Sir?" Ali's voice interrupted Zain's troubled thoughts.

Zain looked up. From the expression on his assistant's face, Ali had been trying to get his attention for quite some time. It had been like this all week. Before then, Zain couldn't remember a time when his mind hadn't been on business.

"Yes, Ali? Make it fast. I'm going to meet Lauren for dinner soon."

His assistant stood straight, hands behind his back, and looked ahead, past Zain. "I spoke to the royal astrologer, and we might have a problem."

Problem? Dread pinched Zain's chest. He didn't need this. What he needed was all the supernatural help he could get.

"There is no auspicious day for you and Miss Ballinger to get married," Ali said in a rush and then hunched his shoulders, as if waiting for an explosion.

Zain frowned. That wasn't possible. "I don't understand."

"He's done Miss Ballinger's chart—"

"Don't ever let her know that." Zain winced, imagining Lauren's reaction if she ever found out.

"And when he compared it with yours, he discovered that you are not a good match."

Zain raised an eyebrow. Some old guy halfway around the world was suggesting he and Lauren weren't a good match? What did he know? He couldn't see what Lauren and Zain were like together. He couldn't see them in bed.

"Astrologically speaking, of course," Ali muttered, as if he could follow Zain's train of thought.

"How can this be?" Zain leaned back in his chair and spread out his arms in protest. "What about the prophecy? It's supposed to work with the stars, not against it."

"I pointed that out to the royal astrologer. He suggested that we could have made a mistake."

Zain went very still. The room went dark as clouds hid the sun. "What are you talking about?" he asked carefully.

Ali nervously cleared his throat. "The prophecy had midnight in mind for our country. You didn't kiss Miss Ballinger when it was midnight over the desert."

Zain jumped up from his chair. "I refuse to believe that," he said in a low, lethal tone. "The prophecy is about the prince and where he is at midnight."

"Of course, Your Highness." Ali kept his attention on the blank wall.

Zain stabbed his finger in the direction of Ali's temporary office. "You go inform that royal astrologer that he is the one who made the mistake. He needs to try again, and this time he had better find an auspicious day."

"As you wish." Ali paused and darted a quick glance at Zain. "Of course," he said slowly, "this does offer you an opportunity to bow out."

Zain tilted his head and frowned. Had he heard his assistant correctly? "I beg your pardon?"

"No one would blame you if you chose not to marry Miss Ballinger." Ali looked away again. "We could accept that we got the prophecy wrong."

Zain stood in shock. Not marry Lauren? Take this excuse and walk away? That night of his birthday he might have given it some consideration. Today the idea was unpalatable.

"Ali," Zain said in a growl. He laid his hands flat on his desk and leaned forward. "Lauren is destined to be my bride."

"But the stars—"

"Forget the stars!" Zain stiffened as his words echoed around the room. Ali looked as stunned as Zain felt.

Ali blinked furiously. "I don't understand. Are you going against—"

Zain raised his hand to stop his assistant from saying it out loud. His superstitions ran deep, which made this all the more difficult. "No, I believe Lauren is going to be my bride."

"Your Highness, think about this." He started to tick off the points with his fingers. "We may have been wrong on the timing of the prophecy. The royal astrologer can't find an auspicious day. Miss Ballinger has shown no signs of accepting your proposal."

"I admit," Zain said as he straightened to his full height, "it doesn't look good, but that doesn't mean it can't happen."

He thought about Lauren and her pursuit of making her dream come true. She had known in her bones that she was going to be a dancer. She hadn't waited for it to happen. She had worked hard and sacrificed to get it.

But she hadn't gone as far as everyone had predicted. Zain sighed hard as he recalled Lauren's bitterness. She regretted giving her all for a dream that she didn't achieve.

Would the same happen to him? Was he so focused on Lauren saying yes that he was heading for a fall? Would he regret the time he spent with her if they didn't get married?

He chuckled and shook his head. He would never regret his time with Lauren. In fact, even if their relationship was doomed, he'd want to spend as much time with her as he could. Make the moments count.

Zain grabbed the jacket from his chair and headed for the door. "Ali, tell the royal astrologer to keep looking."

"Where are you going?"

"Where else? I'm going to meet Lauren." And tonight he was going to take back the ultimatum and make up for lost time.

Ali was at his side. "I'll call for the car."

"Don't bother." Zain tightened his tie. "Lauren is picking me up."

Ali gave him a look, but said nothing.

He didn't need to, Zain decided. Everyone knew that only a desperate man would willingly get in Lauren's car. Zain figured he had passed that point a week ago.

"Okay, Zain." Lauren stomped on the brakes and the rear of her car fishtailed. "You have a problem with women drivers, don't you?"

He dug his hand into the armrest, but kept a calm expression plastered on his face. "I admit you are the first woman I've allowed to drive me," he answered coolly.

"Allowed?"

"You'll probably be the last, as well." He watched the light turn green and said a quick prayer.

"I am a good driver." The tires screeched on the asphalt. "I've never been in an accident. I've never got a ticket."

"Because no one can catch you," he muttered. His security detail was embarrassed by how difficult it was to keep up with Lauren.

"You don't have the right to be a backseat driver," she announced. "You probably don't even have a license."

"Why would I need one when I have a chauffeur?"

"You don't know what you're missing. I like being behind the steering wheel."

"I'm beginning to realize that." Lauren wanted to be the driving force in everything. In the car. In bed.

It was slowly dawning on him that he had given her too much freedom. He had let her set the pace, thinking it was the only way he wouldn't scare her off. Didn't she realize how difficult it had been for him? How much he had to compromise his true nature?

Maybe she did know. Maybe she wanted him to suffer. She liked to torment and tantalize him. It gave her more power.

"Oh! I have to get in here." She made a wild turn. Zain grabbed hold of his seat belt. He closed his eyes, bracing himself for the angry horns and horrendous squeals of tires.

None came. The eerie silence made him even more reluctant to open his eyes. He kept them shut tight until Lauren slammed the car into PARK.

She turned off the engine, grabbed her purse and hopped out of the car. "I'll be right back."

He watched her run into the store, her slim black dress hindering her movements. He liked it when she wore a skirt or dress, and couldn't take his eyes off her long legs.

He missed having those legs wrapped around him. His cock twitched as he watched her lean forward, the skirt straining against her hips and legs. He gritted his teeth, his blood pooling south as she rested her arms on the counter, chatting up the cashier.

He needed to take her to bed. Fast.

What was it about her? She challenged him. Drove him crazy until he didn't know which way was up. And he liked it. He wouldn't take it from anyone else. For someone who preferred comfort and convenience, he should have given up on Lauren a long time ago. But then, what was the fun in that?

Lauren hurried into the car and shoved a slip of paper on the dashboard. "Sorry. I had to get a lottery ticket."

She made it sound like an emergency. He frowned at the ticket and looked at her. "You don't strike me as someone who plays the lottery."

"I will be for the next couple months." She cranked the ignition, glanced behind her and shoved the car into reverse.

"Why?" He rested his head against his seat and braced himself. The woman pulled out of parking spaces like a bat out of hell.

"How else am I going to win a million dollars?"

He could instantly grant her that wish. "Lauren, if you need money, all you have to do is come to me."

Now he was in his element. He liked to be needed. He liked giving and being generous. It was more than gaining control; he wanted to be Lauren's hero.

She pressed the gas pedal a little bit harder. "Thanks for the offer, but I'm okay. I'm playing this for a friend of mine." She briefly explained the pact her friends had made.

"What did you list?" He needed to know. It was a window into her desires, and it could help him win her over.

"Get a job, get a place to live and get a car."

He paused, waiting for her to continue. "Those were your dreams?"

She gave a huff of irritation. "Why does everyone keep saying that? Those are perfectly good goals. And guess what. I achieved them all on my own."

Yeah, they were perfectly good ten-year goals for someone who was playing it safe. Who had suffered too many disappointments back to back and needed an attainable goal. It sounded as if Lauren was too scared to dream, even now. He was going to have to teach her to reach for the stars.

"I like Cheryl's dreams better," he said as he studied her profile. He would never get tired of looking at her. "Winning a million dollars is a lot more interesting."

She made a face. "Not to mention statistically improbable. But here I am, pouring my hard-earned money into her dream."

"Sometimes half the fun is going after the dream."

She gave him a sidelong look. "You're talking to the wrong person about that."

Zain decided he needed to pull back. "What else did Cheryl have on that list?" To his surprise, Lauren started to blush. Her jaw tightened, and she fidgeted in her seat.

"This should be interesting," he murmured.

"Not really." Her fingers tapped nervously on the wheel. "I'm supposed to win a million dollars and kiss a prince."

He blinked and stared.

"Not that I didn't want to kiss you," she insisted.

"Of course." He turned and looked out the window. The small town rushed by, but he didn't notice. She hadn't wanted to kiss him. It hadn't been impulsive. It hadn't been her desire. It had been a task she'd had to fulfill.

She was torn between looking at him and at the road. "I mean, I could have kissed you on the cheek and met my goal."

"You can't imagine how that eases my mind," he said dully. He watched as she almost missed her turn. He could have sworn two wheels didn't touch the ground, but he didn't care.

"Zain, are you okay?"

"I suddenly understand how you feel about the prophecy." And he didn't like it.

She gave a quick glance at him. "What are you talking about?"

"You think I'm stuck with you because of the prophecy. And it turns out you were stuck kissing me because of that pact." It hurt. It shouldn't, but it did. He had been drawn to Lauren, driven to touch her, claim her. She hadn't felt the same.

"It's not like that at all. I've kissed you when it had nothing to do with Cheryl's dreams."

That was true. She hadn't told him to get lost for a while, either. "But you still think I'm hanging around because of the prophecy."

"Aren't you?"

"I can't take it away and prove otherwise." The frustration blurred his words. But then, he could take it away. Right here, right now. All he had to do was tell her that the royal astrologer thought he had messed up.

He didn't want to tell her. He didn't know what would happen once he did, and he wasn't prepared to take the chance.

"You're awfully quiet, Zain."

He looked around. They had stopped. She was parked behind her apartment. Zain threaded his fingers in his hair, not bothering to hide his agitation. "I don't know what you want from me."

"Nothing."

Why was he not surprised? "That's the problem. You don't want to hear any marriage proposals. You don't want my money. You don't want me in your bed."

She scoffed. "I never said that."

"I can give you anything. Everything." He raised his voice in frustration. "All you have to do is say the word."

"You'll give me whatever I want? No matter what?"

"Yes," he said, riding on a wave of relief. They were finally on the same page. He would show her how good their future would be. How he could provide for and protect her. "Dream big."

She looked away. "I don't think so."

"Go for it," he insisted. He wanted her to ask for the moon so he could dazzle her by getting it for her. "I can give it to you."

She slowly turned and faced him. "Okay, this is what I want." She gnawed on her bottom lip. "The next time you give me a marriage proposal, I want it to be straight from the heart."

That was dreaming big? He opened his mouth, but she motioned for him to remain silent.

"The next time you ask, I'll know it isn't because of the prophecy. It will be because you want to get married, and you want me as your wife."

"But . . . but . . ."

She looked him in the eye, daring him to rescind his offer. "You said you can give me anything."

"I did." He had been thinking in terms of a fabulous lifestyle and multiple orgasms. But he gave his word. He wouldn't back down. As tempting as it was to propose at this moment, they both knew he wouldn't have given her what she wanted.

But he didn't know how long it would be before he could give a heartfelt proposal. He didn't know if it would ever happen.

"Don't worry, Zain," she said with a wry smile as she studied his face. "I know the probability of that happening is as strong as winning a million."

"Don't be too sure."

"And one more thing . . ."

Zain closed his eyes. "Yes?" He prayed she wanted something simple. Something that wouldn't require him to suffer, rip his heart out or stay away from her.

"Would you please lift your ultimatum?"

His eyes popped open as relief swelled in his chest. "Well"— he gave an exaggerated sigh and ripped off his seat belt before bounding out of the car—"if you insist."

CHAPTER TWENTY

LAUREN COULDN'T BELIEVE she had made that wish out loud. Her cheeks were still hot from blushing, and she was keeping her mouth firmly shut in case she made another ridiculous wish.

Her request hadn't been fully formed in her mind until that moment, but once she'd said it, she didn't want to take it back. Now she was worried that her wish had revealed too much.

She gripped Zain's hand, enjoying the feel of his solid strength as he led her to her apartment. Did he know that she wanted his love? That she didn't want to be the only one falling in love?

No, probably not. Men didn't usually pick up on those subtle messages, Lauren decided as she fished for her keys in her purse. But she shouldn't have made the wish. She knew better than anyone that wishes didn't come true.

Zain plucked the keys from her fingers and opened the door. He guided her inside quickly. She wanted to laugh at his indecent haste, but she knew exactly how he felt. She heard the jangle of her keys and the thump of her purse hitting the floor before he pulled her close.

She closed her eyes and parted her lips as he kissed her, inviting him in. His touch was urgent and fierce, as if he needed to claim her before his luck ran out.

Lauren pushed off his jacket and loosened his tie, placing quick kisses along his chin. She inhaled his scent, which buzzed through her bloodstream. She nuzzled against his neck, wanting more.

Zain didn't touch her. His hands were clenched at his sides. She realized he was trying to slow down. She didn't think she could handle that. After his ultimatum, she needed him fast and hard. It was the only way to ease the ache inside her.

Could she break his iron control? She smiled against his jaw as confidence bloomed in her chest. She knew she could. Zain was already shaking with need, barely holding on, and she hadn't taken off any clothes.

But, if he wanted it slow, she aimed to please, Lauren decided as she hid a wicked smile. Very, very slowly, she unbuttoned his shirt, kissing a path down his chest. And then up again, in case she had missed a spot. She parted his shirt and laved her tongue against his nipple.

Zain's muscles bunched as he tried to steady himself. She swirled her tongue along the hard nub and then bit down. He flinched, hissing between his teeth.

She slid her hands along his chest and abdomen before gliding them along his back. She loved the feel of his muscles under the palms of her hands. As she roamed her hands along his spine, Zain reached for his belt and whipped it out of the loops of his pants. He kicked off his shoes and stopped abruptly when she gave him a love bite along his collarbone.

He arched back, and a groan rumbled deep in his chest. It was like something had snapped inside him. Zain grabbed her, lifting her off her feet, and strode to the bedroom. She held on tight, rubbing her body against his, unable to hold back the naughty thrill that swept through her.

Zain tossed her onto her bed, and before she could catch her breath, he was on top of her. His hands were everywhere, teasing and demanding as he removed her clothes. Lauren didn't need words to know that he wanted her, and he wanted her now. It promised to be hard, fast and wild, just as she wanted.

She looked up in his face, and her heart gave a funny little squeeze. His eyes glittered with a blatant need that mirrored her yearning. His body appeared hard and tight, while hers felt soft and yielding. She didn't think she could take over this time. Tonight she would be surrendering.

And she wanted to surrender to Zain and please him. No one had ever looked at her like this before. She was desired, wanted. It was as if she was his deepest wish, and he couldn't believe it had been granted to him.

Lauren reached out and slid her hands down his chest before grasping his fully aroused cock. She wanted to give him everything he wished for. Her muscles clenched in anticipation, and she wiggled her hips.

Zain reached for the drawer in her bedside table. She barely paid attention until he stopped. The tension in his body was different. Darker. He moved away and Lauren gave a murmur of complaint.

"What is this?" he asked in a low, rough voice.

Lauren looked at what he held in his hand. She blinked and tried to focus. Oh, *that*. Surely Zain knew. He was sophisticated and unbelievably sexual. Maybe he hadn't seen the latest design. "It's a vibrator."

He turned to stare at her. For a moment he didn't say anything as his eyes slowly narrowed into slits. "Have you been using this for the past week?"

Nonstop, actually. It was as if Zain had uncovered a raven-ous sensual side of her that she hadn't known existed. But the look of displeasure on Zain's face stopped her from saying that. "Yes. What of it?"

Lauren winced. That had probably come out a little more defiant than she wanted it to. She didn't know why she was feeling defensive. She hadn't done anything wrong. She wasn't the one who had made the stupid ultimatum.

But the look on Zain's face had her holding her tongue. He looked at her as if she had cheated him out of something. Which was ridiculous. She hadn't. She knew she hadn't.

It wasn't as if she had picked the vibrator over him. Like that would ever happen! Who cared if it was top of the line and designed to give a woman the ultimate pleasure? So what if it had more speed than a mortal man? The vibrator didn't satisfy her like Zain did.

All this week she couldn't avoid making the comparisons. The vibrator took the edge off, but it wasn't enough. She missed the emotional connection, the intimacy, she had with Zain.

He handed her the vibrator. The sex toy felt heavy and foreign after she had been touching Zain's hot skin. "Show me how you play with this."

"Uh, no." That was revealing way too much. She tried to hand the sex toy back, but he wouldn't accept it.

"Why not?" He towered over her. She felt at a disadvantage, splayed naked on the bed while he stood, still wearing his pants and an unbuttoned shirt. "Do you do exactly the same things that you do with me? Or do you do something entirely different?"

Okay, she could see the traps that lay ahead. Either way he would think she was holding out on him. She wasn't, but he wasn't going to believe that.

It wasn't as if she'd had a one-night stand with the first man she'd found after Zain's ultimatum. Which she could have, considering they hadn't made a commitment. Destined to be his bride didn't count as a commitment as far as she was concerned.

But the very idea of having sex with another man felt wrong. She wouldn't have done such a thing. Somewhere along the way she had made an unspoken commitment to Zain.

"Come on, Lauren," he said softly. "Show me."

His voice was like a caress. He really was interested in how she used the vibrator. Fine. She'd show him. She'd give him a performance he would never forget.

She took the phallic-shaped vibrator and stroked it upward with her hands. She glanced at Zain. His pants concealed his cock, but she could tell he was aroused. Did he imagine being in place of the silicone?

Lauren placed the tip against her lips and looked into Zain's eyes. She darted her tongue along the crown, licking it as if it were melting ice cream. She wanted to touch Zain like this right now, and from the tight expression on his face, he wanted it, too.

Sliding the vibrator between her lips, she closed her eyes halfway. The direct eye contact was too much. It didn't matter if Zain was fascinated by her performance. Her movements were too revealing. She wasn't used to this kind of attention, although she liked showing off for Zain. She felt naughty and desired, and his hot gaze turned her on.

Lauren removed the vibrator from her mouth and turned it onto the lowest setting. The gentle hum seemed to echo in the bedroom, mingling with Zain's harsh breathing.

She slid the vibrator along her neck and shoulders before gliding it along her breasts. Lauren gasped as the pulses radiated inside her. She rolled the vibe in circles. She started wide, and the circles gradually grew smaller and smaller, until she placed the vibrator directly onto her puckered nipple.

Lauren arched her spine as the pleasure forked through her. Her eyes grew hazy, but she could tell that Zain wasn't as removed from her display as he pretended. A muscle bunched above his clenched jaw. His nostrils flared as his chest rose and fell rapidly. She wanted him to touch her. Taste her. Take her now.

"Turn it up higher," he demanded.

Her core clenched at his words, her nerve endings dancing with anticipation. He wanted more? He didn't want to take the vibrator from her and take over?

"If you insist," she said in a purr and turned it up a couple of speeds. She rolled it along her stomach, her body quivering with anticipation. After slicking the vibe along her pelvic bone, Lauren rested it against her mound.

The heavy vibrations were almost too much for her swollen clit. She moaned as the intense pulsations rippled through her. It was hard to keep her eyes on Zain. She wanted to close her eyes and surrender to the flood of sensations.

Lauren bit her lip as she stroked the folds of her sex with the vibrator. She widened her legs, wanting to show Zain that she was glistening, pink and ready for him. She was inviting him to come join her and play.

Yet he stood before her, spellbound. He had no idea that he was an essential part of her pleasure. She had never felt this good, never experienced a sensual overload like this when she was by herself. Every move she made, every touch was heightened sharply because he was watching.

Watching, but not joining her.

"Touch me, Zain," she whispered before biting down on her lip as her body throbbed for completion.

"You don't need me to."

She tossed her head side to side. "Yes, I do. Please."

Zain's hand covered hers, and he took the vibrator. She sighed with relief, prepared for him to toss the sex toy aside and enter her with one swift thrust. Instead, he pressed the vibrator against her clit.

Lauren bucked her hips as the pure pleasure took on a biting edge. She stretched out her arms and gripped the bedsheets, pulling them off the corners.

Zain cupped her breast with one hand as he ran the vibrator along her wet slit. Her breath came out in little pants as her heart pounded in her chest. Lauren turned and twisted against the sex toy. It was too much, but still, she wanted more.

As Zain caressed her with one hand, he slid the vibrator in her. Her vaginal walls clamped on the sex toy. Lauren's eyes rolled back as he thrust the vibe in and out.

"Zain," she moaned shakily. She closed her eyes as wave after wave of pleasure pulsed through her.

Zain set the vibrator to the highest level.

Lauren's mouth sagged open as the intense pleasure stormed through her. Her legs went limp, and she couldn't fight it anymore. She surrendered just as the ecstasy became torture. Her climax shattered, and her body went numb.

Zain removed the vibrator and tossed it to the side. She heard the zip of his pants and the crinkle of foil. Lauren was exhausted and overwhelmed; she didn't think she could take any more. She gasped when he entered her in one long thrust, and her body welcomed him eagerly.

She raised her hips to meet him. He was a snug fit as her swollen flesh squeezed his cock, drawing him deeper. She opened her eyes, compelled to meet his gaze. He wanted to claim her body and soul. At this moment, the way he held her so possessively, she was about to surrender.

Zain didn't move. She felt his cock pulsing inside her, but he didn't thrust. Lauren whimpered, rocking her hips as the heat poured through her body. Her clit throbbed for his touch, and her nipples stung for attention.

She watched him place his index finger in his mouth to wet it. Lauren stared at his gorgeous face, his eyes narrowed and his expression intense. She shivered and squirmed, ready for a rough, wild ride.

Zain removed his finger from his mouth and cupped her ass with his hands. He lifted her slightly from the mattress and Lauren moaned as his cock slid deeper inside her swollen, juicy core. Her breath became choppy as pleasure filled her.

Zain slid his finger along the crease of her buttocks and pressed it against her anus. Lauren stilled, her breath caught in her throat. She tried to relax, but her heart was pounding against her chest. Her skin was hot and tingly.

But she didn't pull away. She wanted whatever he would give her. She gasped as he dipped his finger into her rosebud. She felt a moment of discomfort and wiggled, discovering a kind of pleasure that stunned her.

He thrust his cock in her hot, wet core, each move deep and powerful. Zain continued to slowly sink his finger deeper inside her. The white-hot sensations held Lauren immobile. Zain made her feel so good that it should be a sin. She was afraid to move in case she broke the spell.

Zain continued to thrust as her vagina clung to his cock. He drove into her to the hilt and withdrew until he couldn't hold back any longer. One wild thrust triggered an orgasm that took her by surprise. It grew slow and hungry as he teased her anus, lighting up a cluster of nerve endings she didn't know existed.

She opened her mouth and screamed with pleasure. Her mind went blank as her body went numb. The climax wrenched everything out of Lauren, leaving her dazed and breathless as Zain pulsed hotly into her.

He collapsed on top of her, his chest crushing her breasts. He slowly withdrew his finger, but his cock was still sheathed inside her. Their legs dangled limply over the edge of the bed. Neither had plans of moving.

"Lauren," Zain said against her sweat-slick throat, "don't use a sex toy without me."

She bit back her response. She could use it anytime, anywhere, and with anyone she chose. But she knew she wouldn't. As long as she was with Zain, she'd compromise on this one issue.

Lauren gave a long, drawn-out sigh. "Well, if you insist . . ."

Zain lifted his head and looked deep into her eyes, as if searching for her sincerity. He gave a nod. "I do."

He bracketed his arms at her sides and leaned on them, giving her a chance to breathe. A wicked gleam entered his eyes. "Now let's see what else you have in that drawer."

CHAPTER TWENTY-ONE

CROWN PRINCE RAFAEL
East Coast of the USA

WHEN HER PHONE RANG, Shayla was reluctant to answer it. She didn't look at the phone or move toward it. She was too uninterested, too lethargic to do anything. She'd been that way since Rafael left a week ago.

She hadn't seen him leave, but it was like she knew the moment he passed the gates of the university. The sparkle in the air evaporated, and her world felt small and claustrophobic. Since then, the routine that usually brought her comfort was now boring her to tears. The antics and dramas of her fellow students didn't fascinate her anymore. They irritated her.

It was all Rafael's fault, she decided with a scowl as she moved away from her apartment window and walked to the phone. She had been doing just fine at the university. Had even toyed with the idea of becoming a professor so she didn't have to leave her perfect life. Why had Rafael had to show up and ruin everything?

Now she knew that she had confused an effortless routine with perfection. She had been comfortable with the student life, intimately knowing the campus along with all its rules and idiosyncrasies. But it was way past time to move on and venture into the real world. She had to stop treating life as a spectator sport and get into the game.

She picked up the phone and didn't get a chance to speak.

"Shayla?" Luca asked, urgency pulsing through his voice. "I need a favor."

She rolled her eyes. "What have I been doing for the past few weeks?" And where had it gotten her? Depressed and confused.

"You don't understand. Cathy just dumped me."

Good for her. Shayla couldn't find any sympathy for Luca, and that made her feel worse. "You sound surprised."

"Of course I am!" Luca's voice rose. "Doesn't she understand what I've been doing for her?"

And didn't he see that Cathy was fed up with hiding? No favor or intervention was going to make that disappear. "I'm not talking to her for you."

"You don't have to," he hurriedly assured her. "She has no way of leaving campus, so I know she's around here somewhere. I have to find her. I can't lose her."

Did he want her to go look for Cathy? He was on his own. "Good luck."

Luca paused, and Shayla didn't know if he was trying to interpret her mood or if he was bracing himself. "But there's a hitch."

Shayla closed her eyes. "Of course there is."

"Rafe is back."

She stiffened as the traitorous fireworks went off inside her body. Energy coursed through her bloodstream, and her heart beat faster. "When did he come back?"

"Just now. I heard him knocking on my apartment door but I'm hiding out. He'll be at your place soon."

Shayla looked at her door. He was coming here? A part of her wanted to make a run for it, but she knew she wouldn't.

The need to see him again was too strong. "So?" Shayla tried to sound breezy, but her voice was too high and tight.

"Can you stall him?" he asked hopefully. "Just long enough so I can find Cathy."

Her mouth sagged open. "That could be hours!"

"I owe you one."

"You are asking too much from me. I am not going to occupy him for hours in my apartment." The last time he had been there, she had been clinging to him, naked and hot from afterglow. And he had only been there for a few minutes!

"I swear this will be the last thing I will ever ask from you."

She clenched her teeth. "Not good enough."

"And I promise that once I find Cathy I will tell Rafe that I broke up with you."

Once he did that, Shayla would never see Rafael again. That should make her calm, but instead it felt like a punch to her heart. "And then you'll introduce him to Cathy?" she asked. "No grand entrances? No hide-and-seek?"

"Yes. Absolutely. I promise."

She jumped when she heard the knock on the door. "Your brother is here," she whispered.

"Please, Shayla, I'm begging you."

She gave a deep sigh. "I don't believe I'm doing this," she muttered.

"Thank you, thank you, thank you. I'll call you when it's all clear."

"You better not forget." She hung up the phone and stared at the door.

If she was alone with Rafe, she knew she would wind up making love to him. It didn't matter if they were together for a couple of minutes or an hour—she couldn't keep away from him.

In the past, Rafe had called it to a halt because he thought she was Luca's woman. If she kept him here, locked away from the outside, she would have to distract him so thoroughly that he didn't care. Was she up to it?

The logical side of her was always relieved that Rafael called it quits before it got too far. She knew that making love to him would be a life-altering moment, and she shied away from it because she liked her life just fine.

But her body longed for him until she couldn't concentrate on anything. Today that was going to change. She was going to make love to him and walk away with no regrets. It was the only chance she was going to get.

Because once Luca "broke up" with her, she wouldn't be the center of Rafael's attention. She would no longer be seen as a threat or a dangerous woman. She would once again be ordinary Shayla, and a man like Rafael wouldn't be aware she was in the same room.

Shayla smoothed her T-shirt and tugged at her ancient denim miniskirt, wishing she had worn something different. After all, this was the last time she'd see Rafael. If she was lucky enough for this to be a footnote in his memories, she would have liked to be stunning.

She gave a shake to her hair and squared her shoulders back before she unlatched the lock. She swung the door open, and her gaze collided with Rafael's.

Her small world suddenly expanded, unable to contain the buzz of excitement. The colors brightened, and she hadn't realized how gray her days had been. She thought she had been an expert when it came to love. It was supposed to be warm, happy and easily controlled.

She had been so wrong. It was a roller-coaster ride. You never knew what would happen next. Sometimes it was scary, and sometimes it could be an amazing experience. There were times when you didn't want it to end, and other times you hoped you were in one piece by the time the ride stopped.

She was in love with Rafael, and she was lucky to have met him under the guise of a dangerous woman. It allowed her to be bold and audacious, but her mixed-up emotions felt just as extreme. She wanted to be this wild in real life, but she wanted a strong man by her side. She needed someone who would keep her from crashing and burning. It was a shame that man wouldn't be the one standing in front of her.

"Hello, Rafael." She leaned against the door and slowly took in his appearance. He wore a black T-shirt that skimmed over his lean, muscular chest. The black jeans emphasized his powerful thighs and long legs. Shayla had never seen Rafael this casual, and she liked it a little too much.

His gaze flickered on her bare legs. Her skin tingled, and she did her best to stay still. "Is Luca here?"

"No, but I'm expecting him. Won't you come in?" She stepped back and gestured for him to come in.

He cast a suspicious look at her. "Such a warm welcome compared to the last time."

She flashed a brilliant smile. "I try to be accommodating."

His eyebrow arched, and a gleam entered his brown eyes. He didn't say anything but she knew he caught her reference to the last time he was at her apartment.

She felt the blush heating her cheeks and tried to control it. Bad girls didn't blush. "My neighbors are nosy, and I would prefer you were inside."

He stepped across the threshold and it felt like her apartment shrank. His commanding presence overwhelmed the small room. How was she going to keep him here if he didn't want to stay? Shayla silently closed the door and locked it, knowing the flimsy chain wasn't going to do any good. She had her work cut out for her.

"You didn't tell Luca about us." She immediately wanted to cringe. That was not a good way to start. If anything, Rafael would turn around and walk out.

He looked at her with hooded eyes. She couldn't tell what he was thinking. "I decided it wasn't necessary."

"Is that right?" Why didn't he tell Luca? It didn't make sense. He had the proof he needed to keep his brother away from her.

Shayla tried not to show her confusion as she strolled away from the door, hoping Rafael would follow. The farther away he was from the exit, the better. "You like to share women with your brother? Good to know."

"There's something you need to know about me." His voice was low and lethal. "I don't share my woman."

A wicked curl of heat invaded her body. *My woman.* Wow, she liked those words a little too much. She sat down on her bed, which doubled as her couch. The movement felt too suggestive, but if she got up now he'd know she was nervous. "I don't need to know that because I'm not your woman. I'm Luca's."

"Not anymore." He walked toward her.

Her stomach took a dip, and she gave Rafael a quick look. Did he know the truth? She couldn't tell. "What do you mean?"

He folded his arms across his chest. "You're mine. Exclusively."

Shayla went still. Rafael wanted her.

She wanted to take him up on his offer, but that meant she had to be as bold as ever. She didn't know how to handle a man like Rafael, and it wouldn't take long for him to realize that she was about as dangerous and exciting as a nun.

She crossed her shaky legs and leaned back, resting her hands on the mattress. "I don't remember that kind of agreement," she said softly as her heart galloped wildly in her chest. "I'm not an exclusive kind of girl."

"Get used to it."

A shiver of pleasure swept through her. "Oh, I get it." She tilted her head up. "You think I'm a bad influence for Luca, and you've decided to hook up with me in order to keep me away from your brother."

He didn't say anything. She got the feeling that he was watching her very closely. Was her bad-girl masquerade showing some cracks?

Shayla bobbed her bare foot, trying to appear as though she had nothing to hide. "That's not a good enough deal for me, Rafael. Luca treats me like a princess. He shows me a good time and showers me with gifts."

"Oh, yes"—he looked around her sparsely furnished apartment—"I can see that."

Oops. Panic flashed inside her. Next time she said something like that, she had better have the luxury items and grand gifts in evidence. "And then there's the sex," she continued. "I like my men younger. They can keep up with me."

Rafael didn't seem offended by her claim. He wasn't rising to the challenge either. His eyes were gleaming as if he were secretly smiling. "But can you keep up with me?"

She didn't think so. She had never met a man like Rafael. But she certainly would like to try to keep up with him in bed. "What's your offer?"

"My offer?"

She gave a small shrug as every muscle in her body strained to jump him. Only one thing held her back. She wanted to be the woman he thought she was: someone who was an equal match to him. But she didn't know how to pretend to be that person. "If I'm going to give up a prince who is wrapped around my little finger, then I need something to compensate for my loss."

"Stick with me, and you won't think you've lost anything."

"That's big talk," she said. She slowly rose from the bed, her knees still feeling a little shaky. She stood in front of him, her feet almost touching his. She tipped her face up to meet his gaze head-on. "Show me what you got."

Shayla was stunned by the words coming out of her mouth. She couldn't believe her audacity. She hadn't planned to say that. Where had those words come from?

"I'm making the offer," he reminded her with a slanted smile. "Don't you think you should show me what *you've* got?"

Show him what made her dangerous and wild? He'd laugh. Give him a taste of how she supposedly seduced men who would give her anything she wanted? She didn't know where to start.

But maybe she was approaching the situation in the wrong way. She shouldn't try to shock or amaze him with her alleged sexual prowess. That would only make her freeze up. If this was her only chance, she should go with whatever felt good.

She reached out for him, linking her arms along his shoulders, and did what she'd wanted to do since she'd opened the door. She kissed him. Gently at first, exploring the shape and taste of his mouth, uncertain how he would respond.

He didn't show surprise or resistance. She drew him closer, licking his lips with the tip of her tongue. Her heart tripped a beat when Rafael cupped her face with his hands.

Shayla tightened her hold on him. Rafael was hers. She felt the tears prick beneath her eyelids as her heart skipped a beat. She felt the kick in her bloodstream, and a colorful, swirling celebration erupted inside her, pressing against her skin, ready to break free.

Rafael deepened the kiss, delving his tongue in her mouth. His kisses grew hungry. She wanted more, longing pulsing through her.

Shayla dipped her hands under the hem of his T-shirt. She caressed his warm, bare skin, allowing her fingers to tangle with the dark hair that dusted his chest. Her nails raked along his nipples, and she smiled when he growled.

She pulled away from him, just long enough to tug off his shirt and toss it onto the bed. Shayla barely suppressed the sigh of pleasure at the sight of Rafael's bare chest. His skin was golden brown. She wanted to rub her hands all over him.

"Lie down," she told him huskily. It was only a matter of time before her wobbly knees would betray her.

He hesitated. Indecision flitted across his face.

"Backing down?" She hadn't meant for the words to come out so aggressively. The truth was, she was worried he would call it quits like he had in the past. She should have known she wouldn't have this one chance with him. It had been too much to hope for.

Rafael's eyes were hot and smoky. Almost knowing. "Why would I?" he asked as he gathered her closely against him. He lay down on the bed, taking her with him. She sprawled over him and quickly moved to straddle his hips. Her bare legs grazed against the denim of his jeans, but she was more aware of his hard cock pressing against her wet slit.

He reached for her shirt, and she caught his hands with hers. "No, I'm in charge."

His mouth tightened. "That remains to be seen."

She wasn't sure if she liked the sound of that. If he participated, he would take the control. Worse, he would have the power to stop whenever he wanted. She couldn't let that happen.

She had to make him relinquish control. But how? She tried to think fast. "Uh, there's something you should know about me."

He tensed. His hands clenched hers. "Tell me later."

"No, I need to tell you now." She looked down at his hands. Her fingers were small compared to his. He could easily slip out of her hold. How could she keep him in bed? At this rate, she would have to tie him up.

Bingo! Her eyes lit up. That was what she would do. It would be perfect. He couldn't leave, and she would have her way with him. "I'm into bondage."

He blinked. He showed no expression, but his eyes twinkled. "What a coincidence," he drawled. "So am I."

Oh, God. She hadn't expected that! Now she'd really gotten herself into a mess. "You don't understand," she said, just in case he was getting the wrong idea. "I need to tie my man down to the bed."

She studied his face. Had she gone too far? Was he going to hightail it out of her apartment?

He probably was thinking about it. He was a strong, powerful male. He was a crown prince. There was no way he would let her tie him up. At least that was her guess. She couldn't tell what he was thinking. If she didn't know any better, it looked like he was trying really hard not to smile.

"It's amazing how much we are in sync," he said as he moved his arms above his head. "Go for it."

She didn't know if she should be relieved or if she should start freaking out. At least she had got her way. She looked around the bed. What was she supposed to tie him up with? A bondage enthusiast would have something nearby, and she had nothing!

Shayla frantically snatched Rafael's discarded T-shirt and wrapped it around his wrist. She tied the cotton shirt to one of the brass rails.

That still left his other hand. She would have to use her T-shirt. She grabbed the hem of her shirt and whipped it off. Her white bra suddenly felt small and tight under Rafael's gaze.

Her nipples hardened and pressed against the thin material. She was tempted to preen and tease him, but his other hand was still free. She grabbed Rafael's wrist and leaned forward. Her breasts dangled just above his mouth as she quickly tied his other hand to the bed.

She leaned back, rocking against his hard cock. She had Crown Prince Rafael underneath her, half-naked, and tied to her bed. It wasn't the time to be nervous. It was the time to make every one of her fantasies come true.

CHAPTER TWENTY-TWO

THE FIRST THING SHAYLA wanted to do was get Rafael naked. Her belly gave a funny flip. She had dreamed about his body enough, and she wanted to see the real thing. She hoped her imagination hadn't exaggerated.

When Shayla got off the bed, Rafael watched her very closely. "Where are you going?" he asked.

"Trust me. I'm not going to leave you here." She walked to the foot of the bed and quickly stripped off his shoes and socks. She then reached for his jeans.

"Aren't you going to tie my ankles?" Rafael drawled.

Shayla paused, her hand on his zipper. Was she supposed to? Even if it was standard procedure, she was running out of things to tie him up with. "Not this time," she said breezily.

She slowly pulled down his jean zipper and removed his jeans and underwear. He was gorgeous and sexy, lying sprawled on her bed, his hands bound to the farthest bedposts. His golden brown skin was dark against her pale bedsheet.

Shayla felt like she had caged a wild beast. Her heartbeat pounded in her ears as an insistent throb gathered between her legs. She gave a quick glance at his face. He was aroused, his eyes shining with need. He looked comfortable. Too comfortable. Did he do this stuff often?

She caressed his chest and stomach. She enjoyed the freedom of running her hands over his body. She watched his expressions and knew exactly how to touch him. The sharp intake of breath, the tension in his jaw, even the darkening of his eyes told her how to give him the maximum pleasure.

When she firmly clasped her hands over his erection, Rafael hissed between his clenched teeth and arched his hips off the bed. She tightened her hold on his cock, enjoying the heat in her hands as she stroked him. Shayla moved one fist upward slowly, past the tip, and then gripped the base of his cock as the other hand moved upward.

She repeated this caress over and over, mesmerized by Rafael's responses. His eyes were squeezed shut, his breathing labored as he murmured encouragement for her to touch him harder, faster, or to press down right there.

He abruptly rolled his powerful legs to the side, blocking her hands. Shayla cast a quick glance, wondering what she had done wrong. His chest rose and fell as a ruddy color spread across his cheekbones. His eyes glittered with an almost feral emotion.

"Join me on the bed," he said in a gravelly voice. "I want you on top of me. I want you naked."

She shouldn't give in to his request. Didn't he know that she was in charge? But she wanted her skin touching his. She didn't want any barriers.

Shayla pushed the bra straps off her shoulders. She arched back and reached for the hooks, then slowly revealed her breasts to Rafael. Her breasts felt heavy and tight as her skin tingled. Her nipples puckered under his hot gaze.

Her fingers weren't as nimble as she unsnapped her denim

skirt and let it slide over her hips. Her panties followed. She stood before him naked. For a brief moment she wished his hands were free, just long enough to caress her.

No, it was better this way, Shayla decided as she looked at his big hands. She was in control. She would have him any way she wanted.

She crawled onto the bed, the bedsprings squeaking as she straddled his hips again. This time she didn't lower herself onto his body. She was barely touching him. She crawled up, flattening her hands on the mattress next to his head. She dipped her back until her bare breast was above his mouth.

Rafael lifted his head and licked her nipple. The tip of his tongue curled and flicked against her, sending a sparkling shower through her chest and belly. Shayla rose slightly, just out of reach. He made another attempt to capture her breast in his mouth, but failed.

"Shayla," he warned.

Who was he to warn her? She wanted to laugh. If she wanted to do this, she could. He couldn't stop her.

She moved again, offering him her other breast. Rafael greedily sucked her nipple. The hungry pulls went straight to her wet, swollen core. Shayla groaned, tempted to sink onto his cock and ride him until she climaxed. She shakily moved away from his mouth, smiling at Rafael's growl of displeasure.

That sound excited her, and she wasn't sure why. There was something about Rafael. He brought out the dangerous side of her that lurked underneath her ordinary face. She wanted to torment him. She wanted him to beg.

But it was more than that. She wanted to take whatever he offered. She wanted to be greedy and rough, and she knew Rafe could take it. He would want it from her.

She leaned down and kissed him hard. He tried to draw her

deep into his mouth, but she resisted. She pulled away, noting the treacherous gleam in his eyes. He didn't like to be teased. He would have to get used to it.

Shayla kissed and touched him, guided only by what pleased her. She bit down on his nipple and drew a line down his sternum with the swipe of her tongue. When she reached his lean hips, she cradled his cock in her hands and took him in her mouth.

He surged against her, his hips rising from the mattress. She sucked him until his hard cock was wet and slick. He thrust in her mouth, his breathing harsh and choppy.

"Get back up here," he ordered savagely.

She smiled at his authoritative tone, which was ruined by his husky voice. His self-control was slipping, yet he still thought he was in charge. She'd have to prove him wrong.

She licked, nipped and kissed her way back up to his mouth. She barely touched his lips with hers when she said, "I want to ride your mouth."

If he was shocked, he didn't show it. His eyes glowed wickedly. "What's stopping you?"

Excitement coiled in her chest as she carefully straddled his face and gripped the brass headboard in front of her. Shayla lowered onto Rafael until his solid jaw pressed against her soft thighs. She shuddered and closed her eyes at the first flick of his tongue.

Shayla tightened her grip on the brass railing and gently rocked against Rafael's mouth. She moaned low and deep as the intense pleasure whipped through her body.

She rolled her hips, gaining speed as he licked her. Shayla missed having Rafael's hands on her. She imagined him grabbing her hips and directing the rhythm. She wanted him to cup her breasts and squeeze her nipples hard.

Letting go of the brass railing, Shayla grabbed her breasts, squeezing and kneading them the way she imagined Rafael would. She pinched her nipples and shuddered as the white-hot sensations zipped through her.

Rafael burrowed his tongue deep inside her. The climax rushed to her hot center, swirling fiercely until it exploded deep in her belly. She cried out and grabbed Rafael's hair in her fists. She thrust wildly into Rafael's mouth until she shattered.

Her arms and legs shook weakly as she slowly moved away and stretched her body on top of his. She sought his heat and strength. Shayla placed her hands on his chest, listening to the hard beat of his heart. It matched the one drumming in her ears.

"I need to tell you something," he murmured in her hair.

She lifted her head up and looked at him. "What?"

He smiled slowly as he slipped his hands out of the bindings. "You could use more practice tying knots."

Her mouth dropped open. Instinct told her to get away. She didn't move fast enough. When she felt his big hands on her, she knew it was too late. She was suddenly underneath him.

Shayla stared at Rafael, but she couldn't tell what he was thinking. He looked dark and menacing. Her heartbeat fluttered wildly against her ribs. "You could have slipped out of those at any time?" Her voice was squeaky.

"Yep," he said as he knelt between her legs.

"Why didn't you tell me?" She glared at him with indignation.

"That wouldn't have been nearly as much fun." He threaded his fingers through hers. He held their hands above her head and flat against the mattress.

"You . . . you . . ." She tried to get out of his hold, but he wasn't budging. She dug her nails into his hands. He didn't flinch.

"Tell me later," he whispered as the tip of his cock pressed against the folds of her sex.

He entered her with one sure thrust. Shayla gasped and tilted her hips to meet him. It was a snug fit, and she parted her legs wide, inviting him to go deeper.

It was Rafael's turn to torment her. He drove into her steadily before he retreated and gave a shallow thrust. He did this over and over.

She wanted him to go hard and fast. She needed him deep inside her, but Rafael was deaf to her pleas. Shayla rocked her hips, silently begging him to sink into her. His muscles began to shake as sweat dripped from his hot skin. He was beginning to weaken, but he continued to tease her.

Shayla clenched his hands when she wanted to claw his back. She moaned when she imagined grabbing his ass and slamming him into her. Need coiled tightly in her womb as her body throbbed for completion.

Rafael tensed above her before bucking wildly. The fast, hard thrust sent her over the edge. His guttural groan echoed in the room as he found his release.

He sagged against her, exhausted. He was on top of her, and while she found him heavy, she didn't complain. They lay in silence, their hands still joined.

"Why were you pretending to be into bondage?" Rafael murmured in her ear.

Shayla ducked her head and looked away. "I don't know what you're talking about."

He lifted his head and caught her chin with his hand. Rafael gently turned her head so he could look into her eyes. "You wanted to keep me in bed. Why?"

She hesitated, wondering how he suspected something. She decided to give him half of the truth. "Because you keep walking away when things start to get good."

One side of his mouth hitched up in a sexy smile. "And that's the only reason you wanted to tie me up?"

She jerked her chin from his hand and made a move to get up from the bed. "I can't imagine what you're thinking. Why do you always assume that I have an ulterior motive?"

"Because you always have one."

"I do not." She sat up, keeping her back to him. "I wanted to have sex with you, so I had sex with you. End of story."

What must he think of her? She shouldn't let it get to her. This is what she wanted, and she had to face the consequences. She might come across as brash and opportunistic, but if he couldn't handle that, then he didn't deserve her when she was generous and soft.

His fingers tightened against her waist. "You're not doing a favor for Luca?"

Her spine stiffened and fear, cold as ice, ran through her veins. "I think it's time for you to go."

Rafael propped himself up on an elbow. "I'm getting close, aren't I?"

She shook off his grasp and got up from the bed in a hurry. "Forget your offer," she told him as she hunted for her clothes. "I think I prefer Luca."

"Don't ever tease me about that." His voice was low, but she heard the edge. She wouldn't make that kind of comparison again. "I know that you have not dated him."

She found her denim skirt and hopped into it. "Date is such a euphemism for what I really do with Luca."

"Drop the act. I know he's dating Cathy."

Shayla froze. How did he know about Cathy? She stared at him, unable to hide her shock. "Who told you?"

"Does it matter?"

"Yes, so I can go hunt that person down." Who would have told him? It didn't make sense. A thought occurred to her, and she almost didn't want to ask. "How long have you known?"

His eyes shuttered, as if he knew she was going to fly off the handle. "I found out right before I left."

"And you decided to play the game." She wrestled with her bra, unable to put it on.

"I decided to change the rules."

"And you won. Congratulations." She tossed the bra back on the floor.

"This is not a competition."

"Sure feels like one." She stomped over to the brass railing and grabbed her T-shirt before he did. "You've had your fun. You can go now."

"You're the one who had fun. You flirted and came on to me, knowing I wouldn't touch you. You enjoyed torment-ing me."

"Tormenting you. Yeah, right." She thought she'd had the power over him, but she was only kidding herself. An ordinary woman was no match for someone like Rafael.

"You did."

She tugged the shirt over her head, refusing to respond to the odd note in his voice. "You were only interested in me be-cause I was an inappropriate choice for Luca."

"That's not true."

"And when I resisted you—"

"Resisted?"

"It just made you more determined to have me." She yanked the shirt down and realized she had it on inside out. Shayla clenched her teeth and took it off again.

"You have it all wrong."

"You're right." Her movements were sharp and angry as she

fixed her shirt. "I did everything wrong. This is what I get for playing the other woman."

She jumped when she heard the knock on the door.

"That's Luca," Shayla whispered. She quickly put her shirt back on. "Get dressed."

"Ignore it."

"He knows we're here." She looked at Rafael and wanted to groan. He was still naked and rumpled, and he looked like he had just had mind-blowing sex. She grabbed Rafael's shirt and threw it at him.

"That doesn't mean we have to let him in."

"Shayla?" Luca's voice was loud and clear from the other side of the door. He sounded excited and happy. She shouldn't have been envious of his mood, but she was.

"I'll be right there." Her voice cracked as she called out to Luca.

"This is not over," Rafael told her as he reluctantly got up from the bed.

"Guess again, Rafael." It had been over the moment she'd met him. She never had a chance to find her happily-ever-after with this prince. Too bad that hadn't stopped her from falling for him.

CHAPTER TWENTY-THREE

PRINCE SANTOS
West Coast of the USA

SANTOS GLANCED AROUND the grand salon of the billionaire's home and wished he were anywhere else. Jefferson Craft was a generous host, and he had invited a lot of interesting people. Santos knew he should take this time to network and make good contacts for his future projects, but he would rather be alone with Kylee.

He shouldn't have accepted the invitation, Santos decided as he half listened to the conversation around him. He was sure the topic was fascinating, but he couldn't keep his attention focused. Why was he there?

He caught Kylee's eye from across the room. Her smile warmed him before she moved out of his vision. He knew exactly why he was here. He was doing this for Kylee.

Santos nodded as the man in front of him continued talking about— He wasn't even sure. Something about his winning a Nobel Prize. Or was it a Pulitzer? He couldn't remember.

The cocktail party was not his thing, and he didn't think the embassy dinner he had to attend would be much better. But he'd been through worse. Nothing was as torturous as Kylee's intensive course.

The past few days had been hellacious, as Kylee set her intensive course on demonic speed, but he hadn't complained. If he could face hurricanes and man-eating sharks, he could take whatever Kylee dished out. He knew he had to turn into Prince Charming, if not for his country's mission, then for Kylee's reputation.

Santos absently tugged his ear. It felt strange not wearing his earring. He should have felt emasculated without it, but he had noticed the way Kylee looked at him when he took it off. She understood what he was giving up, and that made the small sacrifice worthwhile.

He liked how Kylee looked at him during the preparations for this dress rehearsal. He still got the wry amused glance and the prim set of her mouth. He also got the heated gaze and bold appraisals, but there had been something more: reluctant admiration for how hard he was working, surprise and awe when he mastered a lesson quickly. And it was difficult not to notice the covert looks she gave him when he wore a suit.

Problem was, he hated the image she had created for him. Hated it more than being cooped up on a sunny day. Hated it more than the time he was bedridden from a skiing accident, and he hadn't thought he could hate anything more than that.

What was so wrong with the way he used to be? Couldn't Kylee fall for a surfer? A guy who preferred action over talk? It wasn't likely. He would stick with this image if it meant keeping Kylee. Unfortunately, his Prince Charming routine was a masquerade, and he couldn't keep it going for much longer. He didn't think it was going to last another minute.

The dark suit he wore was like a death shroud. His silk tie was trying to strangle him, and it just might succeed. He didn't care if Kylee found the best tailors and designers. Nothing would make him feel better other than being back in bed with Kylee, naked and alone.

He had been prepared to send his regrets, but Kylee wouldn't let him. Not only would that action be the height of rudeness, according to Kylee, but they needed to use this party as a dress rehearsal for his big dinner. She would study him, analyze what went right and what needed improvement.

Even though he had worked hard for this moment, that reason hadn't been enough to get him out of bed. In fact, he was ready to pin Kylee to the mattress and stay under the covers until the sun came up. Nothing would have distracted him from that mission other than Kylee's promise of a naughty reward when they got back from the party. That offer had lured him out of bed.

He decided he'd had enough of the party. He'd been on his best behavior, and it was beginning to slip. Where was Kylee? He scanned the room for her. He wished she had stayed by his side, but she always found a reason to drift away. It bothered him more than it should have.

He spotted her, and his heart gave another kick. She looked sexy and elegant in the one-shoulder cocktail dress. The soft black fabric emphasized her blond hair and sun-kissed skin. The dress hinted at her feminine curves, and the flirty hem drew his eye to her long legs whenever she walked.

He liked the dress even more because he had picked it out for her in one of the resort's boutiques. She wore it with a confident smile, no jewelry, and a daring pair of stiletto heels. Santos was unreasonably proud with his choice.

He tilted his head to the side to see whom Kylee was talking to so animatedly. He frowned when he saw it was their host.

The billionaire oozed with charisma. He could make anyone feel like whatever they had to say was the of utmost importance to him. He was also handsome, Santos reluctantly admitted, if one liked the crinkles at the eyes and the graying at the temples. Santos knew that most women did.

The billionaire could afford the best clothes, but he also knew how to wear them. His manners were impeccable and he put everyone at ease. A man of the world, he could discuss anything from dead languages to a video that was making the rounds on the Internet. Women were dazzled by him. Men wanted to be like him.

Jefferson Craft was the real Prince Charming.

Jealousy bubbled in Santos's chest when Jefferson lightly touched Kylee's bare shoulder. He didn't remember the billionaire being a touchy-feely kind of guy. Santos also noticed Kylee didn't object. He watched as she opened her small evening purse and handed Jefferson her business card.

A flash of panic gripped Santos. He remained perfectly still. Was Jefferson Craft going to be her next client?

He didn't like that idea. Not at all. He and Kylee were a great team when they were focused on the same goal. He knew she wouldn't jump in bed with another man while she was with him, but Santos wanted it all. He didn't want her to work this closely with another client, but he also knew that he had no right to complain.

He had made this transformation, as thin as it was, to help Kylee's reputation. She needed to prove to the world that no matter what kind of woman she had been in the past, she was the best image consultant. As much as he was happy to help her, Santos hadn't considered that she would work with the real Prince Charming. His days were numbered.

Don't worry, he told himself. *She made you into her ideal man.* The argument didn't make him feel any better. But as long as he kept up the image, he got to keep Kylee.

Jefferson's hand glided down Kylee's arm, and Santos saw red. Prince Charming or not, the caveman inside him wasn't going to take much more. It was time to reclaim Kylee.

Santos quickly excused himself from the group and headed straight for Kylee. Their host had disappeared by the time he reached her. When Kylee smiled at him, Santos's dark mood lifted.

"Guess what." Excitement danced in her eyes. "You won't believe it."

"Jefferson Craft wants to hire you?"

"Yes!" She quickly lowered her voice. "For his personal assistant. He says she's his best employee, but she needs a sophisticated image to help her do her job."

"That's great." He should have suspected that. Jefferson Craft didn't need to change his image.

"I'll find out more when I have dinner with him."

Warning bells clanged in Santos's head. "Dinner? With Jefferson?"

"And his assistant."

"You want me to come along to lend you some moral support?" He would also add his services as guard dog, but that didn't sound Prince Charming–ish, so Kylee didn't need to know that.

"Thanks, but it's going to be the same night as your dinner. But enough on that." She looked around the room and absently rubbed the crease between her eyebrows. "You are doing great. We only have a half hour more before we can leave."

"Relax," Santos whispered into Kylee's ear.

Relax? Kylee would have snorted if she didn't think the sound would echo in the grand salon.

"This is a dress rehearsal," he reminded her, slowly stroking her back. The gesture should have calmed her down, but it made her more aware of Santos. "It's not the main event."

"True, but we're doing a dress rehearsal in a billionaire's home," she added and then realized it probably didn't matter to Santos. He dealt with the top one percent all the time. She, on the other hand, had never rubbed elbows with this kind of power. It was a goal she'd had since she transformed herself, but now she found the reality of it very intimidating.

"The cream of the crop in attendance," she said softly through her fixed smile. "I should have known, but I didn't prepare for that."

"Who cares what the guest list is?" His fingertips brushed against the scooped top. "By the way, there's something I've been meaning to ask you."

"What's that?"

He looked down at her, his fingers splaying against her back. "How did you get into the dress?"

She wanted to laugh. Only Santos would ask her that at a very stuffy cocktail party filled with VIPs. "You don't know? You bought it for me."

"I wasn't sweating the details. Forget it." He rested his hand on her waist. "What I really want to know is how do I get you out of it?"

"I'll give you step-by-step instructions when we return to the hotel," she promised. "Now focus. These guys can spot a phony. If you step out of line, they will crucify you."

"Thanks for the pep talk," he said drily.

"Sorry." She bit her lip and looked away. She shouldn't dump her worries onto Santos.

His hand glided up and down her hip. "Are you wearing anything under that dress?"

"Oh, God." She went rigid as full-blown panic wrapped around her bones and squeezed hard. "Is that Coco Collins? She's the publisher of all those celebrity magazines."

He shrugged. "I don't talk to the tabloids."

"This is different." She leaned against Santos, seeking the strength she could really use right now. "What she says about a public person has far-reaching influence. It doesn't matter if you're a politician or a Hollywood starlet. If you impress her, you have it made. Unfortunately, if she thinks you're a hypocrite or a liar, she'll ruin you with just one news item."

Santos dropped his hand from her and moved toward Coco.

Kylee grabbed Santos's arm. "What are you doing?" she whispered fiercely.

"I'm going to talk to Ms. Collins." He patted Kylee's hand. "It's the quickest way to solidify my new image."

Kylee didn't let go of his arm. In fact, her fingers dug in deeper. Coco would find out in minutes that Santos was a fraud. Kylee had to protect him from that.

It didn't matter that he was a prince; Santos was no gentleman. He was doing his best and Kylee believed he would one day succeed. It wouldn't happen overnight, and it wasn't going to take hold by the time he met Coco.

Santos didn't care about her history, and she felt safe with him. But she wasn't comfortable in this glamorous world. It was a nice place to visit, but she didn't think she wanted to live in it.

"Don't talk to her," she pleaded. "It's too big of a risk."

The corner of his mouth tilted up in a slow, sexy smile. "In case you haven't noticed, I like taking risks."

"Talking to Coco Collins is not an extreme sport," she insisted. "It's social suicide. One misstep, one mistake, and it's all over."

She knew she should have had more faith in Santos's abilities. If anyone could achieve the impossible, it was he. But she also knew he had a maverick spirit. It was one of the things she adored about him, but it could get him into trouble. She only wanted to protect him.

"So you want me to ignore her and let her think I have something to hide?" he asked.

That was not an option. "Maybe this wasn't such a good idea." She tried to think of an alternative that would make everyone happy. "You know, I can fake a fainting spell, and we'll be out of here in five minutes."

"Pass out and people will think you're pregnant." His smile made her toes curl. "Guess who they'll think is the father."

"Good point." She gave his arm a shake. "Okay, you pass out."

He laughed at the suggestion. "I don't need to. You've prepped me for this night. I am your Prince Charming."

His words jolted her. Kylee looked at him from beneath her lashes and offered a shy smile. "That you are."

He looked wonderful. The sight of him in a suit made her go all hot and soft. Yet, she was dissatisfied with Prince Santos's transformation. She missed the long hair and the board shorts. To her, Santos wasn't slick and sophisticated. He represented the sand and the surf. He was fun and carefree, and she needed that more than she needed tuxedos and tiaras.

It shouldn't matter what her opinion was. The assignment was to tame the prince. She had done exactly what she had promised. Now if only she could shake off the nagging sense of regret . . .

At least she hadn't tamed him in bed. She didn't think that would ever happen. Santos was too sensual, too insatiable. And she would like to keep it that way.

"Keep staring at me like that," Santos said in a low, intimate tone, "and I'm going to throw you over my shoulder and take you back to bed."

Maybe not one hundred percent civilized. *"Shush."* She quickly looked around. "Someone might hear you."

"I'll risk it."

She had a feeling that he would risk a lot more. "Go talk to Coco, and I'll stay here. Do it before I lose my nerve." She gave his arm a push, but he didn't budge.

He captured her hand and kept it on his arm. "I want you to come with me."

"No, bad idea. I'll get nervous and say the wrong thing. I'm more of a behind-the-scene consultant. You are better off on your own. Go work some of your magic. Show her just how amazing you are."

"All right." He let go of her hand and cupped her cheek.

She dodged his hand. "What are you doing?"

"A kiss for luck?"

She shook her head. "Absolutely not."

He narrowed his eyes. "Kylee . . ."

"Kissing is not allowed," she told him as she backed away. "That will cause a scene."

He followed her. "You're the one causing the scene."

Her foot hit the wall. "You can't touch me. At all."

His eyes glittered with anger. "Say what?"

"You mean, 'I beg your pardon,'" she automatically corrected as she looked around to see if anyone was watching.

He placed his hands on the wall above her shoulders, effectively caging her in. "A billionaire can have his hands all over you, but I need to keep my distance?"

She almost squawked at the accusation. "He did not have his hands all over me."

"Kylee, I will wear a suit for you. I will remember all the rules you crammed into my head and actually follow them. But there are a few things I expect from you."

She hunched her shoulders. "What's that?"

"You will stand at my side proudly. You will not be ashamed to touch me—"

Her mouth sagged open. "I am not ashamed!" How could he have thought that? She simply didn't want to indulge in public displays of affection.

"And you will back me up if I get into trouble."

"I can guarantee you will find trouble. And you know that I have your back. I can't believe you would think otherwise." She scowled at him. "Anything else?" she asked, glaring at him.

He swooped down for a kiss. It was fast, hot and hungry. When he pulled away, her lips clung to his, eager for more.

"No matter where we are," he said softly, "and no matter how much I aggravate you, when I kiss you, you kiss me back."

"I will, Your Highness," she promised as she tucked her hand into his arm and led him to Coco. "You can count on it."

CHAPTER TWENTY-FOUR

Prince Zain
Deep in America's Heartland

LAUREN SAT IN HER usual booth at Renee's bakery. She had her cup of coffee and her glazed doughnut, just like every other morning she came in to visit her friends. And just like clockwork, her friends were late, and Renee was behind the counter, taking care of her customers.

Lauren took a nickel from her coin purse and grabbed one of the scratch-off tickets, which she was buying as systematically as her morning coffee. Lauren scratched the nickel against the silver coating, hoping to come up with a winner.

"Are you still playing the lottery?" Tanya asked as she approached the booth.

Lauren barely glanced up at her friends as they settled into their usual spots. The jostling and bumping didn't distract her. "I haven't won a million yet."

"You're not going to," Stacy informed her. "That lottery doesn't go up to a million."

"So?" Lauren tucked her tongue in the corner of her mouth and scrubbed the nickel harder. She sighed when she realized she didn't win. Again. Lauren grabbed the second ticket in her purse and gave it another try.

Tanya cast a haughty look in her direction. "You have become addicted."

"No, I still have to win a million before Cheryl's birthday. Remember the pact that we made?" It seemed like no one else was trying as hard as she, and she had the most difficult tasks to complete. At least, it seemed that way to her.

"You're not going to make a million playing those."

"It'll add up." Eventually. All right, it probably wouldn't, but she was going to give it her best shot.

She looked down at the scratch-off. She hadn't won anything. Again. Lauren shook her head and shoved the tickets aside before returning the coin into her purse.

"Have you won anything since you started playing?" Stacy asked as she took a sip of her latte.

"No," Lauren admitted, "but I will soon. It's just a matter of time."

Tanya and Stacy gave her the strangest looks.

Lauren replayed her words in her head and grimaced. "Okay, that may have sounded a bit addictive, but seriously, I have just as good a chance of winning as the next person. You know what they say: you have to be in it to win it."

Stacy coughed and put down her coffee mug. "You think you have a chance of winning a million dollars?"

Lauren shrugged. "Anything is possible."

Stacy blinked and gave a vigorous shake of her head. "Wow, Lauren. That is the most optimistic thing I've heard you say in a long time."

"Prince Zain has been a good influence on you," Tanya said.

Lauren knew her friend was right. Before she met Zain, she'd thought hoping and dreaming were dangerous pastimes. Now she viewed the world differently. There were opportuni-

ties and adventures everywhere. It was simply a matter of rec-
ognizing them and taking action.

Like Zain's proposal. At first, she had thought he was crazy.
Then she thought he would give up the moment he found
resistance. Now she knew if he asked her again, he would mean
it. He had made a promise, and he would keep it.

That was the risk he was taking, not knowing how she
would respond. If Zain asked her to marry him, she wouldn't
compare the pros and cons. She would go with her gut instinct
and her heart's desire. She would take a risk and accept.

If he asked. *No,* Lauren thought with a smile. *When
he asks.*

"Look at her," Renee said, smiling at Lauren as she came to
the booth and sat down. "She's positively glowing."

"Lower the wattage, Lauren," Tanya said. "You're making us
green with envy."

Lauren stopped smiling. "I don't know what you're talking
about."

"Don't play it cool," Renee advised. "You can't hide the fact
that you're head over heels in love."

Lauren sat straight up as horror pierced through her
heart. "What?"

"It's written all over your face."

"Is it?" She pressed her hands to her warm cheeks. Oh,
God. Could Zain tell?

"Don't worry," Stacy said. "We can tell because we've
known you forever."

Lauren closed her eyes and groaned. Great. Now her friends
were reading her mind. She was more transparent than she
thought.

"I don't see what the big secret is," Renee told Stacy. "She's
in love. Why hide it?"

Stacy rolled her eyes. "Because she's in love with a guy who wants an arranged marriage. That puts her at a disadvantage."

"That's one way of looking at it," Renee said. "Or you could look at it this way: she is in love with a guy who makes her happy. And—get this—the guy wants to marry her no matter what."

Lauren looked at Stacy. "I kind of like her spin on the events."

"Wow, you have changed," Stacy said.

Tanya slammed her coffee mug onto the table. "I don't know why you keep saying no to the man. I mean, hello! He's a prince and a millionaire."

"I have a few other requirements in a husband," Lauren added drily. "I want him to love me. I want him to think that the prophecy is the best thing that has ever happened to him."

"What makes you think he doesn't?" Renee asked.

Lauren opened her mouth and stopped. She had been about to say it was because he never said the words. In all fairness, neither had she.

"If you ask me," Renee continued, "you have to take a man's actions into consideration. I think Zain adores you and is happy with the way the prophecy turned out."

Lauren wanted to believe that, but she needed proof. "Why do you think that?"

"It's in the way he looks at you and always finds a reason to touch you. It's like he can't get enough and wants to spend every waking moment—"

"In bed with you," Stacy inserted.

Renee glared at Stacy. "Yes, it's obvious that he can't wait to be alone with her, but it doesn't matter. When they're together, no one else seems to exist. They are in their own little world."

"That's just sexual satisfaction," Stacy decided.

"No, it's not," Renee said irritably. "We've all been around long enough to know the difference between adoration and satisfaction."

That wasn't enough proof for Lauren. She wasn't looking for a grand gesture, but she needed to know that she was special to Zain. "What do you think, Tanya?"

"I think that if I had picked that scrap of paper, I would be Princess Tanya by now."

Renee and Stacy groaned. "Not this again," Stacy muttered.

"Not necessarily," Lauren replied. "You didn't come up with my research or my plan of action."

"I could have."

"I doubt it."

"And I don't know why you're playing the lottery." Tanya gestured at the scratch–off tickets. "You've already won the lottery when it comes to finding Mr. Right. Your problem is stubbornness. You refuse to claim your prize."

"It's a little bit more complicated than that," Lauren said.

"It's actually very straightforward," Tanya said. "You're making it complicated. You don't realize how lucky you are."

"Everyone thinks that I am so lucky for getting the marriage proposal. And you know what? I am. Zain could have any woman he wanted, and he picked me. But he didn't really pick me. He got stuck with me."

Lauren pressed her mouth as the words reverberated in her head. No matter how well things were going for them, she couldn't erase the simple fact that Zain hadn't chosen her.

"But has anyone thought that Zain is the lucky one?" Lauren asked. "Do we think he won the lottery when it comes to his destined bride? Of course not. I don't think Zain does either."

"Stop putting yourself down," Stacy warned her.

"Don't you think you're expecting too much?" Tanya asked. "Zain is a hot, rich prince. You are a commoner."

"She's not common," Renee said, jumping to Lauren's defense. "Lauren is one of a kind."

Lauren wasn't sure how to take that. "Thank you?"

"She's not taking advantage of Zain's situation," Renee said to Tanya. "She's not interested in his wealth or title. Lauren wants to make sure that Zain is happy, and not many women would do that."

This makes me a grand prize for a prince? Lauren thought. What about her dazzling personality? Her . . . Hmm, she didn't have much of a list. Why didn't Renee just add kindness to animals? Punctuality? Good penmanship?

"Speak of the devil," Stacy said in a low voice as the bell on the door chimed. "Zain's here."

Renee smiled. "I told you he can't get enough of you."

Lauren's heart skipped a beat when she saw him enter. Then she saw his expression. It was like a blank, controlled mask. "Something's wrong," she murmured. "Excuse me."

She got out of the booth and hurried to Zain. She liked how his face brightened when he caught sight of her. She greeted him with a kiss. She leaned into him, brushing her mouth against his, her lips tingling from the brief contact. She wanted to deepen the kiss, but she didn't trust herself. It wouldn't take much before she was clinging to him and begging for more.

"What's wrong?" she whispered.

He cast a sharp glance at her, surprised that she had picked up on his mood. "Let's talk outside." He placed his hand on the small of her back and turned her toward the door.

Dread congealed in her stomach, but she kept a brave smile on her face. "Sure."

They stepped outside, and she looked around. There weren't too many people out on the sidewalks yet, and his bodyguard would prevent anyone from interrupting. Lauren kind of wished one of her friends would disrupt them right about now. Call it a hunch, but she knew she wasn't going to like what Zain had to say.

"Is there a problem?" she asked.

"I have to leave." He placed his hands behind his back. "There are some urgent matters I must attend to."

"Oh," she said, her voice breathless as disappointment crashed around her. "When are you going?"

"Tonight."

She flinched as if someone had hit her in the stomach. "Tonight," she repeated in a dull, flat tone. She wished she had known that the previous night was really their last time together. "When will you be back?"

"I don't know."

Lauren stared at him. She didn't need a translation on that answer. He didn't have to spell it out. He had spent as much time as he could, but time was running out. He wasn't coming back.

Her budding optimism was suddenly nonexistent. She might have been considering the worst-case scenario. He might be back as soon as he could. He might not be able to stay away from her. But what were the odds of that? She had a better chance of seeing him the next time he was running away from a prophecy.

Lauren should have known. She blinked rapidly as the tears stung her eyes. After all, why should he come back? She had shown no interest in his marriage proposal. That was why he was there, why he hung around for as long as he could.

Lauren dipped her head and studied the cracks in the sidewalk as if her life depended on it. She wanted to kick herself.

She should have jumped at the first proposal. Who cared if he had come across as slightly insane and wildly superstitious? So what if she had no intention of leaving everything she knew to go live across the world with a stranger?

Her motto was to always accept the first offer on the table. Never hope for something more or something better. Why had she ignored that when Zain coldly told her they were to marry? That would teach her.

"I'll miss you." She might feel vulnerable letting him know how she felt about him, but she wasn't going to be stingy with her emotions. She needed him to know that she wouldn't be the same without him.

He seemed surprised by her confession, and she realized she had been holding out on him. She had never told Zain what he meant to her, because she was always too afraid that it would put her at a disadvantage. Now she regretted that decision. She should have told him how important he was to her, maybe even risk saying the L word.

Zain hesitated. It looked like he wanted to say something, but was wrestling with the words. "Lauren, I would like you to come with me."

Hope lingered inside her like a wisp of smoke. He wasn't walking away without looking back. "I can't." She hated having to say that, but Zain didn't understand the realities of her life. "I don't have any vacation time. And even if I did, I would have to get permission—"

"No, not for a vacation. I want you to come live with me."

She stilled as the hope billowed inside her, zooming through her veins and lighting her up from within. She had gotten it all wrong. He wasn't leaving her. He wanted to live with her.

Wait. He wanted to *live* with her? He wasn't asking her to

marry him? She studied his face. Caution had replaced the gleam in his eyes. His expression was unreadable.

"Live with you?" she finally dragged out. "Is that allowed?"

He chuckled. "Of course."

No marriage proposal. That could only mean that he wasn't ready to have a wife—or, more important, have her as a wife. He wasn't prepared to make that kind of commitment, but it was better than what they had now. It was a step in the right direction, right? She wanted to think of it in those terms, but she couldn't ignore the fact that he wanted her to drop everything and go live in the desert kingdom of Mataar with him.

"I'm not sure about this," she admitted, her heart thumping hard against her chest. "It's a big move."

She decided that that was the understatement of the year. It was a big risk for her. Probably the biggest gamble she'd ever made. Loving him was a gamble, but this was putting that love into action. It was testing how strong her love was.

He wanted her to quit the job where she was awarded benefits by how long she had been there. He wanted her to leave her friends, whom she had known since she could remember. He wanted her to move away from everything she knew.

In return, she was expected to live in a place she didn't understand, where she knew no one, and to stay with him with no guarantee that they would become husband and wife.

It didn't sound like a good deal. He went from we-must-get-married to let's-live-together with no guarantees on how long it would last. So why was she considering it?

She knew why. Love had something to do with it. It was also because she felt alive when she was with Zain. She was excited about what the future had in store for her.

"I realize that I haven't given you enough time to think about it. I am sorry about that."

Because if she didn't go with him, she was probably going to stay in her dead-end life.

"And if you decide not to," Zain continued, "I will understand. I will come back for you. I promise."

When she was with Zain, she felt like anything was possible. She was powerful and amazing. She felt beautiful in his eyes. Marriage or not, being with him was the best thing that had ever happened to her.

"I've been asked to return tonight but I will do everything in my power to postpone my departure for a few—"

"I'll do it." She looked up and met his gaze, her heart racing. "I'll go live with you."

CHAPTER TWENTY-FIVE

CROWN PRINCE RAFAEL
East Coast of the USA

RAFE NEEDED TO FIND SHAYLA. He had to talk to her. He couldn't remember a time when he had felt this nervous, but then, he usually could predict the outcome to any problem he faced. He had one chance to make it right with Shayla, and he probably would blow it.

Rafe would not stop until he found Shayla, but she had pulled a great disappearing act. While he looked for her on campus, his plans and strategies didn't work. He had even asked Luca for help, but found no assistance. His brother had spent nearly every day for a year with Shayla, and he had no concept of what she was about. How was that possible?

No one had seen Shayla around the past two days. Some of her friends suggested that she had already left because summer school was winding down, but Rafe knew she was somewhere on campus. The place was her haven, her cocoon from the real world. She wouldn't leave, especially when she was upset.

He haunted her apartment, but never saw her. He made frequent trips to the office where she tutored. He realized that was too easy of an answer. Anyone looking for Shayla would go there first.

Rafe leaned against the wall of Shayla's office and tugged at his tie, the only hint of the frustration storming through him. He was not going to let her get away that easily. The clues to where she might be hiding were right in front of him. It was a matter of ignoring the urgency pulsing through his blood and the nagging feeling that he was losing her as every minute ticked away.

He scanned the study but saw no clues. His gaze rested on a romance novel lying on her desk. He remembered the crammed shelves in her apartment.

I like the fairy tales. Reading had been her escape when she was growing up, and it was her escape now. She would find refuge in books.

Going on his gut instinct, Rafael headed for the library. He had tried the building before, but now he was going to search every inch.

Hardly anyone was in the library, and it was so quiet it felt as if time stood still. When he reached the top floor, he was beginning to wonder if he had made a mistake. As he passed one of the private study rooms, he caught a glimpse of her in the door window.

Relief whooshed through him. He gave the door handle an experimental turn and found it wasn't locked. Rafe quietly opened the door and stood on the threshold, watching Shayla.

Slouched in a chair, her feet propped up on another chair, she wore a pair of old sneakers, baggy jeans and a T-shirt several sizes too big. Her hair was pulled up in a messy ponytail, and she wore no makeup. Rafe could see from where he stood that her eyes were red and puffy from crying.

Why was she crying? She was the one who had lied and pretended. She was the one who had seduced him. He knew she was embarrassed at getting caught, but crying? He hadn't expected that.

"Luca's not here," Shayla said without glancing up from her reading.

Rafe flinched in surprise but quickly recovered. "I was looking for you."

She didn't answer. She didn't look up. Instead she flipped the page of her book and kept reading.

He wanted to snatch the book from her hand, but he knew that was not a good strategy. "What are you reading?" he asked calmly.

" 'How to Castrate a Crown Prince in Three Easy Steps.' "

Rafael smiled. "I'm not the bad guy."

"You're worse," she said, still refusing to look at him. "I thought you were a Colonel Brandon, but you were really a Willoughby. I mistakenly took you for Mr. Knightley instead of a Frank Churchill."

Why was she comparing him to men he had never heard of? He didn't like it one bit. "Are you talking in code?"

She slowly looked up. "Let me put it to you this way," she said coldly. "You are no Mr. Darcy."

He raised his arms in frustration. "Still talking in code." Rafe stepped inside and closed the door. The click of the lock echoed in the room.

"What are you doing?" Her feet came crashing down on the floor, and she sat up straight in her chair. "You aren't invited in here. This is a private study room."

"Then kick me out." He leaned against the wall and folded his arms across his chest. He crossed one ankle over the other in a show that he was just getting comfortable. "Give it your best shot."

She slammed her book shut and glared at him. "Leave me alone. You've had your fun."

"What about you? You led me to believe you were my brother's lover."

"I had a very good reason," she insisted, even though a guilty blush crept into her cheeks. "I was helping Luca and Cathy."

"They didn't need your help."

"Yes, they did." She tossed her book on the table, and it hit the wood with a loud thud. "Cathy is like me: an ordinary woman who doesn't fulfill the requirements of a princess. She has no proper heritage, but she already has a history."

Rafael bit the inside of his cheek. "You have a history?" If she did, it wasn't scandalous or well-known.

She jutted her chin out. "I might."

"You've hidden it well. Everyone around here thinks you are a sweet girl who is always helpful and hardworking." Which she could be when she felt like it, but Rafe was surprised that no one had ever looked beneath Shayla's good-girl image.

Her mouth twisted. "You'll have to let me know who your sources are. I won't ask them for recommendation letters."

"What's wrong with what they said?" he asked with feigned innocence.

"'Sweet'?" She wrinkled her nose at the word. "That's code for 'knows when to keep quiet and can follow the rules.'"

"You can't be accused of that."

"And 'girl'?" She clucked her tongue. "I'm a woman."

His gaze lingered on her, but he was remembering how brazen she had been in bed. "I can vouch for that."

"'Helpful and hardworking.' Sheesh." She shook her head. "Why don't they just add good penmanship and punctuality while they are at it?"

"Don't worry. I know the truth about you." He might have been the only one who did, and he liked it that way. "You aren't a good girl. You're probably the most dangerous woman I know."

"Stop teasing me," she ordered wearily as she slowly rose from her chair. It was as if she didn't have the strength to argue anymore.

"You tied me to your bed and had your wicked way with me," he reminded her.

Her cheeks turned bright pink. "Rafael, I am the woman people say I am. Ordinary. Nobody special."

He held up a finger to stop her train of thought. "No, that's what you pretend to be because you think it's safer."

She started to gather up her stack of books. "You don't know what you're talking about."

Rafael rubbed his chin with his hand, and he pondered why Shayla would hide her true personality. "I blame the fairy tales."

"I should have never told you about those," she mumbled.

"The good girl saved the day and is rewarded with true love. She got the prince in the end." He held his hand up as she started to interrupt. "Sorry. The prince got the good girl in the end."

"Rafael, you have it all wrong. I am not trying to live in a fairy tale."

"Of course not." He stepped away from the wall. "Because you know deep down that you're the enchantress who causes trouble."

Her eyebrows went up. "Enchantress?" she said with a reluctant laugh.

"The wicked woman who casts a spell," he continued as he stepped closer to her, "or the beautiful queen who will use all her power to get the life she wants. I hate to break it to you, but you are not the main character in those fairy tales."

"I'm aware of that."

"You are much more fascinating, not to mention more powerful."

She was quiet for a moment. "I'm not powerful at all."

"Come on, you can tell me," he said in a confidential tone as he brushed the backs of his fingers along her bare arm. "You would love it if the villainess won just once."

Her mouth tugged into a reluctant smile, and she immediately froze. She frowned and took a step away from him. "Are you done?"

Rafe shrugged and sat on the corner of the table. "I'm just saying that the sweet-girl routine is the disguise. You know it and I know it. The reason you are upset is because you showed me who you really are."

She was already shaking her head. "No, I'm upset that you played me."

"*You* played *me*."

"Then I guess we're even," she said with a big, fake smile. "You can go now."

He wasn't going anywhere. He had tried to show that he understood her and that he liked her the way she was. That wasn't working. It was time to put her on the defensive.

"Not until I get the truth," Rafe replied. "I want to know one thing. Did you have sex with me to keep me in your apartment until the coast was clear?"

"No! I've already told you that wasn't the case. How could you think of something like that?"

"You tied me up." Not that he was complaining.

"That doesn't count," she insisted heatedly. "You slipped right out of the binds."

He leaned forward, his gaze colliding with hers. "Why did you have sex with me?"

"Because I wanted to," she responded instantly.

Rafe leaned back as satisfaction welled inside him. He tried hard not to give a victorious smile or have the triumph glitter in his eyes. "What a bad girl you are."

Shayla slid her bottom jaw to one side as she tried to control her emotions. "I also knew it would be the only opportunity I had."

What would she have done with him if she'd had the luxury of time? Rafe broke into a sweat thinking about it.

"I lied about being into bondage, but I tied you up so you couldn't leave like you did every time."

"You really are wicked," he said with a smile.

"No, I'm not," she said with a sigh.

"But you want to be. And you can . . . with me."

Rafe suddenly understood. When she was alone with him, Shayla used to feel safe showing her true nature. He didn't just like her bad-girl side—he encouraged it.

"You have it all wrong, Rafael. You thought I was dangerous because I was a threat to your baby brother. If you had met me any other way, you wouldn't have looked at me twice."

"Don't underestimate yourself."

"And who are you to ask my motives for making love to you." She pointed an accusing finger at him. "I should be asking you that. You knew what I was up to, and yet you went through with it. Why?"

"My reasons haven't changed," he said softly. "I want you. Exclusively."

His words had a visible effect on Shayla. She stiffened and looked at him uncertainly. "Still?"

"Yes." He held her gaze. "Now and always."

"You said that when you felt obligated to protect your brother. But you're no longer taking me away from Luca," she said, her voice edged with desperation. "I was never with him."

"Thank God," he said with feeling and speared his fingers in his hair. "Before I knew the truth, I was ready to fight for you. It wasn't going to be pretty."

She reared her head back and stared at him. "You would have done that? Why?"

"Haven't you heard what I've been saying?" He rose from the table, not hiding the determination and possessiveness he felt. "I want you. Exclusively."

"For how long?" She edged back as he approached her. "A night? A week?"

"I was thinking in terms of forever, but we can work up to that."

Her leg bumped against the chair, and she sat down, her movements abrupt and awkward. "Forever?"

He wrapped his hands around the arms of the chair, trapping her, surrounding her as he leaned in closer. "I won't accept anything less."

Shayla seemed more confused than worried about his warning. "Are you saying . . . ?"

"One day you will be my queen."

Her mouth fell open. "I don't think so!"

Shayla's vehemence caught him by surprise. "Why not?" She might not have blue blood, but he knew she had been born for the role. He couldn't imagine anyone else by his side.

Her eyes were wide with panic. "I don't have what it takes."

"Yes, you do."

Shayla looked prepared to argue about that. "Name one thing that makes me eligible."

He could go into her education, her strong sense of loyalty or her work ethic. He could also tell her that while she was a worthy adversary, they would make an unstoppable team.

Instead he decided to mention the one thing she couldn't argue about. "You love me."

She blushed and purposely looked away. Rafe suddenly found it too difficult to breathe. His lungs felt tightly bound. Shayla did love him. He knew that without her saying the words. He had never thought she would deny it.

"So what?" she finally muttered. "I'm sure it will pass."

The constriction broke free, and he inhaled shakily. "Then I'll have to marry you quickly."

Shayla turned and cast him a withering look. "This is not something to joke about."

"And it's not something to rush into," he admitted. "So we'll go slowly." But not too slowly. Every primitive instinct urged him to claim her. The sooner he could show the world that she was his, the better.

She studied his face with open suspicion. "Why would you want to?"

He dipped his head and brushed his mouth against her forehead. "I want to take you away from here and share my life with you. I want you to rule by my side."

She moved her head away from him to watch him through narrowed eyes. "You mean you want me in your bed."

"That, too," he admitted before kissing her brow. "But it's more than that."

"Why me?" Her eyelids lowered gradually.

He gently kissed her closed eyes. "Do you know that I searched the whole world for a bride, and I never met anyone quite like you?"

"You weren't looking hard enough," she said drily. "Or maybe you were looking in the wrong places."

"I wasn't looking for someone to love." Rafael placed a reverent kiss on her mouth. "I was looking for someone who fit the requirements of a traditional princess."

"Keep looking."

"I don't have to," he said with a smile before he drew a trail of kisses along her bottom lip. "I should have known that once I found the woman I could love forever, she would be the perfect princess. Well"—he gave her a wink—"perfect for me."

"You love me?"

"I see I have some convincing to do." He knew he was moving fast, but he wanted to start their life together as soon as possible. "But, yes, I love you, Shayla."

"And you really want to marry me?"

"Yes," he said as he outlined her mouth with the tip of his tongue. "The first thing we need is to have you graduate. That means you need to turn in your thesis."

"I'm one step ahead of you."

He lifted his head. "You are?"

"I turned it in while you were away," she revealed to him. Her expression grew serious. "After you left, I realized it was time for me to move on, too."

Rafael saw this as a good sign. He had been worried about taking her away from the one place she had loved for years. "We're already at step two: you and I take a trip."

"Where?" she asked as her lips clung to his.

"To meet my parents."

She moved back abruptly, the chair legs squeaking on the floor. "Are you crazy? I'm not ready for that."

"It's okay. They won't bite." And he wasn't going to train or coach her for the official audience, even if she begged. He wanted everyone to see exactly why he had fallen so hard for Shayla Pendley.

"You don't understand," she said as she dodged his mouth. "I am not the kind of woman you bring home to your mother."

"You haven't met my mother." He tried to capture her mouth, but she proved elusive. "Shayla, do I have to tie you up?"

"Here?" Her breath caught in her throat, and her cheeks turned pink. Her eyes glittered with interest before she peeked at the door. "You wouldn't dare."

Rafael smiled and loosened his tie. . . .

CHAPTER TWENTY-SIX

PRINCE ZAIN
Deep in America's Heartland

MOVING, ROYALTY STYLE, was supposed to be easy. Painless. She wasn't supposed to lift a finger or worry about the details.

So much for that idea.

Lauren stood under the bright sun, her feet firmly planted on the hot parking lot next to her apartment. "How many times do I have to say this?" she asked Zain's assistant. "You are shipping my car."

Ali cast a glance at the car and wrinkled his nose with disapproval. "You won't need it."

"Yes, I will."

"You will have a driver," he reminded her.

That didn't matter to her. She held up her car keys and jangled them. "I'm taking the car."

Ali closed his eyes and took a deep breath before he opened them again. "I don't think you understand, Miss Ballinger."

No, it was Ali who didn't understand. She was giving up almost everything of her ten-year goals. She had worked hard to get a place of her own and a full-time job, and now she was leaving those behind. She was not leaving her car.

A troubling thought occurred to her. "Are women allowed to drive in your country?"

He blinked at her. "Of course. Why wouldn't they be?"

She folded her arms across her chest. "Then why can't I bring my car?"

Ali gave her car another once-over. He squinted, as if the vehicle hurt his eyes. "Don't you want a new one? His Highness can buy any one you want."

"He doesn't need to. I want this one."

The assistant knew he wasn't going to win this round. "As you wish." Ali turned around and started to walk away, muttering, "I should have known not to make a move without the royal astrologer's consent."

"Wait a second," she called out to him. The assistant froze and reluctantly turned around. "You don't move until the astrologers tell you?"

Ali seemed offended by the suggestion that an astrologer ranked higher than he did. "We take it into consideration."

"Mmm-hmm." She was sure it was much more than that. "And this is not a good day to move?"

"It's not," Ali admitted. "However, His Highness is in a hurry."

So Zain had disregarded the astrologer's warning. She thought he was really into astrology and fortune-telling. "So he picks and chooses what he wants to believe?"

Ali narrowed his eyes. "It doesn't work that way."

"Looks like it does to me."

"Not at all," he was quick to defend his employer. "For example, the royal astrologers say that they can't find an auspicious day for you to marry. His Highness told them to keep looking."

"The astrologers can't find an auspicious day?" That was

news to her. Why hadn't Zain told her? Probably because she would have made fun of the idea. "How can that be if we're destined to be together?"

Ali suddenly found her car very fascinating.

"Zain and I are destined to be together, right?" She hated having to ask that. All this time she had questioned the prophecy, and now she wanted it to be true.

"About the car," Ali said brightly.

Ha. Ali wasn't going to distract her with her car. "Is there something else about the prophecy I should know about?" she asked as the dread twisted her stomach.

"No!" Ali said. "Of course not. Everything is fine. Nothing to worry about."

The assistant's strenuous denials didn't make her feel better. She felt like the shoe she'd been waiting for to drop since Zain had made his first marriage proposal was about to hit—and hit hard. "What's going on?"

He looked down at his feet. "I think it would be best if we forget what I said."

"Spill it, Ali."

He gave a long sigh, and his shoulders sagged in surrender. "All right, but you didn't hear this from me."

That sounded ominous. Lauren leaned against her car, deciding she might need something to prop her up.

"The royal astrologers think that His Highness made a mistake," he informed her, his expression stony. "They think he got the time wrong with the prophecy."

"I see." Her voice was eerily calm, which was strange since she felt like something hard and sharp had slammed into her. She was a little surprised that her legs hadn't given out on her or that she wasn't sliding into a heap on the hot pavement.

"But Prince Zain doesn't agree," Ali hurriedly assured her.

Lauren wasn't so sure about that. She thought he hadn't made a marriage proposal recently because of her request. What if he wasn't asking because he didn't think the prophecy had been fulfilled? Why bind himself to her if he didn't have to?

"What do you think, Ali?"

"Me?" he squawked, panic shimmering in his voice.

"Do you think he made a mistake?" She suddenly felt very cold, so she rubbed her bare arms for warmth. "You can tell me. Do you think the prophecy has been fulfilled?"

"What's going on?"

Lauren heard Zain behind her, but she didn't turn to face him. As much as she wanted to curl into Zain to find strength and comfort, she needed to find out how he really felt.

"Your Highness." Ali jerked to attention. He looked back and forth at Zain and Lauren. From his expression, he didn't know whether to be relieved or worried by Zain's presence. "Miss Ballinger has been asking some questions about the prophecy."

"Is that why you stopped offering marriage proposals?" Lauren asked coldly, not looking Zain in the eye. "Because you may have gotten the prophecy wrong?"

"Leave us, Ali," Zain said.

Lauren waited until the assistant had walked away before she looked at Zain. Her heart gave a funny little flip. Why had she had to fall in love with him? He was a prince, he was gorgeous and he was way out of her league. But for a short time, she had allowed herself to think that anything was possible.

"How long have you known?" she asked in a low, flat voice, which hid her wild, chaotic emotions.

"It doesn't matter."

She gritted her teeth. "It matters to me."

He rubbed the back of his neck and sighed. "I found out right before you made your request."

Lauren was tempted to look up in the sky and spread her hands out in defeat. It figured. Her timing was always off. She pushed off the car and walked to the driver's side.

"Where are you going?"

"Anywhere but here." She opened the door and got in.

"You can't walk away from an argument," he said, frustrated as he followed her.

"Watch me." She slammed the door shut, locked it and quickly drove off, doing her best not to look at Zain.

When she squealed out of the parking lot, she didn't know where to go. She made a turn, not caring where it led to. She simply needed to get away.

One thought repeated in her mind. *The prophecy might be wrong.* She shook her head as the houses and buildings passed her in a blur. That prophecy had been her insurance. She didn't believe in it, but she respected the power it had over Zain.

Lauren noticed that the path she had taken headed toward Main Street. It was as good a place as any. She saw the sign for Renee's bakery and suddenly parked in front of the building, hoping her friend hadn't closed up for the day.

Lauren hurried inside, the door slapping the frame behind her. She barely heard the door chime or inhaled the scent of baked goods. All her attention was on her friend behind the counter.

"Hey, Lauren." Renee's smile dimmed as she looked at Lauren and then outside the front window. "What are you doing here? I was just about to lock up."

"I needed to talk to someone," Lauren announced breathlessly as she sat down on one of the stools.

Renee tilted her head. "Second thoughts about the move?"

Lauren looked away. "Zain may have gotten the prophecy wrong," she said quietly. Yep, still hurt when she said it out loud.

"He may have?" Renee struggled with the words.

"There's some question about the timing."

Renee grabbed a metal serving tray and started polishing it with a dish towel. "What do you think?"

"I never believed in the prophecy in the first place," Lauren said as she reached for the sugar shaker and held it tightly in her hand.

"Then why are you upset?" Renee polished harder.

Lauren shrugged. "I don't know. Because Zain did?"

"Is he backing out?" her friend asked sharply.

"No." Lauren propped her chin on her fists and stared sadly at the counter. "But he hasn't asked me to marry him."

"Because you told him not to until he was ready."

"Yeah, but it was easy for me to say that, wasn't it? I knew he would stick around because of the prophecy. There was a chance that he would eventually learn to love me."

Renee put down the tray. "He already does."

Lauren really wanted to believe that. She needed to believe it, but that didn't make it so. "You keep saying that, but he obviously doesn't love me enough to marry me."

"Do you love him enough?"

Lauren gave a small smile. "Would I be going through all this if I didn't? I'm sacrificing everything."

Renee rested her elbows on the counter. "Tanya thinks you should stop your bellyaching because you're giving up one lifestyle for something much better."

"Oh, please." Lauren rolled her eyes. "If I wanted that lifestyle, I would get it myself."

"That's true. Or it used to be. If you want something, you

go out and get it. The problem always was that you settled for less than you deserved."

Lauren nodded in agreement. "I was going to go live with Zain."

"Are you still going to do it?"

"Probably." Lauren flopped her head on the counter in shame. "I'm so pathetic."

"No, you're not." Renee patted Lauren's head. "You're taking a leap of faith."

"Not really," Lauren said, her voice muffled. "He's never going to make another wedding proposal."

"I think he will. He's gotten really good at it."

"I've used up all my chances," Lauren said, confessing her deepest worry.

"Then don't go."

She looked up at her friend in horror. "You mean it's all or nothing? I don't like those odds. I think I'll take what I can get. It's what I do best."

"Here's an idea," Renee said as her eyes lit up. "If you really want to marry him, why don't you ask him?"

"Beat him to the punch?"

"Sure. Why not?"

"I won't know if he's ready," Lauren argued. "If he really thinks the prophecy is right—"

Renee gave an exasperated sigh. "Lauren, ignore the prophecy. Act like it doesn't exist."

Lauren sat up straight. "I can't do that. It started everything."

"The prophecy brought him to you. It doesn't guarantee you keep him."

"Yes, it does." Lauren was not going to let her safety net slip away. "The prophecy says that I am destined to be his bride."

"That's a very limited outlook," Renee decided. "You should view this situation the same way you do the lottery. The prophecy is the ticket. It means you have a chance. You might win the jackpot, you might win a little or you might not win anything at all."

Lauren wanted to be more than a bride. She wanted to be Zain's partner, his wife, the love of his life. The prophecy didn't mention it, but that didn't mean it couldn't happen. "Okay, you might be onto something here. The prophecy got me noticed."

"Actually," Zain said from behind her, "it was the way you danced."

Lauren's eyes widened as her heart slammed against her ribs. She stared at her friend, unable to turn around. "How long has he been there?"

Renee winced. "Oh, since about thirty seconds after you came in."

"And you didn't tell me?" Lauren whispered.

"I did! Did you not see the whole eye-contact thing? The motioning of the head?" She gave an exaggerated tilt of her head. "His reflection on the metal tray?"

"You need to work on that. Why didn't you just say, 'Hi, Zain'?"

Renee shrugged. "You were on a roll, and I didn't want to interrupt. I'll be in back if need me."

"Don't leave me." Zain had heard everything Lauren said. She felt exposed and vulnerable.

Renee was already walking backward, ready to make her getaway. "You're going to be just fine."

"What kind of friend are you?" Lauren called after Renee.

"The best," she replied over her shoulder before she disappeared into the back of the bakery.

Lauren wasn't so sure about her friend's claim, but all thoughts of Renee fled when Zain gently placed his large hands against her back. She tried to steel her emotions, but it was a losing battle. Anytime Zain touched her, she became soft and compliant. And he knew it, the rat!

"You know why I haven't asked for your hand in marriage lately?" he asked softly.

"There are a few possibilities. I believe you heard them." She swallowed roughly as his hands glided up and down her spine. If Zain's goal was to soothe her, it wasn't working.

"I didn't think you were ready to hear it again."

Lauren made a face. "Good save." And, in a way, he was right. She would have questioned another proposal, even though she knew he was a man of his word.

He lowered his head so that his mouth brushed against her ear. Lauren shivered as his warm breath tickled her skin. "The prophecy said you were destined to be my bride. I wish it told me how to go about getting you."

Lauren frowned. "I don't come with a set of instructions."

"Tell me about it," he said with a wry chuckle. "But I've learned a lot about you. You are someone who needs proof. I wanted to show you how much you mean to me. I thought my actions would speak louder than my words."

"They do." When she was with him, she felt his support and respect. She knew he cherished her, but she had spent too much time worrying that it was all going to end.

Zain's hands slid to her waist. His grip was possessive, but she didn't try to get out of it. "I have also come to realize that, despite what you say, you would mistrust a whirlwind courtship.

You need a solid foundation so that you can slowly work your way up to it. It's the only way you would feel safe and secure."

She slowly turned around and looked into his eyes. "You might be onto something there," she admitted.

"I want to be with you, but I can't stay here. I have to go back home. I thought asking you to come with me was the best compromise. I didn't mean for you to feel even more uncertain."

"It's okay. I'm still going."

A smile tugged the corners of his mouth. "I heard. For a minute there I thought I had lost you. I wasn't going to let that happen."

"Do you think you got the prophecy right?"

"Yes." There was no hesitation in his answer. "The prophecy said you were destined to be my bride. It didn't say I was destined to love you."

"I know." She also knew that it wasn't something she could wish for on a star or force to follow her time line.

"That happened on its own."

She frowned and stared at him. Her heart twisted and she held her breath. What had he said? Had she misunderstood?

"I love you, Lauren." Zain's voice shook as he cupped her face with his hands and reverently brushed his mouth against hers. "And I'm going to prove it to you every day."

"So," she said as her lips clung to his, her heart beating wildly, "are you going to marry me?"

He lifted his mouth away from hers. "Are you asking?"

Was she? Why shouldn't she? She didn't need to test Zain and how he felt about her. She believed him. More important, she believed in them. "Yes, I'm proposing."

His eyes sparkled. She didn't think she'd ever seen him this happy. "It's about time."

"Is that a yes?" she teased.

"No." He lifted her from the stool and clasped her tight against his chest. "This is." He covered her mouth with his as he circled around, swinging her feet off the floor.

Lauren squealed with laughter, clinging onto Zain's strong shoulders. Hope and love danced inside her. She didn't need anyone telling her what the future might bring. She knew it was going to be great.

CHAPTER TWENTY-SEVEN

PRINCE SANTOS
West Coast of the USA

SANTOS'S LIMOUSINE PURRED to a stop at the curb. He opened
the door and got out before anyone could assist him. Stretching
to his full height as if he had been trapped indoors for too long,
Santos breathed in the balmy air.

He inhaled the scent of the ocean and felt himself relax. As
he walked by a tropical floral arrangement, he found that he
preferred the tang of the flowers over the cloying perfumes and
colognes he had smelled throughout the night.

He heard the strains of chamber music and shook his head.
He had listened to it enough tonight to last a lifetime. Was he
going to be humming it for the next few days?

When he stepped inside the open-air lobby, he realized that
the classical music was coming from one of the gardens outside.
A string quartet, dressed just like he was in tuxedos with tails,
was playing in the shadows for an elegant party.

The event he had just attended was stuffier, but on the
whole, embassy dinners weren't all that bad, Santos admitted as
put his hands in his pockets and walked through the lobby, nod-
ding at the concierge, who greeted him by name. Santos could
have done without the fancy dress and even fancier silverware,

but the people were interesting. They might be formal, but they were essentially people of action.

It was too bad Kylee couldn't have been there. She would have liked everything from the guests to the menu. Santos smiled, knowing Kylee would have been thrilled at the excuse of wearing long white gloves.

He could easily imagine her wearing them. She would look very prim and refined. But he could also imagine her teasing him by stripping them off slowly. As she tugged each off, inch by inch, she would shed her ladylike image and reveal the earthy, sensual woman underneath.

Santos pulled his black bow tie loose and sighed, but it wasn't enough. He still felt chained. Leashed. He took off his tuxedo jacket and rolled his shoulders. Now he felt better. No matter how much training he received, he knew he was not meant to wear a tie and jacket.

He was going to have to fake it if he wanted to keep Kylee. She might be a mix of earthy and elegance, but she didn't want that in a man. Her job was done, and if he wanted to hang on to her, he needed to be Prince Charming.

It wasn't a good plan. In fact, it was destined to fail. He shouldn't attempt it, but every day he kept the guise was one more day with Kylee.

But he was making assumptions, Santos realized with a frown. He hooked his jacket over his fingers and strolled along the meandering walkway to his hotel building. Kylee hadn't said anything about what the future held for them.

As the pathway forked to his building or to the beach, a movement caught his eye. Everything inside him went still when he saw Kylee. She stood on the edge of the sidewalk, which ended where the sand began. She was in front of the small waterfall, the lights casting a soft glow on her.

Kylee looked extraordinarily sexy. She tilted her head back and laughed, the breeze ruffling her short hair. She wore an off-the-shoulder black dress that made a man think about tugging the dress down and dragging it off her curves.

Her dress had long sleeves, and the skirt floated below her knees. The flirty sandals with the killer heels got his pulse racing. Where had she got that outfit? And why hadn't he seen it before? Maybe she knew it was safer not to wear it around him. He would have it off her in a minute flat.

And then he noticed that Kylee wasn't alone. The shadows almost hid her companion. She was with Jefferson Craft. By herself. Next to a romantic waterfall. In the dark.

Santos wasn't going to put up with that. He clenched his jaw as the urge to invade roared through his blood. He knew Kylee's focus was gearing toward her next big project, but she wasn't done with him just yet.

He strode over to them, letting his footsteps sound loudly in the hushed darkness. Kylee glanced over, and he knew the minute she saw him. It was as if a light had been turned on inside her. Santos's chest tightened as he wondered what he had done to deserve her warmth and affection, and what he could do to keep it.

Jefferson looked over his shoulder. "Good evening, Your Highness."

"Craft," Santos said with a nod, barely looking at the other man. He cupped his hand on Kylee's elbow. It was a sign of possession, and although a flash of annoyance crept into Kylee's eyes, she didn't move. He leaned down and gave her a hard, brief kiss.

True to her word, she kissed him back. He was tempted to deepen the kiss and clasp her tightly against him, but he wasn't going to push his luck.

Santos lifted his head and looked into Kylee's sparkling blue eyes. "Am I interrupting?"

Kylee narrowed her eyes as Craft replied, "Not at all. I was just saying good night."

Santos acknowledged that the billionaire might get points for his good manners, but he didn't care about that. The most important thing was having Kylee at his side tonight.

Craft captured Kylee's fingers, and Santos instinctively tightened his hold on her elbow. The billionaire gave a courtly bow over her hands before touching his lips against her knuckles. "I look forward to hearing from you, Kylee."

Her cheeks turned pink, and she ducked her head shyly.

Santos watched Kylee's pleased response, and his stomach gave a sickening twist. Damn. The guy got major bonus points on that one.

"Good night, Jefferson," she said softly.

Jefferson? Santos felt his blood boil because of that one word. Kylee was calling the billionaire by his first name? In front of another person? She still wouldn't do that for him.

Santos knew he had to face the facts. He had stiff competition for Kylee. It didn't matter that he was a prince or that he could spend the rest of his life working on his image. He was never going to be as sophisticated as that billionaire.

Kylee waited until the other man walked away before she extracted her elbow from his grip. "I was going to take a walk on the beach before I went inside. You want to join me?"

"Jefferson?" The word came out in a low growl. "You're on a first-name basis with him?"

She looked down as she removed her high heels. "Commoners follow different rules than royalty. How was your evening?"

"Fine," he answered tightly. "How was yours? With *Jefferson*?"

"That's all I'm getting? 'Fine'?" She curled her hand around his arm and guided him to the beach. "I worked for a month nonstop on this night. I need to hear something more than 'fine.'"

"You want to hear that I caused a food fight?"

She gave him a sharp look and then chuckled. "You did not."

"You're right. I didn't." He saw her shiver from the cold ocean breeze and tenderly draped his jacket over her bare shoulders.

She smiled and thanked him before burrowing into his jacket. She looked small and fragile, but he knew better. The woman had the strength to transform herself into anything she wanted to be. He didn't have that kind of power, and he felt like he was letting her down.

"Everything went smoothly," he said as he looked away and stared at the ocean, "thanks to you."

"I'm glad, but I want to hear more." Her shoulders bumped against his arms as they walked toward the big rocks that had shielded them the night they went skinny-dipping. "I expect a full report."

"Not tonight." A full report would have been the final act of her job. He wasn't ready for that.

She pressed her lips together, reining in her impatience. As he guided her past the rocks, she gave up the fight. "Okay, not tonight." She dug her toes into the sand and looked out to the ocean. Leaning her head against his shoulders, she gave a heartfelt sigh.

"Oh, before I forget"—she opened her small evening bag and retrieved his earring—"I wanted to give this back to you."

"Thanks." He silently put it back on, wondering what it

meant that she was returning the earring she disapproved of so much. Was this a sign that her assignment was done, that she was moving on?

"What do you think?" He tilted his head to show off the uneven pearl. He studied her face, wanting to catch every nuance.

Her face softened, and she gave a small smile. "It's you."

What did that mean? It probably wasn't good, but then why was she smiling?

She looked back at the resort and tilted her head, listening to the string quartet. "I love this song. I wish I knew what the name was."

He couldn't help her there. He didn't know anything about classical music, and he wanted to keep it that way. But that didn't mean he couldn't use the music to his advantage.

Santos wrapped his hand along Kylee's waist and pulled her close. Her breasts pressed against his chest, and his cock pushed against her lower belly. He placed one of her hands on his shoulder and held the other before he began slow dancing with her on the sand.

Santos would be the first to admit that he wasn't much of a dancer, but tonight he was simply holding Kylee and swaying to the music. He didn't want to perform any tricky moves or hold her at an appropriate distance. He only wanted to savor the moment.

When the music stopped, she tilted her head up and linked her hands behind his neck. His attention zeroed in on her mouth. His lips tingled with anticipation. If he was going to be a gentleman, he would keep the kiss brief.

If he was really going to be a gentleman, he should probably step away from her and refrain from all body contact. One kiss wasn't going to be enough. One kiss, and before he knew it, he would strip her bare and take her against the rock. That kind of behavior had got her in trouble before.

He brushed his lips against hers, his body humming for more. The music started up again, as fast and powerful as the beat of his heart. Kylee parted her lips and Santos hesitated. He shouldn't deepen the kiss, not when he wanted to claim her here and now.

The tip of Kylee's tongue darted along his lips. A shudder swept through him. He was going to be a gentleman, not a caveman.

And then she dipped her tongue into his mouth. Santos groaned and clasped his hands against her jaw. He drew her in deep, his mouth grinding against hers.

Kylee kissed him fiercely, clinging to his shoulders. He dropped his hands to her waist and pressed her against the rock. He abruptly stopped when his hand grazed the hard surface.

He had messed up again, and after only one kiss. Santos stared at her, breathing hard. Did he really think he could make love to her with finesse? He couldn't even show her the courtesy of waiting to take her to bed.

He was never going to be the Prince Charming she wanted. She needed to know that. Santos pushed away and rubbed his hands in his short hair.

"What's wrong?"

"I'm sorry, Kylee," he said, closing his eyes with regret. "I can't do this anymore."

"Can't do what?" Kiss her? Be with her? Was he ready to call it quits, moments after his all-important dinner?

Well, what had she expected? Kylee held his jacket tighter around her, as if it could ward off the inevitable. She knew how a princess should act, but that didn't mean she was an appropriate match for a prince.

"This." He gestured at himself. "I'm not the guy who wears tuxedos. I don't kiss hands. I'm not going to be as suave and debonair as Jefferson."

Was that what he was worried about? "I know." She had tried to make him into her vision of Prince Charming. It was no wonder he had fought her every step of the way.

His shoulders dipped at her words. "I didn't want to disappoint you."

"You haven't." Once he was willing to be made over, he had gone beyond her expectations. He was the man she had envisioned, but she always knew it was skin-deep. "I tried to fit you into an image people have when it comes to royalty. I should have only softened the rough edges and let you be you."

"No, I wanted the chance to be your Prince Charming."

"I don't need Prince Charming." She took a step away from the rock. "I prefer you."

"Yeah, now." He flicked at his unmade bow tie.

"I have a confession to make." She placed her hand where she knew his primitive tattoo lay underneath his shirt. "I like your tattoo and the earring. I even miss your long hair."

He studied her, as if he was trying to determine her sincerity. "You tell me this after I get a buzz cut?"

She winced. "Sorry."

Santos held his hands out wide. "Why did you keep going if you liked the way I used to be?"

"I was going by what worked for me. Or what used to." She looked down at her bare feet and dug her toes deeper into the sand. "In the past I was stuck with a beach-babe image, and I wanted to get rid of it. That meant avoiding anything that had to do with the beach. Even when I transformed myself and no one knew about my past, I made a point to stay away from the ocean. I was afraid this image was skin-deep. And what happens? I meet you, and you drag me to the beach and I'm back to my former self."

"Not quite. You haven't completely abandoned it. You're probably the most regal person I know."

She hadn't realized that was what she'd needed to hear from him until he said it. Santos knew how indecent she could be, but he had also seen how prim she could act. He accepted both sides of her equally.

"It's back to the drawing board—for you and me," she said. "I want to see the real you shine at these formal functions."

"What about Jefferson's project?"

"I'm not going to accept the job." It was probably the worst thing she could do in her professional life, but the decision gave her a sense of relief.

"Why not? Jefferson is known for paying top dollar, and any project you do for him is good for business."

She shrugged. "I think I'm going to take a break from work and figure out who I really want to be."

"You already know." He reached for the jacket draped around her shoulders and grabbed the lapels. He slowly drew her closer until she could feel his heat. "You just haven't figured out your strategy to reassemble Kylee Dawes."

She gave him a sharp look. "You know me too well."

Santos pressed his mouth against her forehead. "It's going to be your best project yet."

"I don't know. I might be a work in progress for a long, long time."

"I know a great place to figure it out," he said as he guided her backward to the boulder. "There's this amazing island—"

"Your island? Isla de la Perla?" Hope flared in her chest. "The place where women swim naked?"

"Half-naked," he corrected as her back rested against the rock. "And you're only allowed to skinny-dip with me."

Kylee's eyebrows rose. "Is that by royal command? Do I really want to visit a place where you make the laws?"

"I'll make it worth your while," he promised as he nibbled along her lower lip.

"We might need to negotiate," she teased.

He leaned in and kissed her leisurely. His slow pursuit was at odds with his hard cock pressing against her mound. When he placed his hands on either side of her head, Kylee felt surrounded and protected by him.

She speared her hands through his hair as she kissed him, demanding and urgent. Santos's hands drifted along her neck and bare shoulders before he pulled down the top of her dress.

A groan tore from his throat as he kneaded and squeezed her bare breasts. Waves of pleasure rippled through her before Santos bent down and took one puckered nipple in his mouth. He sucked hard and Kylee moaned loudly.

Santos pulled away. "We shouldn't do this here."

She grabbed ahold of his shirt, refusing to let him stop. "I don't want to wait." When she thought of Santos, she thought of wide-open spaces, the roll of the ocean waves, the warm sand and the stars above her.

His hand cupped her breast, and he brushed his thumb against her hard nipple. "What if someone sees us?"

"I don't care." It was big talk. She didn't want anyone other than Santos to see her unguarded moments.

"Or takes a picture of us?" He caught the nipple between his thumb and forefinger and pinched it until she gasped. "Makes a video?"

"Can't we act as if we're the only two people around?"

If someone saw them, then she'd deal with it at that time. She didn't want anyone to intrude on her private moments, but she wasn't going to hide how she felt because someone might use it against her.

"You might regret it," he said softly.

"Why should I be embarrassed about making love to you?" He was the man she loved, and she didn't need to hide it. She wanted to express it.

Kylee pulled his shirt open, and her stomach took a funny little dive when she saw the markings of his tattoo on his brown skin. She reached for his pants and hurriedly unzipped them. Although he looked gorgeous in the tuxedo, it wasn't him. Santos, the real Santos, was rumpled, casual and half-naked.

Santos gripped the back of her legs and tilted her until she was sprawled against the rock, her thighs cradling his hips. He pushed her dress up her bare legs, and his fingertips grazed her panties. He stripped them off her legs and tossed them onto the sand before he sought her wet heat.

His fingertip rubbed against her clit, his eyes colliding with hers. She felt the coil of need twisting faster in her belly. She couldn't catch her breath as her sex throbbed for completion.

She lay in front of Santos, her dress scrunched at her waist and his jacket underneath her back. Her breasts were bare, her legs splayed for him. She was naked and open for him, looking at him straight in the eye, but she didn't feel vulnerable. She felt free and wild.

Santos grabbed her waist, held her still and surged inside her. She gasped as he filled her. Kylee met his thrust with the rolling of her hips. She tightened her legs around his waist, encouraging him to sink deep inside her.

Santos retreated and thrust again. His rhythm drove her

wild. She didn't know half the things she said to him as she clawed his shirt, wanting him to go faster and harder. The coiling need swirled inside her, ready to burst.

The heat erupted with a force that stunned her. It streaked through her arms and legs, pressing just beneath her skin. She didn't think she could contain it.

Kylee stiffened and closed her eyes as the white-hot fire scorched through her. Santos leaned forward, capturing her mouth with his and swallowing her hoarse cry. Her body pulsed and shook as he thrust wildly inside her. He arched his back, every muscle shaking. Santos called out her name and gave one hard, deep thrust before he came.

Santos sagged against her, his head falling on her shoulder. Kylee let her legs weakly drop, but her feet didn't touch the sand. Santos still held her pinned to the rock.

Santos looked into her eyes and gave her a lopsided smile. "I think I like this look of yours the best."

"You do?" She gave a small laugh and brushed her hair from her face. Her heart was still pounding fast, and her sex pulsed. Her dress was bunched up and ruined, and she felt the whisker burns he had left all over her skin. She knew she was a mess, but Santos looked at her as if she was perfect. "Because I'm naked? On a beach?"

His expression softened. "And in my arms."

EPILOGUE

One year later

"WHY ARE THEY TAKING pictures of us?" Crown Princess Shayla muttered to her friends as they browsed the upscale lingerie boutique in London. The store was closed so they could shop in privacy while the princes went to a gentlemen's club, but the paparazzi crowded the storefront windows, snapping pictures and yelling questions through the glass.

"It's the fact that we're looking at lingerie," Lauren said, tossing on a short robe. She stroked the coffee-colored satin and hummed with pleasure. "Princesses aren't supposed to wear sexy things."

"You'd think they'd be used to us by now." Shayla wasn't about to wear a tweed set anytime soon. She was a sensual woman, thanks to Rafael, and there was no need to hide the fact. The jeans, sweatshirts and sneakers had been replaced with flirty dresses, scandalous evening gowns and stiletto heels.

"Ooh. Perfect." Kylee gave a triumphant squeal and held a full-length silk nightgown against her. "What do you think?"

The pearls and crystals twinkled in the lights, but it was the aquamarine silk that did wonders for Kylee's sun-kissed skin. She looked like the island princess that she was.

Kylee conveyed the perfect blend of casual elegance, and she was a media darling, thanks to her professional expertise, which she used to help the kingdom. It was obvious that living in paradise with Santos had done wonders for her.

Lauren tilted her head and frowned at the nightgown clasped against Kylee's chest. "It covers up too much, don't you think?"

"Exactly," Kylee said with a smile and twirled around with the nightgown as the camera lights went off like fireworks. "I wear bikinis and sarongs all the time on Isla de la Perla. If I wear this, it will be too proper for Santos. He'll rip it off me in a minute flat."

"Then you might want to add the matching kimono to go with it," Shayla said, pointing to the sumptuous silk robe. "Make Santos work for it."

Kylee's eyes lit up. "Good thinking."

"Well, I'm going to try this on." Lauren held up a short black babydoll. The sheer mesh nightie left nothing to the imagination.

"Naughty," Shayla said with a smile, noting that while Kylee tried to conceal, Lauren found every opportunity to reveal.

When Lauren had invaded the kingdom of Mataar a year ago, it had been something of a revolution. Most of the countrymen didn't know what to do with an outgoing princess who became a powerful patron to their arts. And Lauren and Zain were always shocking the country. The royal couple couldn't keep their hands off each other. It was obvious that Lauren and Zain were living a fantasy life in the desert.

Lauren looked at the matching boy-short panties. "Do you think it needs something else?"

"Maybe thigh-high black stockings with lace trim?" Shayla suggested. "Add some black heels while you're at it."

"Yeah." Lauren's lips tilted up in a naughty smile.

Shayla turned to the hovering store manager. "Excuse me. Do you have any costumes?"

The woman blinked and did her best to show no expression. "This way," she said in strangled voice, before she escorted them to the collection in the back of the store.

Shayla didn't know why store managers always acted that way. Did she still look too innocent? Or did they believe that princesses had no need to play dress-up?

There was a small collection of sexy, expensive costumes. Shayla was disappointed to see that it was the usual French maid and nurse uniforms. "Anything that screams conquering warrior princess?"

"No, no, no, Shayla," Lauren said as the store manager's eyes widened. "You're supposed to find a costume that is the opposite of what you are."

She was a conquering warrior princess? Ha. "I don't see myself like that at all." She was an academic who was living out her dream. Rafael was the one who had conquered her body and captured her heart. And she was enjoying every minute of it.

The phone rang, and the boutique manager quickly excused herself. Shayla felt a spurt of relief to finally be alone with her friends. As much as she enjoyed the personal service a princess received, she just wanted to hang out with her friends.

"You may not be a warrior princess, but you're close to it." Kylee leaned against a mirror as she watched Shayla browse through the rack. "Didn't you read the magazine article about us? That one that said we were rewriting the rules?"

"They said we were dangerous women only because they can't figure us out," Shayla replied. "We're princesses, so they think we're supposed to be proper and pregnant all the time."

"Hey, here you go." Lauren pulled out a red velvet robe

with faux-fur trim. It came with a black lace nightgown and a crystal tiara. "It's called the Wicked Queen."

Shayla took the hanger and studied the outfit. One day she would be a sexy, powerful queen who had her wicked way with the king. "I don't need a costume for that," she said with a smile. "I'm already on my way."

She was about to replace the outfit back on the rack when she looked at the robe again. She imagined sitting on the edge of the huge bed she shared with her Rafael. The red velvet robe would be fanned out on the bedspread.

Her husband would kneel before her. Naked, of course. He would place his mouth on her foot, kissing a trail up her bare leg. He would go higher and higher, following her commands for more.

She would push her luck, just she like she always did, and watch Rafael transform from an indulgent tutor to a fierce lover. He would strip off the nightgown and bind the robe tightly around her arms, determined to teach her a lesson.

"Then again"—Shayla held the outfit against her, her heart skipping a beat as heat uncoiled deep in her belly and spread through her body—"I could always use the practice."

ABOUT THE AUTHOR

Susanna Carr lives in the Pacific Northwest. Visit her Web site at www.susannacarr.com.